PERIL OF THE STARMEN

By
KRIS NEVILLE

ARMCHAIR FICTION
PO Box 4369, Medford, Oregon 97504

For more information about Armchair Books and products, visit our website at…

www.armchairfiction.com

Or email us at…

armchairfiction@yahoo.com

SPACE SHIPS OVER WASHINGTON D. C.

They came from the deepest regions of outer space. In three "spider ships," they landed near our nation's capital, Washington D. C. And when they descended from their ships they met the people of Earth with broad smiles and promises of inter-galactic friendship. It was truly a great day for all the people of Earth. Unfortunately, it all proved too good to be true, as Earth was soon faced with a seemingly inevitable doom…

Veteran science fiction author Kris Neville spins a taut, exciting tale of alien invasion, mind control, political intrigue, and the blatant betrayal of mankind. "Peril of the Starmen" takes you on a relentless, wild ride that will keep you on the edge of your seat.

FOR A COMPLETE SECOND NOVEL, TURN TO PAGE 89

CAST OF CHARACTERS

HERB

He was a simple Starman, a technician. All they wanted him to do was blow up the Earth…and himself along with it!

SENATOR BUD COUNCIL

A Junior U. S. Senator with delusions of grandeur. He resolved to seal a bond with the visiting Starmen—but at what price?

NORMA COUNCIL

She was in favor of the Earth welcoming the Starmen with open arms—until she learned of their secret purpose.

THE OLIGARCH

This alien leader held the minds of his fellow Starmen in a grip of uncompromising control—but to what sinister purpose?

FRANK COUNCIL

The idealistic brother of a U. S. Senator. He found out that good old family values weren't all they were cracked up to be.

SENATOR STILSON

As head of a powerful Senate committee, it was up to him to determine the fate of the visiting Starmen.

WILLIAM

He was the first of the visiting Starmen to openly question the purpose of their mission—and it cost him dearly.

CHAPTER ONE

"I CALLED you three in," the Oligarch said, "because I have some very important news."

Herb—he would later be assigned that name—was one of the three. He hated the Oligarch, and he had no doubt that the Oligarch knew it.

"There are," the Oligarch said, "people on the planet. Unfortunately."

Dull rage and frustration and despair and helplessness bubbled up in Herb. His face remained calm.

"We'll have to keep them from interfering with us," the Oligarch said.

Herb wanted to cry: Find another! Not this one! Not the only one we've ever found with people on it!

But he said nothing. His anguished thoughts whirled like a dust storm, handling and rejecting ideas like bits of paper. The remote and inaccessible Scientists were beyond accounting. Perhaps only this planet would serve. Perhaps there was insufficient time to locate another of suitable mass. Perhaps... But one could not know. One could only submit to authority. The storm died away, and Herb acknowledged bitter reality with helplessness. There even seemed a nightmare inevitability about the selection.

"It would be dangerous to try to work secretly," the Oligarch said. "If they were to discover us in the midst of planting the explosive, it would be fatal. We'll go down and ask their permission."

No one protested.

"To that end," the Oligarch said, "I have selected you three competent, trustworthy men. You will learn their language and when we land, lull their natural suspicions. It will be your responsibility to see that we blow up the planet on schedule."

The crush of the responsibility was terrifying. "I don't need to tell you," the Oligarch said, "that you can't fail."

And it was true. Herb *believed*.

Unless the planet Earth was exploded, the ever-unstable Universe, itself, would collapse. Already the binding force was dangerously diminished. If new energy were not released

Peril Of The Starmen

By

Kris Neville

Their space ships landed near Washington, and they met Earthmen with friendly smiles. It was a great day — and quite possibly, our last!

within a month, disintegration would begin. The Universe would alter and flow and contract and after the collapse, slowly build itself into a new form—that form itself containing the inherent stresses of change and mutability. Only the arrival of starmen to space flight at the critical time—only their continued vigilance—prevented disaster beyond accounting for.

Herb *believed.*

CHAPTER TWO

WELL inside the solar system the huge space ship plunged on, released from the warp drive and slowly braking to establish an orbit around the third planet.

Herb came up from the deep stupor of the drugs. He had been under their influence for the last twenty hours while the sleep tapes hammered information into his unconscious brain.

"All right," said Wezen, their private custodian, "time for exercise. Two hours of workouts, and then you eat."

Herb sat up and felt his head. It ached dully. "Give me a minute. Time to think, Wezen. I'm—"

The other two Starmen were also recovering.

"None of that! No time to think! Get up! Get up!"

Herb got reluctantly to his feet. Cold air washed over his nude body, and he trembled. He wanted to return to sleep, not the drugged sleep of the sleep tapes, but the genuine, untroubled sleep. Something frightening and alien was taking place in his mind.

He looked around for a dream form. It was a subconscious response. He realized with relief that it was not necessary to fill one in. Technically, he had not been asleep.

The Oligarch came to witness the first awakening. "How goes it, Wezen?"

"Fine."

"I don't know," Herb said. "My mind, it's…I can't think…"

One of the others said, "There's all kinds of information, but I can't get at it. I…can't…get…at…it." He looked around desperately. "Every time I try, something new comes up. It's like a volcano. I can't control it. I think, the name of a river is Mississippi—and then I know that leaves are green, and…"

"The sun is 93 million miles away…"

"The day is divided into twenty-four equal periods of sixty minutes…"

"The largest ocean is the Pacific…"

"The Federal Government of the United States of America is composed of three independent branches…"

They were all talking at once.

"It's awful. Not to be able to control…"

"Good, good," said the Oligarch. He was satisfied with the progress. By the time they landed, they would be little more than mechanisms designed to answer questions; they would not be able to think at all, they would *respond*. Stimuli-response.

"Freedom," said the Oligarch.

"Is," Herb found himself saying, "is the basis of any government that governs justly."

Wezen made a little intake of air that was loud in the shocked silence.

"I said that," Herb said unbelievingly.

"Excellent," said the Oligarch. "The proper reaction."

Wezen relaxed, but he was visibly shaken. He had *heard* the heresy. What might happen to him later, when this job was done?

"The indoctrination is beginning nicely." The Oligarch nodded. They would be able to sooth suspicion and dispel fear when they arrived on Earth. They would speak of love and assistance when the time came. "But you still have much to learn."

"You have a lot of information about them," Herb said. "Their history…their… You got it just in the last few days from their radio and television shows? I don't see how…"

"We extrapolate; there are machines," the Oligarch said.

He regarded Herb narrowly. "I believe we better step up the pace." He was not going to give Herb time to rest, to think, to understand, to correlate the mind staggering mass of information he was receiving. "Let's hurry to the recreation room for calisthenics."

In the corridor, Herb glanced around for microphones and saw he was in an unwired stretch. He turned to the starman beside him. Their eyes met. Identical information had been fed simultaneously to both of them. "You heard what I said?"

"Yes."

"What kind of a place is this, this Earth?"

The other strained to think. "It's…it's…I don't believe it."

"All men are created equal," Herb said.

"And they hold these truths to be self evident…"

"Nor make any laws abridging"

"Shhhhh!" the third starman whispered. "Microphones up here."

They fell silent.

THE Oligarch went to his stateroom and ordered a meal. He had been indoctrinated by the sleep tapes about Earth well over a Brionimanian year previously. The tapes had been brought back by an extensive scouting expedition composed solely of Oligarchs.

He found them a naive race. Weakness, of course, was their shortcoming. As was often the case. He imagined his hand touching the lever that would trigger the explosive. He saw, in imagination, the planet fly asunder.

He had destroyed before. Five races had died beneath his hands. And now—

Perhaps, he thought, I am growing old. Why is it I do not want to destroy this race myself? Am I becoming weak?

He was angry with himself. Weakness! He thought. I'm acting like a subject, he thought. *I'm an Oligarch.*

Oligarch, he thought.

Five races, and now the sixth…

Where will it end? He thought.

It will never end.

Slowly the smile came. We are supreme, he thought, the lords and masters, and it will never end.

His scalp prickled with destiny.

Five races. He saw his hand reach out for the sixth.

He shuddered. Weeks ago he had reached his decision.

Bleakly he thought: I can't do it.

Perspiration crept down his spine. If a planet were not blown up, the whole fabric of his society would collapse. Brionimar must never learn.

But Brionimar *would* learn. Earth was on the verge of space flight. Within a generation they would be listening for radio and television extension-waves in hyperspace that would indicate the existence of another civilization. In two generations they would be in the skies of Brionimar. And then the subjects would see salvation: here (they would reason) is another race capable of preserving the Universe. And there would be no appeasing their blind and mindless wrath until the last Oligarch was dismembered and bloodless.

His hand reached out and curled around an imaginary lever. It must be done, he thought. But not by me. Not by me. Not this hand. He looked down at his hands: white and immaculate and always clean. He washed them frequently.

Someone else must pull the lever.

I must leave a man behind at the bombsite to do it, he thought.

Psychology was a science on Brionimar; and he was a scientist. There was only one man he could be sure of out of all the crew. There were several fanatics, but he distrusted them. There was one idealist who would, of a psychological certainty, pull that lever and blow himself up along with Earth in the belief that his action was necessary to preserve the Universe.

Herb.

CHAPTER THREE

WHEN the starmen came, they made headlines in the newspapers all over the world.

They sat down on the east-west runway of the Washington National Airport.

MEN FROM STARS LAND!

And shortly:

FIRST CONTACT REVEALS STARMEN HUMANOID!

GENERAL SAYS ARMY READY IF STARMEN MENACE!

EARTH WARNS VISITORS!

And on the heels of these:

UNEASINESS SPREADS!

STARMEN SAY PEACE THEIR MISSION!

NO INVASION, SAYS WILKERSON!

PEACE, SAY STARMEN!

And a few hours later:

CONGRESS TO MEET!

CONGRESS FORMS COMMITTEE: WILL REPORT FINDINGS TO AMERICAN PEOPLE!

STARMEN SAY PEACE BETWEEN WORLDS!

Fear and faith combined; courage and cowardice; hatred and optimism. The great ground swell of popular approval was to come much later. At first there was naked uncertainty. Could the starmen be trusted?

And suppose they could be trusted?

Suppose that.

What then?

What?

Many were afraid.

Bud Council, freshman Senator from the state of Missouri, was one of them. In the course of events he was to be assigned to the Committee to investigate the Starmen. A weak man, a fearful man, and as such, a dangerous man...

CHAPTER FOUR

FROM his initial statement it was obvious that Bud sided with the group determined to oppose all contact with the starmen. His reaction was more frantic than most. He awoke at night from a soggy dream of terror. *Let us alone*, he sobbed, trembling. *Let us alone.* The future, once so secure, was now a veiled menace. Go away, he whispered into the night, *let us alone. We don't want you. Go away.*

He appeared sleepless for the first hearing. The three starmen filed in. He hated them.

They testified.

Herb, in the witness stand, peered out at the swarm of white faces; his head turned automatically from interrogator to interrogator.

"Our government is a modified democracy, much as your own, containing strong safe guards for individual liberty and civil rights," Herb said. One would need to look deeply into his eyes to detect the dullness and the depersonalization that was the true index to the words.

His thoughts were fuzzy, floating upon the periphery of his immediate existence. A detached part of himself seemed to observe and record the proceedings without understanding them; there was a fever of information inside of him.

"We believe in the mutual exchange of knowledge. As proof of our good will, we will be glad to send in a team of scientists..." And later; "Our aim is mutually profitable trade."

He rested. One of the starmen took the stand. The drone and whine of voices lulled Herb. He wanted to relax, to sleep, to recover, to become master of himself once again.

After a recess, he found himself once more on the stand. Senator Rawlins, a thin, nervous mid-westerner, began a line of inquiry. Herb tested his fingers, feeling the comforting reality of the hard chair arm. He explored the surface with childish wonder while his voice responded and waited and responded. Dimly, persistently, doggedly, stubbornly the ego, the self—that small spark of assertiveness and awareness— struggled to arrange and order, to reason and make sense of—to unify and master—the knowledge it possessed. The consistency with which his spoken lies appealed to human prejudice should have made him realize the extent to which the Oligarchy was experienced in dealing with alien civilizations and the extent to which they had prepared specifically to confront this one. But he was aware only of the sound of his voice. The words fell away into some lost abyss of confusion.

"But the theory behind this, now?" Senator Rawlins said.

"I'm sorry, sir. We are technicians aboard this expedition. We have very little to do with the theoretical aspects. That's up to the Scientists."

"Well, you are, sir, familiar with the idea that—we'll say— that light has limited velocity?"

"Yes, sir, that is correct. It wouldn't make sense for it to have infinite velocity, to be instantaneously everywhere." A tiny sense of urgency formed in his mind.

"Are you familiar with the fad that the speed of light is a limiting factor? Nothing in the natural Universe goes faster than light."

"I couldn't say, sir, I really don't know. At an extremely

high speed our space ship makes a, a *transition*, but…I guess, sir, yes, sir." The answers weren't coming now. The Oligarch had not dared permit him scientific knowledge. There was a little vacuum where there should be information.

"You'll pardon me, but aren't you unusually ignorant, for a technician, about physical theory: about the action of gases that we were talking about a moment ago in fact, even about astronomy?"

Herb did not say that such pursuits were the exclusive prerogatives of the Oligarchs. He did not say: I am inferior in mental capacity to an Oligarch; I can never become a Scientist. That was not to be mentioned. "I am a technician, sir."

Senator Rawlins shook his head and made a few notes.

There was fear somewhere inside of him. What more could he say? Suppose…suppose… Had he answered wrong? It was as if his knowledge was a river rushing his ego toward the great waterfall of defeat, and he was powerless to control anything. He must not fail. Must not, must not, must not fail.

The imminence of collapse made the very sky terrifying, to know that this apparent order could crumble, and planets fly from suns, and suns themselves spin blindly nowhere. Every word before the Committee was vital. The whole wheeling order of existence turned upon it.

He felt the wood beneath his fingertips, smooth and cool and solid.

THE second day of the open hearing, Norma flew down from Vermont to reason with Bud.

Bud was gracious. Years in politics had taught him to mask his real feelings; taught him so well that he was no longer at all sure what his real feelings were.

The outbursts of anger and suppressed sadism he

unleashed on those closest to him always the morning after, confused him and left him feeling that the person of the previous day had been someone distinct and separate from his genuine self.

"It's good to see you," he said. A warm, brotherly and artificial love flattered his sense of rectitude. He considered her the baby of the family. He remembered her as a gawky, frightened girl giving a last long glance at the security of the living room before venturing into the night of her first date. "I've been meaning to get up your way." His hands signaled the extent of his confinement to Washington. "There's so much to do, you can't imagine. I have to take work home with me. I'm sometimes up half the night with it...I've been hearing about you. Very fine, Norma, very fine."

Norma was tense and uncomfortable and, Bud thought, a little overawed to be sitting across the desk from her own brother in the rebuilt Senate Office Building.

She blinked nervously. "Frank will be in this afternoon."

"Yes. Yes?" A trace of petulance haunted Bud's voice. "Terribly busy just now, but..." Hollow enthusiasm conquered. "That's just fine. I can always find time to see Frank."

"He thinks it's important that he see you," Norma said.

"Has something happened?" Bud always sought ways to escape from the anticipated responsibility of sharing a family crisis.

"We want to talk to you."

"I don't quite understand, Norma. What are you talking about?"

"These hearings, Bud."

Instantly the Senator felt the crush of the whole family arrayed against him, and he wanted to snarl at her in shame and anger and shout, "Leave me alone! Leave me alone! Leave me alone...*please!*"

"They've got space flight. We can't even begin to guess what else they've got. What does Senator Stilson do? And you're there on his side, right with him."

Bud puffed his cheeks and his skin grew hot and prickly. *It's none of your damned business,* he thought viciously.

"They have space flight," she repeated doggedly. "Think what that would mean to us."

"I haven't time to discuss it right now, Sis. We'll have to talk this out later." He stood up, anger pounding in his temples.

She stood with him. "Tonight. You and I and Frank."

"I don't quite see how…" His voice was weary, and he let the sentence hang short of blunt refusal.

"Tonight, Bud. We've got to see you tonight. He's flying in."

"Well…" he sighed resignedly. My place, then. I'll see you at, nine o'clock there."

"That will be fine."

"Nine, then. I've got to rush. My place at nine."

"Goodbye, Bud."

LESS than an hour later flash bulbs popped from all corners of the room as the starmen entered for their second session of questioning.

Chairman Stilson, in a peevishly thin voice, limited the photographers to ten minutes and ruled against pictures during the questioning. After nearly half an hour, the hearing got underway.

Herb was first on the stand. He continued in the same fashion as yesterday. His answers were polite and informative. Senator Stilson's attempt to get him to contradict himself proved unfruitful. Herb surrendered the chair to one of the others and returned to his seat at the long table reserved for the starmen.

The hearing droned on. He no longer listened. He wanted to sleep.

"Yes," said the starman who was testifying, "that is correct. One of our main reasons for making this expedition is to offer you technological information: space flight, medicine..."

"...eventually trade..."

"Initiate a cultural exchange at the first practical moment..."

Herb heard someone say: "But we have limited facilities on this expedition. A larger one, with your permission, will be dispatched for Earth within a year." He was not even sure whether it was he who was speaking. "In the meantime, we would like permission to conduct certain scientific tests on the surface... A mineral analysis, sir, primarily. But we are interested in geological evidence..."

"...whether or not," someone said, "the physical similarity of our two races is due to parallel evolution or to a forgotten, prehistoric cycle of colonization by a common ancestor..."

"...These tests can be completed within a few days..."

"In return, sir, we offer..."

"...We must leave within a week. We must have an answer before then."

They described their own planet and their own civilization. They made an excellent impression.

When it was Bud's turn to question, he asked Herb: "How do we know—here, you've learned the language, so much about us and all—how do we know that this isn't a fabrication, a tissue of prevarications you're telling the American people here today? We have to take everything on faith. Now, you know so much about us, you have studied us..."

"We have only a week..." Herb replied.

THEY were waiting for Bud at nine o'clock. He was late.

"I'm sorry," Bud said. "Came as quickly as I could. I was at a secret session...but for a brother and sister, well...I just had to leave..."

"We appreciate it, Bud," Norma said.

"Drink, anybody?"

"No, thanks," Frank said.

Norma shook her head.

"Mind if I have one? I'm rather upset today—the hearings and all, the meeting tonight..."

He went to his bar.

Frank was on the sofa. His gaunt, heavy-boned body waited motionless. His blunt-fingered, surgeon's hands lay unmoving. His skin was tanned from the Oklahoma sun. Norma sat stiffly erect in the overstuffed chair.

"I guess you know what we want to see you about," Frank said.

Bud poured carefully without looking around. "Norma said something about the starmen. Terrifying thing, terrifying thing. You think they'll really leave when we tell them to?"

"I don't see there's much we can do about it if they make up their minds to stay," Frank said.

"Look, Bud," Norma said, "think how far ahead of us they are. They must be friendly, they must be sincere in their offer to help us."

Bud shook his head. "My deep and sincere conviction on this is that it's a matter of our pride and our independence and our freedom. They're all at stake. I mean—" He waved helplessly. "You know how I feel. I mean, my views are in all the papers, in the *Record*. With me it's a matter of principle. I don't see how we can accept that sort of offer. It's degrading."

"If we tell them to leave, to go away, to leave us alone, we've lost the greatest opportunity in history." Norma insisted.

"Norma," Bud said. "You know how I feel about you. You know I'd do anything in the world for either of you. Anything within my power. All you need do is ask. Money, anything. But this…this… We're proud. Mankind is proud." His heart swelled with the beauty of renunciation and righteousness. "We're too proud, too independent, too *free*. I would not be willing to sacrifice those great, eternal truths, those historic principles that are the foundation of our way of life, that have made America great: dignity, pride, self-reliance…"

"I think they have about the same metabolism as humans," Frank said. "Speaking as a medical man, I believe if they'd give us their medical knowledge, we could conquer disease on Earth. And with their technology—"

"We are a proud race," Bud said. "We must cling to that. That is more precious than gold."

When Frank spoke, there was a mixture of contempt and terror in his voice. "Bud, you're a monument to the basic anarchy of the American people."

"*Frank!*" Norma cried.

"He is. If the people paid any attention to what they were doing, do you think they'd elect a man like that?"

Bud's mind darted frantically. What was happening here? What was behind this? Why was Frank, his own brother, out to get him? What sinister motive—?

"You underestimate them, though," Frank said, "There's a little trickle of maturity in this country. For every aberration like you it gains a drop of experience and knowledge. The war is over. We've had our emotional jag. We're about to go into one of our rational periods. We're about to wake up to our responsibilities. Your day is passing. I don't know if there's enough of you left to keep out the starmen. The people are coming around. But—I—do—know—this. I know…"

"Stop—" Norma cried. "You don't understand Bud. You're trying to make him into something dishonest and cynical..."

"I've watched him come up. I've watched him for years. I've seen all the rotten deals he's pulled. I've seen him smear innocent people—ruin their careers—and all not for patriotism but for himself. To advance his career. Keep his name before the public. He doesn't care for anything but Bud. Bud, and any means to the end that he moves up, gets power—power for power's sake—power to create and destroy—power to change and control. I've watched him—I know him. I'm talking the only language he understands."

Bud was trembling. The sense of indignation, horror, and innocence was blunted by the shallow dryness of his breathing.

"Frank...stop this...you're out of your mind!"

"I'm going to see you defeated in the next election, Bud. I'm going to dig up dirt; I'm going to find out who your mistresses are. I'm your brother. I'm going to hound you, disgrace you, drive you from office. You know me. You know I mean what I say. You know me. You know I mean what I say. *You know I will do it.*"

"What do you want? My gosh, Frank, what are you after?"

FRANK'S hands were shaking. His mouth worked nervously. "For once in my life, for once in my life I've got something all-the-way decent to fight for, and I mean to fight just as dirty as I have to in order to get it. Bud, you're coming over to my side on this starmen hearing. You're going to vote for cooperation with them. Do you hear me? Do you hear what I say?"

Bud, his eyes bulging with shock and disbelief, shook his head dumbly. His own brother—this terror raging before him—impossible, his own brother... His heart pounded.

His will was gone. "What do you want?" he repeated dryly.

"I told you."

"I—I—I'll have to think. I—I—"

"No you won't," Frank said. He stood before him now. "No, you won't."

Norma jumped between them. "Leave him alone…"

Bud snaked from behind her and fled to the bar. His unprotected back a crawling mass of chill, he poured himself a drink. "You're…you're upset, Frank. You've been, been overworked." He drank the drink in a feverish gulp. "Now…" his voice fluttered nervously. "I'll forget what you've said here tonight. I understand." His breathing was still tight and frightened. "About the starmen. I haven't, I haven't really given the matter too, too much…attention. I still have an… I was just today thinking of…"

Frank started to speak.

"I can see both sides of the argument," Bud said rapidly. In the depth of his stomach he lived with the cold knowledge that Frank would stoop to anything—any lie, any distortion—to defeat him. Frank could defeat him. It wasn't as if Frank was a stranger. It wasn't as if Bud had been in the Senate for years. No, he was a vulnerable freshman, and unscrupulous politicians back home were already. This was terrible. All his dreams of the future trembled on his words. He was physically afraid.

"Frank is just upset," Norma said frantically.

"Yes, yes," Bud murmured.

"Frank, you apologize. Do you hear me…apologize!"

Frank and Bud found their eyes locked in a moment of silent communication, and seeing victory in the dull defeat inside of Bud, Frank said hoarsely, "I apologize, Bud. I shouldn't have said those things. I lost my head. I'm sorry."

They both knew it was no apology. The threat was still very much there.

CHAPTER FIVE

THE spider ships towered above the surrounding aircraft. Their construction was utilitarian; their living quarters were cramped; entrance was achieved from the ground by means of a retractable ladder from the base platform.

The underbelly dome contained the cutting ray. It could strike deep into the Earth, burning through shale and granite with equal efficiency. The portable casing could be sunk almost simultaneously; it would seem to contain the ray as a hose contains water. While like a giant rig, the ship would poise on its triple legs above the operation. As rapidly as the crew could section the casing, the drilling would proceed.

The three ships would form a triangle. Like insects sending down stingers they would, when the time came, lance three deep shafts into the Earth. Then down the casings would plunge the identical charges. Technicians could compute the point where the three shock waves would meet. A fourth ray would enter the Earth to the proper depth; and at that point would be buried the deadly atomic seed. At the proper time, the charges would be detonated. And where their waves met, under incredible heat and pressure, there the chain reaction would begin, to explode, in an instant, the whole of the Earth.

The Oligarch summoned Herb. "You may sit at my table," he said.

Sleep laden, Herb sank down across from the Oligarch.

"The necessity for rushing them into a hasty decision is unfortunate," the Oligarch said.

Herb sat hating. The words scarcely penetrated into his confused being. The turmoil was worse than ever.

"…I have been studying the reports. Three members of

the Committee, as it stands now, oppose us. And listen…"

"Yes."

"They will be sure to try to end the hearings tomorrow."

"Yes," Herb repeated dully.

"It will go to the full Senate. We have requested a decision within a week. That may not be sufficient time for the popular sentiment of the country to crystallize in our favor. A few determined men may be able to defeat us."

Herb felt a little shudder crawl along his mind. Then his thoughts whirled away.

"It will be infinitely more difficult to win the crucial support of Senators Klein, Stilson, and Council after the Committee hearings end. We must bring them to our side. They have become the focal point of the opposition. We must prolong the Committee hearings until we have convinced them. If we can convince them, the full Senate will go along. We'll have ripped the heart out of the opposition."

Herb tried to concentrate on the reasoning. "Yes," he said.

"They will press for an immediate vote. They have known, even if they don't realize it consciously, that the longer they delay, the surer they are of being defeated."

"If we don't…can't…"

I don't know, the Oligarch thought. *I don't know. Threats? Try to plant the charges secretly?* "We'll have to convince them. And we've got to do it within a week—maybe a little more, a day or two more."

"What do we do? How? I mean, what do we tell them?" Herb's thoughts were like fog. He wished he could go back to sleep.

The Oligarch knew he was wasting his time explaining to Herb. He wished that he could go before the Committee, himself, but he dared not. Automatic reactions were far more consistent and convincing than his calculating deceit would be. *He* could conceivably be caught in a lie. Not Herb.

"I'll…I'll try…"

The Oligarch analyzed Herb's potential. *Ten days. Ten days. If he becomes unreliable, where shall I find another?*

"We have almost three weeks," Herb said. "We could give them fifteen or sixteen days. We could plant the charges in one day…"

"You may as well go back to sleep, Herb."

"Yes."

Herb stood up and stumbled away.

The Oligarch returned to his cabin, washed his hands, and went to his desk.

He fumbled at the newspapers. He saw an editorial: "Council Makes Starmen Hearing Political Football." The people were slowly coming to the starmen's support, but how long, how long…? He saw another headline: STARMEN POSSIBLE MENACE TO EARTH SOCIETY.

THE first thing Herb did upon arising the morning of the third hearing was to fill in his dream form. He had filled in thousands of them during his life, and yet it was always a frightening experience.

A chill of the Unknown confronted him.

Watchful eyes were, in a way, reassuring; planted microphones could be circumvented; spies could be recognized. But the dream form could not be cheated.

What awful secrets did it reveal? Life and death hung in the balance. Somehow they could tell from the fantasy fiction of a dream how you felt about the reality around you: about the Oligarchy, about your job, about your family.

And they could tell when you lied.

And if you said you didn't dream.

Everyone on Brionimar dreamed.

If they didn't like your dreams, they shot you...

Even into his numb and information-filled mind, terror crept as his pencil moved across the dream form.

He breakfasted in the mess hall and then left for the hearing. As usual, there was a group of humans standing outside the guard lines, marveling at the three starships, standing upon spider legs, looking ready to whirl skyward at any sign of hostility. Far above, the interstellar ship waited in the coldness of space for the shuttle ships to complete their mission and return.

There was an unexpected buzz in the Committee Room when Herb and his two companions arrived.

An ugly television camera squatted across from the Chairman's desk.

Bud had changed his vote on televising the hearings.

Herb watched Bud cross to Senator Stilson. Until this morning the two had seemed very friendly.

"Let's get together later," Bud was saying. "I'll explain my position. I'm sure you'll understand."

Senator Stilson refused to acknowledge that Bud was there.

"Look, Eddy," Bud continued, "don't act like that. Listen, I was thinking this over last night, and I think it's only right..."

"The Socialists have gotten to you, Bud. That's all there is to say."

Bud swallowed in shocked disbelief. "Oh, now..." More than anything else in the world Bud wanted to refute this slander. Desperation gripped him: *the socialists have gotten to you!* No! Damn you! Take that back, you son of a bitch! His hands clenched.

He swallowed again, stiffly, with difficulty. Relax. For the love of God, relax. "Oh, now..."

Senator Stilson walked away.

Bud sat down weakly. I'll show him, he thought. I'll…I'll… It was frightening to have Senator Stilson call you a socialist.

Bud tried not to think about Frank's face…Frank's threats had nothing to do with him changing his mind. A man can change his mind. That he *had* changed his mind seemed to Bud a measure of his honesty and fairness. It was nothing less than that.

One of the other starmen whispered to Herb: "That one's changed sides."

Herb nodded. The Senators were beginning to respond to pressure from their constituents. But even as the tension was sinking, even as elation rose, a second emotion swept through him. It was not enough to deceive those in this room. Now he must also lie to innocent watching millions all over the planet. His fists clenched. He hated Bud.

Early in his testimony he noticed a girl in the audience. There was something in her face that made his eyes return to it time after time. Gradually he came to concentrate exclusively on her and try to explain everything to her alone. He smiled uncertainly, and she smiled back encouragement.

And Norma—this situation suddenly became immediate and personal to her. She watched Herb, listening intently, wanting desperately to communicate her encouragement to him and her belief in him.

BUD caught a taxi to attend the executive session of the hearings that had been set for eight o'clock that evening. The starmen would not be present.

Bud was ill at ease. "Hurry up, damn it," he snapped at his driver.

Telegrams from all over the country had been pouring into his office. They had awakened him to certain possibilities. His changed vote on television had brought him unprecedented publicity, even from normally hostile newspapers. He realized that the longer the hearings continued the more familiar his name would become.

He was convinced by now that the majority of the people (even as himself) were inclined to approve an agreement with the starmen.

Surely they weren't thinking of ending the hearings and taking the matter to the full Senate? They wouldn't dare flush headlines down the drain like that.

Would they?

He grumbled to himself. Of course they wouldn't. Here was a fulcrum, a lever... Look at the publicity... After all, another Missourian had made it from a Congressional Committee. Perhaps the starmen hearings had really seized the imagination of the American people... Harry S. Truman had made it...

He experienced a moral awakening, a sharp clear call to duty that transcended morality. All things changed. The world was suddenly portentous and thrilling, and secret enemies lurked and unseen disasters hovered.

His mind was humming with the exultation. He thought of himself dying someday at the end of his... sixth...eighth...tenth...term of office. He pictured the universal sorrow. He wanted to cry. They would mourn for a year; for two years. They would build huge monuments to his memory. Monuments bigger than any monuments ever built.

The taxi stopped.

Perhaps after forty years in office, he would be assassinated. The public wrath...

"Here we are," the driver said.

Getting out, he knew that he would fight to see the hearings continued.

He was late. Already the other four Senators were seated. Bud nodded to them and took his place. He put his brief case (it gave him a sense of importance to carry one) on the table before him and unzipped it as if to be ready to delve into its contents to document his every statement.

The atmosphere was tense. Bud looked from face to face. Senator Stilson was granite hostility. Senator Gutenleigh avoided his eyes. Senator Klein glared at him truculently.

"It was called for eight," Senator Stilson said icily.

"Good evening, gentleman," he said. "Sorry I'm late."

"Good evening," Senator Rawlins said. "These gentlemen here," he included everyone but Bud in his gesture, "intend to dispense with a report and merely issue the Committee's recommendation. They've already decided to close the hearings and present the matter to the Senate tomorrow."

Bud was stunned. This was unbelievable. That meant…that…the friends! Somehow they had gotten to Gutenleigh, the Senator from Hawaii. Bud had counted on him—on the basis of his television vote—to oppose Klein and Stilson. What outrageous, un-American pressure had been exerted to cause him to surrender?

"But…but…Senator Guten—"

"Has," Senator Stilson said in his thin, peevish tenor, "reconsidered."

Enmity and hostility flared silently from the Chairman. An almost baffled look crossed his face as if the implications had finally arrived in his consciousness: here was a Senator, Senator Council, a member of—as he thought of it—his *team*, who had had the temerity to transgress his leadership. One would expect opposition from a radical like Rawlins. But from a Council! He had always felt that Bud was one of his. The insult was compounded by heresy.

"I feel," Senator Rawlins said, "that two questions require further exploration: how is it that the starmen are so ignorant of basic scientific principles; and for what reason do they insist that we reach such a momentous decision in such a limited time? To ask the Senate to vote now would force an honest man to perhaps a hasty decision. For myself, until these points are clarified, I would be very reluctant to reach any sort of an agreement with them. I want to ask this Committee to reconsider its decision, and I hope the Honorable Senator from Missouri will join with me, and that between us we can prevail upon the other gentlemen."

A sincere democrat, he spoke with quiet desperation, "In order to expect the people to choose wisely, we must be sure that they are given an opportunity to receive all the pertinent facts."

Bud was howling inwardly with the fury of a thwarted child. Headlines were flying away from him. His stand in the full Senate would command only one one-hundredth of the attention it would receive here. He arose, trembling with rage.

Shaking a quivering finger at Senator Stilson he cried, "You have bribed Gutenleigh!"

Gutenleigh looked uncomfortable.

"What did they promise you, Sam?" he thundered, wondering wildly what counter promises he could make.

Even Senator Stilson was shocked by Bud's violent outburst. Bud was famous for his rabid thundering against subversives, but no one had expected him to have the courage to open such hysterical fire on his Senate colleagues. Senator Stilson said, "I resent your attitude, sir!"

"Gentlemen, Gentlemen," Senator Rawlins said. "A little moderation, please."

"I'm for them, damn you!" Bud cried. "You're all in a conspiracy a filthy conspiracy—against *me*."

"If you don't sit down, I will summon an officer and have you removed bodily from this Chamber," Senator Stilson said.

They were all looking at Bud. With a great display of reluctance, he sank to his seat. He refused to look at Senator Stilson. He sulked and plotted revenge. And remembered Frank and hated everybody.

The vote proceeded routinely. Three members voted to recommend that the Senate reject the starmen's offer. Senator Rawlins abstained, and Bud voted that the Senate accept it.

The committee meeting broke up. Senators Klein and Stilson went out to gather up opposition Senators. They lobbied far into the night.

Nor was Bud to be outdone.

CHAPTER SIX

THE three spider ships waited in the late evening darkness. Only a few spectators loitered. The television cameras were quiet. Army sentries patrolled the area to keep the starmen inside and the curious out. Norma's heels clicked sharply on the runway as she approached. At the ropes she stopped and showed the guard the entry permit her brother had obtained for her.

"Come under," the guard said, lifting the rope.

"The one called Herb?"

"He's in that one over there."

She moved in the indicated direction. A moment before, the night had been warm. Now an uncomfortably chill breeze whispered around her as she moved in to the starship's shadow. The thought of the distance it had come, the countless millions of miles of space its hull had shed, was enough to dwarf her into less than insignificance. She wanted to run back to the guard, and to the protection of the familiar.

The ladder was down, and when she reached it, the door above opened and a starman looked out.

"I'd like to come up."

The starman went away. In a moment, he was back with one of the three who could speak English.

"I'd like to come up," Norma repeated.

"We've already given the official tour for today."

"I have an authorization from our government. I'd like to talk to Herb. You tell him I'm from Senator Council. It's about the report."

"Just a moment." He disappeared inside. Norma teetered nervously back and forth. Wonderingly she put out her hand to touch the hard, icy metal of the ladder.

"Come up."

She began to climb toward the opening. Looking behind her, she saw Washington, real and solid and reassuring.

The starman at the top helped her inside.

Herb was coming down the narrow corridor. She smiled at him. "Hello."

"Hello"

"I want to talk to you a moment."

He gestured her inside.

In the first room off the main corridor, Herb stopped. Several starmen hovered nearby to listen.

"Can I talk to you for just a couple of seconds alone?"

"Why—why, yes, I guess." He looked around for permission.

The Oligarch, towering imperiously on the fringe of the group, said, "Why don't you interview her in my office, Herb?

"Come along," Herb said.

In contrast to the Spartan plainness of the rest of the ship, the Oligarch's office was richly furnished. Its private corridor led past the mess hall and opened upon the main corridor that led forward to the second level. It was strategically located. From its doorway one could interdict entrance and escape.

It was the first time Herb had been in the room. Automatically his eyes searched the walls.

"Senator Council asked me to talk to you," Norma said. "He wants you to understand about the report. You've heard? It's going to the full Senate tomorrow. We'd like you to…"

"I'm only a technician, Miss."

"My name is Norma."

"Norma." His emotions were tangled beyond solution. He wanted to say, I'll stay behind when the others leave, will that make everything all right, you won't blame me, you won't blame me for it if I stay behind, will you?' His mind hurt with the confusion.

"We thought, if you'd go away, if the people thought we'd actually lost you…"

"It's not for me to make any kind of decision. I'll have to ask. Would that be all right, sir?"

Norma blinked. She did not understand to whom the question was addressed. Her eyes followed his to the wall, a concealed microphone? She felt a little prickle of fear.

The Oligarch stood in the doorway behind her. "That will be agreeable with us."

She whirled guiltily.

"Bud wanted to, to see Herb tonight…" Norma felt resentment against this man in the doorway. "I was told to bring Herb."

"I will be able to speak for my government."

"I was told to bring Herb," Norma said stubbornly. Bud had not specified, but she told herself that she would not yield to a stranger. She did not consider Herb a stranger. "Isn't it all right to take him?"

"He may come, too, if you wish." He smiled. "Whatever you wish."

His voice was not reassuring. "Thank you." She modified her tone. Some of the iciness went out of it. "I'll leave now. Bud will send two CLD men over for you."

SITTING at his desk in his Georgetown apartment, Bud looked through a stack of letters.

Norma, waiting, tried to become interested in a *Saturday Evening Post* story and failed. She put the magazine aside.

The knock they were waiting for came.

Bud rose and crossed quickly to the door.

"Ah, hello," he said with a genial smile. "If you gentlemen will wait downstairs, I'll call you when they are ready to leave." The CLD men withdrew. "Hello, young fellow. Herb, I believe? And?"

"George...how would George be?"

"George," the Senator said, pumping the Oligarch's hand and drawing him across the threshold. "I like your people's way of using first names. Very democratic. Just call me Bud."

They arranged themselves around the room.

"I don't suppose you'd care for a drink?"

"I'd be delighted," George said.

Bud, solemn faced, mixed the drinks, talking over his shoulder. "I hope you haven't taken our Committee report as a rejection of your generous offer... You understand? I want to explain my position—what we, you and I, can do... There we are." He turned from his labors and handed the drinks around.

"Norma, Herb, I wonder if you'd mind if George and I stepped in there?"

"It's all right with us," Norma said.

Bud and the Oligarch went into the study. Bud closed the

door.

"Now," he said. Ambition was a sickness in him. *This is the boy I've got to sell*, he thought. That's all I've got to do—sell him. Once he's sold, the rest will follow. Ambition was like a hunger, and success hung in the air like smoke. "We can have a nice, private talk. I'm sure you'll appreciate my rather delicate position."

George swirled ice and smiled.

"Norma tells me you can speak for your government?"

George nodded.

"Let's sit down."

"Thank you."

"Now here's the way I feel about it. I'm on your team. We're both on the same team. I want to help you all I can, and I know you'll want to help me."

George nodded.

"I was thinking: If you would leave...not tell anybody...leave tonight. I don't mean for good, but make it look that way. You see?"

"Our leaving would serve as an emotional shock?"

"Yes, exactly. Your leaving might be just what the people need to wake them up and get them on our team. I don't need to tell you that the Senate is likely to reject your offer. I mean, right now. The way things stand now. My first mail is coming in. It's predominantly unfavorable. But from some of the telegrams I've gotten...well...I think the people are coming around. But they're still not all the way around yet. We need a couple of weeks. My idea is, I'd like to be the one that—more or less—handles it."

"You want us to work through you?"

"You have put your finger on it, George. If there's just one Earthman you can trust and work through, who knows the ropes..."

"I believe I understand."

"And when you come back, you make it plain that it was Bud Council who brought you back—it was Bud Council who really convinced you to return."

"You and I," George said, "will probably be able to work out a deal."

Jubilation rang in Bud's ears. This was it. The talk of working out a deal was an assurance of victory. President Bud—no, perhaps it would be better, more dignified, to be President Phil. He would write it out and see which looked best: President Philip Council or President Bud Council... History lay heavily upon his thoughts...For the first time he actually felt at home with a starman.

"Perhaps you would do something for us?" George said.

Bud found himself looking deep into George's eyes. Instinctively he knew that George knew him better than he knew himself, and that George had carefully studied him according to no one could tell what alien science.

"Why...why...yes, yes, of course."

"Well," George said, rising and going to Bud and dropping a hand across his shoulder, "just to be sure that you really are on our team, perhaps you could give us a little token of loyalty."

Bud grew cold in anticipation. But the crowds cheering and the banners waving... No. Not now, they couldn't snatch it away now. What was it George wanted? Money? A signed agreement? Patronage? "Why, yes, naturally."

George's hand tightened in friendly reassurance. He knew that he had found his man. "Your brother's head. I believe his name is Frank. His head. We'll expect you to have it for us when we return in two weeks. Two weeks from to-morrow."

He no longer needed to count on Herb.

CHAPTER SEVEN

THE starmen had vanished into the night that is deepest just before dawn, when the sky is black and most mysterious. They had ordered the guards away, their lifts had whirled, they rose, and far above the Earth there were ruby tongues of jets and the volcanic roar of power.

The airport lay desolate.

…In his ship, Herb could not sleep. He kept reviewing the time he had spent alone with Norma. It was difficult to remember clearly. What few things he could remember would, he was afraid, be lost forever in the jungle of confusion that was his mind, unless he went over them again and again and planted them firmly and deeply into his being.

What an alien and lovely name…Norma. Something about her was so quiet and reassuring. He wanted to bury his head against her breasts and whisper, "I wish I could save your planet, but I can't." He had wanted to confess to her, but he could not. If she had discovered… But now, in the darkness, on the narrow cot, he thought about her and buried his head against her soft breasts, and he smelled the cool darkness of the perfume, and he spoke to her and told her the truth, and she understood his hurt and knew the necessity and forgave him…

*   *   *

The trouble began one week after the take off. The Oligarch read well the signals of its arrival, but he did nothing. A scene would be bad for the crew's morale. He thought it would be a tonic to his own. It would prove the validity of his conclusion: that the indoctrinated starman called Leslie would crack up on the seventh day.

It happened, as he imagined it would, shortly after Leslie had filled out his dream form.

It was in the mess hall.

Without warning Leslie kicked over his chair. His face twisted. His hands whitened at the knuckles. There was an insane expression in his eyes. He looked slowly around the table.

With his first movement there came silence; it was instantaneous; it was as though the clock had stopped in a parlor of corpses. No one moved.

He screamed a great, searing curse. The word was English.

The crew waited. No one breathed.

Leslie began to break things with mounting fury. He shattered his plate by slamming it savagely to the table. He threw his cup against the far wall.

They waited. Many of them cried inward encouragement to insanity.

"Lies!" he screamed in English. "Lies! *There is no Universe!*

He fell to his hands and knees and growled and snapped like an animal.

The Oligarch felt his detachment shatter. Hurriedly he left his table and went to Leslie and killed him.

Breathing with difficulty, he arose and addressed the crew. "This is what happens to a man who lies on his dream form." They rustled uneasily. "Go back to your meal."

One by one they resumed eating. Slowly conversation grew and expanded from whispers to abnormal loudness and then back to whispers again. The ubiquitous microphones peered up eagerly from the tables and the hungry record tapes consumed the sounds.

The food lodged in Herb's throat. There seemed no moisture anywhere in his body. He fought down an irrational impulse to get to his own feet and scream forever.

Once again at his private table, the Oligarch was amazed to find that the complete justification of his own logic left him feeling empty and unsatisfied and disappointed. The matter was behind him. In the future could he expect equal success? Insatiable doubt grew.

He stood up. The compulsion to wash his hands was irresistible. He left the mess hall hurriedly.

As he watched the cool cleanness of the water flow over his hands, he felt at peace.

He was a god, playing with men, knowing them as they would never know themselves, seeing into their inmost souls, moving them to his will.

He was tempted to greater accomplishment. Could he— could he—? Unsure of himself, he was doomed to seek endless reassurance.

Herb. Now Herb. There was a dangerous man. At least, he would become one, in another three days. It would be like playing with fire to play with Herb. It would be exciting, too.

He dried his hands. His heart was beating faster.

Herb would soon begin to doubt. William was already doubting. He should have done something about them both before now. About Leslie before now…

I will see that Herb…that Herb…what?

His mouth was dry. Excitement swelled and made his breath catch. His throat ached.

He would help William to doubt. N one of them must return to Brionimar.

It was intensely rewarding to play God, if you could get your hands clean.

The Oligarch rang the buzzer.

He would leave the mike tapes and the dream forms until this afternoon.

He would interview William now. He was washing his

hands when William entered.

AFTER the interview, William came in and sat on Herb's cot.

In recent days, their common knowledge had drawn them together; before, they had scarcely spoken. Whenever they talked now, they used English, partly as a recognition of their kindred uniqueness, partly as a futile subconscious attempt to outwit the spy tapes.

"It's a ridiculous planet, Herb said.

"Yes, a ridiculous planet," William agreed.

"Freedom," Herb said. "That is nonsense."

"Equality," William said. "Equality. They are down right silly."

"You wouldn't think a place like that could exist, a silly place like that, where a man can actually say whatever silly idea pops into his mind."

"Yes," William said. "They should be destroyed—even if it wasn't necessary, they should be destroyed."

Herb was silent for a moment. The microphones listened. Then: "Imagine how awful it would be to live down there, with no one to do your thinking for you."

"The natural leaders aren't even recognized. You can't tell an Oligarch from a Subject."

"I'd never like to live in a place like that," Herb said. *I dreamed of it, he wanted to say, and I dreamed that Brionimar had been changed into Earth, and there was no Oligarchy, and a man was free.* "It's like a nightmare," he said.

They fell silent.

William wanted to say: *If only we could take that dream back with us, if only our people could see.*

"Yes," Herb said suddenly. "Yes, yes…yes."

"Eh?"

"…nothing."

"He called me in today," William said.

"Oh?"

"We talked."

"What did you talk about?"

"Not much…I don't see what he was trying to get at." William stood up. He looked at the microphone. He felt courage grow in him. "I've been…*thinking…*"

Herb nodded. He dared not speak.

"You know what I mean?"

Herb nodded.

"We'll talk later."

AFTER the fourth daily meal, William came once more. He took Herb's arm and gestured with his head that Herb should follow. Herb arose; his heart stood wildly beating in the cage of his chest; his blood ran with conspiracy and excitement.

They walked down the corridor until they were in a section free of microphones. It was, although they did not know it, intentionally unwired. It provided the crew a harmless escape valve for their emotions. It was not (as any Oligarch could have told you) necessary to watch a Subject all the time. Most of the spy tapes, as a matter of fact, were never even inspected.

William was sweating. Herb could not account for the intensity of emotional strain he seemed to he under. Herb imagined they would talk briefly—and plan vaguely—about ways to carry some of the idea and the feel of freedom back to Brionimar. They would hear a message of hope, they would tell that Earth had not been destroyed in vain, that a civilization could function in freedom without chaos. And perhaps, someday, not in their time, but someday…

"It's not perfect," Herb said, "We dream of perfection, do you understand, but even Earth is not perfect. I think we ought to remember that. I can feel it, I can tell it. I... We want to take that back with us, too."

William was scarcely listening. His muscles were tense and crawling with danger. He had to speak, to confide, to know that he was not alone. To have Herb help him. Herb, too, must know.

"Listen," he hissed. "You know what I meant when I said I've been thinking?"

"Yes," Herb said, "So have I."

William licked his lips. His heart seemed to stop. He took a deep breath.

"How can we stop him from blowing it up?"

The Universe wheeled. Herb could not believe what he had heard...a Destructionist!

"He dropped some hints, he didn't mean to, but he did," William said. "I finally realized. You must have known longer than I have. It's all a lie. He as good as told me so."

Herb took half a step backward. His skin crawled with horror.

William, oblivious to everything but his own words, said, "We've got to stop and plan carefully. I will kill him myself, and then you get to the control room... We'll have to hold the crew off. They might not believe us. Not at first. That will be the big trouble..."

Herb continued to back away. All the training of a lifetime surged into his mind. There is scarcely a way to express the detestation that any starman—when properly conditioned—felt toward a Destructionist. His reason was destroyed. He wanted to leap at William and tear at his face with his, naked hands.

I've got to warn him! Herb thought.

He turned and ran. The Oligarch! I've got to warn *him!* Breath sobbed in his throat.

William watched the fleeing figure. He reached out a hand

to stay him. He could not believe his own miscalculation. He stood, limp and defeated. There was no will left in him. Bleak betrayal was a heavy winged vampire.

There was no place to go.

He sat down.

It was all very logical for the first time in his life. Some where in time the Oligarchy had invented the menace as a device to gain (or to retain) power. They had saturated the people with ignorance, ridiculed thought, and eliminated freedom until the menace could not be challenged. They had established a closed and consistent system that could justify anything. And now that he had gotten outside, stepped beyond it, by denying its ultimate premise, the immensity of the fraud was mind staggering. There was no combating it as long as one lived inside. There have, he thought, been other Earths. Nothing outside the system must be permitted to intrude.

He put his head in his arms and began to cry.

That was how they found him when they came to kill him.

HERB did not watch the kill. He went straight to his cot and lay down and waited for the news to come. He heard the rustle of voices in the corridor as the hunt was being organized.

He was still trembling with disgust. A Destructionist—the very word sent a shudder through his body. To think that William, of them all, that William, would have been one seemed impossible. Still, you could never tell. A neighbor, a friend…you could never tell who might be.

How could they think? What sort of creatures could they be? Herb's imagination shrank from the task. It was one thing to hate the Oligarchy, but it was quite another to favor the end of the Universe.

The rustle of voices diminished. They were after him.

They would get him.

Herb thought: Perhaps with this one action I have saved the Universe. When this becomes known on Brionimar, when it is learned how I, single-handed, exposed the menace, then they will…

But suppose William was right?

Never before had such a thought even fought for recognition, and now, without warning, it erupted in naked completeness. It was an electric shock.

"No!" he shrieked quietly, "no!"

He was sitting erect. He was clammy with icy perspiration. His whole body was suddenly silent and listening, every muscle and nerve strained in the direction of the hunt.

He lay back.

No, he thought.

THE next day the Oligarch called him in.

"I want to thank you again, Herb." He watched his words sink into naked flesh. "If you had not told me, I would never have suspected. But for you, he—he might have succeeded."

Herb refused to look into the Oligarch's face. I did right, he thought. I did what I had to do, what anyone would have done.

"I know it has been a shock," the Oligarch said. "You were very fond of William."

Herb's lips twisted silently.

"I want to tell you a story," the Oligarch said. "Listen, listen carefully. It is about a man called Bud and what he did."

Herb was not listening; and then suddenly he was listening. The Oligarch told the story, and when he was done, leaned forward, waiting. It was as if Herb had just heard the most important story in the world.

"His brother's head," the Oligarch whispered, "he traded his brother's head for power..."

There was something about the idea that reached deep into the ancient folk shadows of Herb's mind and stood as a symbol. But he did not understand about symbols, only their compulsive effects. All his rage and frustration and guilt crystallized around Bud. If he could only see Bud fall and gasp and die, he would have vindicated morality and done all that he could do in the name and cause of justice.

"You may go," the Oligarch said. "Think about what I've told you."

CHAPTER EIGHT

NORMA missed Herb. There was the glamour of the unknown about him and the appeal of the familiar. He was two individuals, a little boy, confused and puzzled land mute and needing her, and a man, strong and wise and belonging to a strange world she could not enter as she had entered all too easily the masculine world of Earth.

She was with Frank when Bud made his television announcement.

Bud beamed happily in the glare of uncounted millions of dollars of publicity. "At my invitation," he said, "the starmen have consented to return."

Frank winced to see what he thought to be a decent cause advancing the personal fortunes of a fool, a hypocrite, and a coward.

Bud—it was a little difficult to imagine (without having heard it) how he managed it—at the high point of his speech inserted a few remarks about home, mother, and the virtues of honesty and hard work. He was, he explained, a poor but honest man, holding certain principles dear to his heart. He was at a loss to account for the fact that he had been chosen to lead this great crusade for the starmen. "We can thank the lord that they have consented to return. *They will return.* I do not believe there are enough Communists in the country today to prevent it."

Frank shuddered to think what might happen now. Suppose Bud should—no! —become President out of all this; suppose the people, in gratitude, or the politicians seeking a popular hero, contrived his election.

Frank felt that he might have erred in using bad means to gain good ends. For Bud, hunting subversives, socialists, liberals, and critics, could rapidly reduce the country to conformism and with native ingenuity, pervert starscience into a political weapon.

The first radio message, on Earth frequency, to the President requested that Bud be given the job of handling all negotiations. If, it said, Senator Council finds it in his heart to accept the responsibility.

Many people did not understand the last.

Bud did.

THE morning of the day the starmen returned, Norma came into Bud's office. She was practically bursting with excitement. Thoughts of what their knowledge would contribute to Earth, the marvelous advances in medicine, in physics, in art that hovered just within reach…

On her way through the secretary's office, she passed a slight, nattily dressed man wearing a hat.

For a puzzled second she furrowed her brow. Then memory came. He had been investigated by the Senate Crime Committee. She bit her lip in exasperation. Why would Bud be willing to see someone like that?

"Wasn't that—?" she demanded, bursting into Bud's office.

He got up with quick awkwardness. His face was

bloodless. "Ohhhhhh," he sighed. "I didn't expect—Hello, Sis."

"Wasn't that—?" she began again.

"It's, it's, it's, he, he…" Bud indicated the box on his desk. "From an old friend."

"What's wrong? Don't you feel well, Bud?"

"Fine, fine," Bud said. "I feel fine…I'm very busy just now."

Norma sat down. The box rested on the desk between them. Warily Bud sank into his chair. She saw his face framed above the box, almost as if the head were hanging suspended and bodiless, and she felt an unaccountable tremor of superstitious fear.

"You poor dear," she said. "You've been worrying so much about the starmen… You're losing, weight. Have Frank give you a checkup, Bud. You ought to take things easier."

" … I will. I've been intending to… I'll have him look me over. Where is he; do you know where he is?"

"He went out last night. I expect him back any time."

He stood up. He was calmer now. He rested one hand on the box. "Yes, I wouldn't worry. He'll show up. I am tired, terribly tired. You saw the Secret Service men out there? They're out to kill me, Norma! *Senator Stilson is hiring them!*"

Norma started to protest.

"I tell you, they are. If the Secret Service weren't out there to protect me, I'd be dead right now. But God has given me a job to do. I can't let them kill me until I have done his will."

"Bud, you're just overworked. Nobody's trying to do a thing like that. Frank says it's just publicity, and I thought…"

"Ahhhhh," Bud said darkly. "Would the President himself have assigned me a body guard if it weren't true? *Would he?* There are extremists in this country—communists and socialists—who would stop at nothing to prevent the starmen from coming back. Even Frank..."

Norma's face grew a shade paler.

"But he's the one..."

"You can never tell! But I'll tell you this. I pray every night, Sis. I get down on my knees, and I pray that God will let me live long enough." Bud's mind suddenly flashed back to his childhood, and he remembered praying that God would let him assassinate Stalin. God needed only to arm him and transport him to the Kremlin. He could have done the rest. He shook his head darkly again. "You don't understand the dangers." He felt courageous. It took *guts* to face the Communist menace.

She wanted to run. She clenched her fists. This is Bud, your brother, she thought. He's just upset.

"I just wanted to see you for a moment," she said. "It wasn't about anything important."

Bud rubbed his hand caressingly over the box. "Yes?"

"I'll let you get back to work." She stood up and started for the door.

"Don't worry about Frank!" Bud said sharply." He's all right. Nothing's happened to him."

Norma was gone.

Bud began to cry, and looking at the box, he whispered, "It's all your fault. You made me do it. You did, *you made me!*"

CHAPTER NINE

HERB knew, even before the spider ships touched ground In Washington D. C., that he was going to murder Bud.

The ships were motionless. Slowly suspense mounted. At last one ship opened its port. The landing ladder spun away.

Down the ladder came the Oligarch, alone, dressed simply

in a solid color double-breasted suit. A businessman's suit. There was something reassuring and normal about him. There was initial silence, and then the cheer rose and thundered.

He went directly to the platform, President Wilkerson advanced to meet him. Their hands joined, and a pleasantry passed unheard beneath the cheering. The Oligarch surveyed the welcoming party of Congressmen, foreign diplomats, and government officials. He saw Bud. He crossed to him.

The cheer became deafening.

They exchanged a few whispered words. Lip readers might have caught the question and the assent. Then, smiling, they turned to the public. Nodding, waving, Bud (visibly upset about something) tried to give the impression of recognizing each face individually. The Oligarch bowed his head modestly.

Herb watched from the port of the spider ship. He clenched his fists angrily. If only he had a weapon of some sort.

The President spoke briefly.

Then, as the Oligarch moved toward the speaker's platform, Herb dropped swiftly down the ladder. His feet touched the ground.

The Oligarch watched from the corner of his eye. Herb moved toward the crowd. The crowd leaned forward to catch the Oligarch's every word.

And he was cleansed. He was free of all responsibility—it was now between Herb and Bud. If Herb succeeded...

"Ladies and gentlemen," he began.

They were hushed.

"Thank you for your reception.

I stand today before..." His voice translated into a billion volts, blanketed the world with supersonic vibrations made audible by millions of loudspeakers.

He needed pay no attention to his speech. His mind was floating free, and his body was light and youthful. There were only a few more things to be done, and then his role would be finished.

"On this momentous occasion," the Oligarch continued.

Herb was free of the worst of the crowd. He resisted an impulse to run. He, too, was wearing a businessman's suit. It was the same one he had worn for the hearings. In it, he was indistinguishable from an Earthman. He pulled his hat lower over his face and pushed his way outward. Faces turned, eyes alerted with curiosity, shoulders shrugged, faces turned away. Herb did not know that Norma had seen him and was now trying to fight her way free of humanity to follow him.

The Oligarch continued his speech. His grim and gloomy reflections vanished. He peered out at the Earth faces with genuine benevolence. *It's not in my hands any longer,* he wanted to tell them. *One of your Senators will make the ultimate decision, unless one of my starmen kills him first.*

And then inwardly he chuckled. Or perhaps, he could have said, *my starman will experience some kind of incident incident, perhaps even a trivial one, that will awaken him to the fact that the universe is not in any kind of danger. In which event, he will not be able to convince you of the real danger to Earth. For in due time, I will announce his escape as a dangerous lunatic.*

HERB'S feet moved rhythmically against the sidewalk. For one moment, there was a sense of freedom and impending loss. No more dream forms, his feet seemed to echo.

No
more
dream
forms...

And coloring it, the perception of the world around him,

the bright air, the hot sun, the colors and the gentle wind. Perhaps the colors were most startling, for on Brionimar there was universal drabness that approached decay. The Oligarchy struck out at all frivolity, sensing danger to itself in all sensuous pleasure.

And then the beauty, the sheer, heart-stopping beauty of freedom and color burst on him; his conditioning collapsed. Earth knowledge surged across his memories.

It must not die, he thought, forgetting hatred in beauty. It must not, because there is so much that is good, that is noble that is sad and mighty…

"Hello," Norma said breathlessly.

He whirled. For an instant he was terrified. He saw that she was alone.

He relaxed. Warmth grew within him. "Hello." Until now, it had not occurred to him that he might have been followed.

"Why did you—?"

A radio was blaring somewhere, and as he looked at her, both of them half-laughing, they both heard the announcement that would be headlined shortly in the papers, as:

RENEGADE STARMAN ESCAPES SHIP. FEAR INSANE, SAYS GEORGE.

EARTH AUTHORITIES ALERTED. (Full description of escapee on page two.)

THIS MAN IS ARMED AND DANGEROUS.

CHAPTER TEN

HERB hunched his shoulders as if to ward off a suspected blow. Norma's eyes mirrored fright and uncertainty, and she moved half a step from him.

Grasping her arm at the elbow, he said, "We have to get

off the streets."

Norma wanted to twist away from him and run.

"You've got to help me hide—" The pressure seemed threatening.

"Let me go!" she said, startled.

He dropped his hand instantly. "You've got to help me."

From the expression on his face, she knew that she had nothing to fear. She felt ashamed of herself.

"We can go to my hotel," she said.

Once in the hotel, Herb's eyes darted around the four walls of the living room.

"There are no microphones," Norma said.

They stood just inside the door. Norma turned and walked decisively to the divan. She sat down. I think you'd better explain."

"I...I need some money," Herb said. "There's something I have to get."

"What is it?"

"I...please trust me, *please,*" he said.

She hesitated; then: "How much do you need?"

"A...hundred dollars... Could you let me have—loan me—that much?"

Norma knew he was not insane. There was something here that she did not understand, but it was not insanity. Her emotions went out to him. She saw the present situation only in personal terms, their own relationship. She saw no wider implications. Intuition, she would have called it. Decisively, she phoned for the bellboy and when he came, gave him a check for the management to cash.

While they were waiting for the money, she said, "Won't you tell me—?"

"I can't. I can't. I wish I could. Please, if you'll—" he hesitated, and then, with sickness and loathing, said, "trust me..."

The money came.

"I'll try to pay you back; make it up to you some way…"

"That's all right. Where are you going? What are you going to buy?"

Perhaps it was the desire to shock her, to destroy her faith in him, perhaps and more probably, it was the need to confess (and hope for absolution) that he said: "I want to buy a gun."

"Why do you want a gun?"

Herb, still standing, tried to memorize her face. He was acutely aware of his isolation. He wanted to go to her side, to talk rapidly, to reveal the cruel and horrible compulsion that was driving him and most of all, to enlist her aid and her understanding. He needed to know that one single individual in the whole Universe could appreciate his attempt to meet his own standard of truth and morality.

"Tell me. Maybe Bud will be able to help you out of your trouble. He's my brother…"

The complexity of emotions that burst upon him was almost impossible to understand. He had thought of her—if he had actually thought of the connection at all—as an employee of Bud's, perhaps, but no more than that. He asked incredulously: "Frank was your brother?"

"You mean… is my brother?"

"Yes…I…yes, of course."

"What did you mean…*was* my brother?" Uneasiness settled deep inside her. "Has something happened to him?"

"No. No. It was a grammatical error." Herb thought the sentence too stiff for credence. But she seemed reassured.

"I'll get Bud to help you. And Frank, too. Perhaps the three of us can get you out of any trouble you're in. I'm sure the starmen will be fair. If it's something you've done…"

"No! Don't talk to Bud! Don't tell him you've seen me. You mustn't!"

"Herb, you're being silly." She stood up…"You make it sound like I've got something to be afraid of from my own brother."

Herb bit his lips in anguish and ran from the room.

Norma heard his feet on the carpet, running, running…

The empty room became a thing of terror. She was entangled in something beyond her understanding, and the world seemed less secure than at any time since her parents had died. Should she go after Herb, or…?

She started toward the telephone, stopped, turned away—and then turned back.

She got the switchboard.

"Get me Senator Council's office. Hello, oh, hello, John…Norma. Is Bud in yet? Oh…still? Have him call me as soon as he—oh. All right. I'll be over in an hour then. And John, have you heard anything from Frank? I'm beginning to get worried about him. He isn't in yet…"

She hung up slowly, wondering if she had done the proper thing.

SHE was early for the appointment with Bud, and she was waiting in the outer office when he came in. His two guards nodded recognition and Bud said, "What is it, Norma?" His tone was irritable, and she wanted to cry.

"Please, may I talk to you a minute?"

Bud shifted his weight nervously.

"Please, Bud."

"Come on. I haven't got all day." Letting her enter the main office before him, he said. "What's it about this time?"

He drew the door to his private office closed after them, and went to his desk where he picked up a letter and pretended to read it. "Well? Well?"

"I've talked to Herb."

Bud's face sagged. The letter began to tremble ever so

slightly. Norma did not notice. He did not look up. How much did Herb know? About Frank? Did he know? "Yes?"

He felt weakness dissolve his arm muscles and dissolve the muscles of his thighs and calves. He was afraid that he was about to suffer a heart attack. He had difficulty breathing. "What—what did he have to say?"

"He wanted me to buy a gun for him."

"What for? What for? What did he want a gun for?"

Norma twisted her hands nervously. "I don't know. He wouldn't say. He's in trouble. I thought maybe we could help him."

"He didn't say anything else?" Bud demanded sharply, feeling the fear fade. "He didn't tell you, he didn't say anything else?"

"No...just that he needed a gun—"

"Where is he now?"

"I don't know."

"You don't know? You don't know? He's trying to get a gun, and you don't know where he is?"

"I—I—"

"No telling what kind of a crazy fool idea he's got. No telling what kind of lies he'd tell about me."

"He's in trouble, Bud. We ought to—"

"You listen to me. You do what I say! Don't pay any attention to anything he says. If you see him again, you call *me*."

"I think I'd better talk to Frank about it, Bud. Have you seen him?"

Bud was on his feet and around the desk. He grabbed her shoulders and began to shake her. Her face drained of color. His nostrils flared white.

"Bud—Bud! What's got into you?"

"Frank's all right!" Bud cried. "Now, get out, get out, GET OUT!" He shoved her away from him. "Get out," he sobbed.

Half dazed, she backed away, opened the door, and disappeared.

Trembling, Bud sank into his chair. It was a long time before his breathing returned to normal. He counted his pulse with intent concentration, feeling it flutter like a wounded bird beneath his fingertips.

CHAPTER ELEVEN

HERB had no real hope of eluding capture. After he fled from Norma, he pulled his hat low over his face and hurried down the street. At the first hotel, he entered and registered and was shown his room.

He fell on the bed; the room was fuzzy and dull. He wanted nothing more than to sleep. His mind was such a searing agony of doubt that he had to escape from it. He curled up warmly and nestled against the softness of the mattress and closed his eyes, trying to drive all thought from him, and he slept...

When he awoke, the room was heavy with darkness and silence, and he lay still, trying to feel the vibration of the ship's motors. The memory of a formless dream clung to his mind, and he tried to clarify it for the dream form.

Awareness of his location came. He relaxed, wanted to sleep again, and thought: no more dream forms, no more... Other memories stirred and returned, and he was uneasily awake. He opened his eyes, growing tense.

He held his breath. The dark around him concealed unknown dangers. He was still fully clothed, and he stood up. He found the light switch.

With the bright flame of electricity he became aware of how heavy his head was; how incoherent his thoughts were; and there was a sour taste in his mouth. He blinked his eyes.

The room was reassuringly normal.

He went back to bed and lay down. His thoughts whirled. Beyond thought there was a great, tugging emptiness in his stomach, a sense of despair that seemed to dwell in every tiny muscle and radiate outward from every tiny blood vessel. The light made him naked, and he could not face his own nakedness.

He turned out the light and returned to the bed. The dark was protective and reassuring now, and he closed his eyes.

Bit by bit the sense of unreality fled.

Dawn came.

The TV set sat squatly on the table across the room. Morning sunshine fell brightly through the Venetian blinds. Herb turned on the set to discover the latest news of his pursuit.

The screen lighted and on its surface formed the deadly trinity of the starships, which had flown from Washington to the Arizona desert. It was a long shot from a sound truck, and the camera panned an expanse of desert beyond to focus briefly on the Arizona sunrise.

An announcer was commenting on the riot of color that was quite obvious to the viewer—the flame of dawn in the sky and the blood red of the prairie flowers that covered the desert.

Herb watched and listened.

The starships were in place. Their cutting beams lanced out, there were puffs of destruction, and the tubings struck into the ground.

The camera near one of the ships observed the operation intently. A scientist was commenting on the technology of the starmen. "The information inherent in one of these ships alone," he said (characteristically underestimating the pace of advancement), "would be enough to thrust Earth a hundred years—in terms of scientific knowledge—into the future."

A shudder spun through Herb's body. He paced the room restlessly. Somewhere at a distance a clock struck the hour. Outside the open window, English sparrows chattered shrill, imperative commands.

Herb was hungry. He phoned the desk and ordered breakfast. He was in the bathroom when the bellboy arrived; he called, "The money's on the dresser." For fear of being recognized, he remained hidden until the bellboy left.

He came out. The tray was on the night table. Eating, he continued to watch the progress of the starships.

The voice of the Oligarch now came from the TV. He fabricated plausible details about what they were discovering of Earth's early physical history.

Sweaty faces advanced and receded from the cameras. The three tubes continued into the Earth, going deeper by the minute.

A sense of urgency and desperation filled Herb. He must hurry to kill Bud. By noon the desert operation would be completed. Earth would be a mined planet. Destruction could then be accomplished by the flick of a switch.

He looked at his face in the mirror. Black stubble pricked his skin in a thousand places, and he ran his hand across his cheek. He shrugged and found his hat.

Until sunset, he told himself, he would have until sunset to accomplish his self-imposed assignment.

Bud, he thought (and revulsion mounted in him) is her brother, and she, his sister; and Frank, Frank is dead and forgotten and hidden somewhere, as soon will be now the Earth and all its beauty.

He was in the street. The sunshine was bright. He walked.

A gun, he thought, for a hand that is hungry for—and he thought: To cup the hand behind Norma's head, and stroke her hair, and look deeply into her eyes. He looked at his hands; strange, hungry hands, he thought. He felt them tighten against the metallic iciness of a gun..."You can't," the man behind the counter said, "buy a pistol without a permit. You'll have to get a police permit before I can sell you a gun." His eyes shifted uneasily from Herb's face, and Herb thanked the man and started back toward the sunshine.

"Wait a minute!" the man said.

The harsh command froze Herb. He turned. He found himself looking into reward-hungry eyes. The hand below them held an automatic. The hand was trembling with greed.

"You're that starman," the proprietor said.

Herb caught his breath. He jerked to his left and spun around. He ran.

THE harsh roar of the automatic burst behind him. The proprietor had taken flight for an admission of identity; but perhaps latent uncertainty had carried the bullet high. It smashed into the windowpane above Herb's head, and glass fragments erupted upon the pavement.

"Stop him! Stop him!" cried the proprietor as Herb fled.

The sunlight was bright. Herb bolted across an intersection, narrowly missed being run down by a car, dodged around a heavy truck and ran to the left.

There was no more shooting.

There was a hub-hub behind him. A policeman's whistle sounded.

Herb jerked around another corner. There was the sound of pursuit.

He ran a block, doubled back, entered a department store, lost himself in the crowd, took the elevator up to the third floor.

He tried to look interested in the merchandise. Each

second cost him an extra heartbeat. He left a counter and went to the stairs. He became inconspicuously preoccupied with distant thoughts. He was once more on the ground floor. He left the building by the opposite entrance.

He hailed a taxi. His heart beat desperately.

Once settled in the rear seat, he felt almost secure. The worst was over. He told the driver, "Downtown."

After a dozen blocks, he got out. When the cab was gone, he walked back the way he had come. He found a hotel, registered, and was shown his room.

He stood at the window. A police car cruised by. For a moment, he was afraid it would stop.

I must get a gun, he thought. Time seemed to be falling swiftly in the bright air.

I must, I must.

He went to the television set and switched it on.

The starships were still occupying the screen. The sun was slanting its rays across the desert.

An announcer spoke in a dryly-excited voice.

Herb sat down, and when at length one starship lumbered in to the center of the triangle and its beam struck out, weariness and futility possessed him. They were planting the atomic seed. Within an hour there would he no hope of reprieve. There was none now; and yet it seemed, doom was not irreversible until this last act was accomplished and the seed in place.

Herb spun the selector. He did not want too witness the climactic moment.

What was the name of Norma's hotel?

He remembered.

He went to the telephone...

When Norma arrived in answer to the call, she found an unshaven Herb nervously pacing the floor.

"Where have you been?" she asked breathlessly.

He seated himself on the bed and wrinkled the coverlet in his hands, working with it furiously.

"They're going to blow up the world," he said.

"Who—What?"

"I helped them. It's my fault. I was a fool. I couldn't know, you see that? I couldn't *know*..."

Norma was ashen.

Herb stood up and crossed to her side and looked down at her. "Out in the desert, they have just finished planting the charge. That's what they came here for. They're going too blow up the world."

"The starmen?"

"Yes."

Norma was on her feet. She was too terrified to ask why. She did not question ... *It was true!*

"We've got to stop them!"

"We can't, it's too late," Herb said.

"Why not, why is it?"

"It's too late."

"We've got to stop them."

'It's too late. There's nothing we can do. Listen. Get me a gun. I want to—"

He loomed wild-eyed above her. She didn't understand what he intended—only that some wild fury was driving him. "You've got to help me stop them. There must be some way."

"Get me a gun! Get me a gun!" Every atom of his being cried out to her—he had to have the gun. His thoughts were warped and twisted. With the gun everything would be clear in his mind. Everything would follow step by step. The gun could spout a great, purifying flame.

He was alone in the room. He looked down. She had dropped her purse, and it had spilled open. He walked to the gun that had fallen from it.

* * *

Norma ran, wild and terrified. To whom could she turn?
Frank! Where was he?
Frank...
Bud?
No. No, not Bud. He—
There was no one else. Bud. Her breath was fire. He
would have to do something. Bud.

She hailed a cab.

"Bud!" she called as she opened the car door. "The
Senate Office Building! Hurry!" Bud, she sobbed under her
breath. He can do something to stop it.

* * *

Herb examined the gun carefully. He weighed it in his
hand. It would do nicely. He pocketed it.

He would need only an instant. A taxi from here to the
Senator's office. A trip in the elevator. Perhaps a slight
wait—and then Senator Council framed in the doorway. He
had—how long? Several hours, he told himself.

He touched the gun again. No hurry. No real hurry.

Several hours.

Norma was hysterical when she burst into Bud's office.
One of Bud's hands darted for the drawer where he had
taken to keeping an automatic. The hand stopped.

Norma's lips were trembling uncontrollably. "Bud!" she
gasped. *"Bud, they're planning to blow up the world!"*

"What are you talking about?" he demanded angrily.
"What do you mean?"

"The starmen! I saw Herb. He told me. I had to come to

you, Bud. You've got to make them stop it!"

"Nonsense," Bud said. "You're out of your mind. You're crazy." He surged to his feet. "Where is Herb? I told you to come see me if you found him. Where is he?"

"It's true!" Norma cried. "I know it's true! They've been lying to us. They spy on each other. They have hidden microphones everywhere. They want to destroy the world, Bud! Oh, please, please, please, you've got to believe me…

Bud came toward her. She was insane, of course. It was astonishing how many people were insane. Sometimes Bud thought he was the only sane person left. "Now, now, you just tell me where Herb is, and I'll go have a nice long talk with him." He pocketed the automatic.

"You don't believe me."

"Oh, I do. Dear, I do, of course, I do. They're going to blow up the world… I'd like to see Herb and talk it over with him." He made soothing motions with his hands.

Bud's face, round and smiling and vacant, peered down. She wanted to throw something at it. She wanted to launch herself upon him and shake him and make him listen to her. He was a monolithic caricature of stupidity. She had to force herself into his mind and make him see.

Bud came no closer to her. "Now, now, everything's going to be all right," he said. "Now, now, brother's little sister is…" He took a half step backward.

She was able to see him for the first time as Frank saw him. A little sense of horror was born and began to grow. She stared at him with slowly vanishing disbelief. How could someone like this be her brother? He was some cold, unfeeling, insensitive thing, wrapped up in a world that embraced no one but himself.

"What have you done to Frank?" she demanded. "Bud, *what have you done to my brother?"*

Bud half snarled.

And the Oligarch stepped out of the little room to the left. "I think it's about time I take over."

Norma felt her heart pulse and stop cold. Ice filled the air.

Bud said, staring at her with fascination, "She's going crazy, George."

Norma turned to the Oligarch. "What did you make him do to Frank?"

"Not here," Bud said softly. "Don't kill her yet. She knows where Herb is."

Norma wanted to scream. She only half opened her mouth when the Oligarch's hand slapped sharply against her neck. Her knees buckled and she dropped unconscious to the heavy carpet.

"She knows where Herb is," Bud said again, "We've got to find him before he tells someone—tells someone else about Frank."

"She was telling the truth," the Oligarch said. "We are going to blow up the world. That's what I came back to Washington to tell you."

HERB arrived at the new Senate Office Building. He paid his fare and dismissed the cab. No one noticed him as he entered the lobby. He took the elevator to Senator Council's office. He was taking his time; he had several hours.

The secretary, John, was behind his desk. The reception room was empty. Herb felt his stomach muscles tighten, and his hands clenched the pocketed gun tightly and grew damp.

"Yes?"

"I want to see the Senator."

"What is the nature of your business"

"I want to talk about, about some private matters. I can wait until he can see me." Herb felt the gun, heavy and reassuring.

"The Senator isn't in right now. Perhaps I can help you?"

"No," Herb said sharply. "My business is with him. It's just between the two of us."

"He just left with his sister and George, the starman."

Herb bent forward intently. Time telescoped. An hour was no longer a practical infinity. "Where did they go?"

"I don't know, sir."

To the spider ship, Herb thought. They came back to Washington. They came back—to give Bud his reward for betrayal...

Herb was at the door. He almost tore it from the hinges when he jerked it open.

John picked up his telephone and placed a call to the CLD. "The starman, Herb," he said, "has just left Senator Council's office. You can pick him up outside. If you hurry."

BUD dismissed his bodyguard, and he and George supported Norma between them as they left the building by private elevator and subway to the garage. Bud's face was Grey, his lips bloodless.

The Oligarch had presented him with a choice. Tomorrow morning, some high government official would receive in the mail Frank's head, along with Bud's signed confession. If Bud did not, before then, speak the key words that would blow up the planet. Bud, in the first stunned instant, cried: "Take me with you!" But even as he spoke, he knew that he was doomed. Knowledge did not prevent appeal, but it helped develop resignation. Bud thrust out with entreaties and debased himself with cowardly promises, and seeing them fail, tried threats that failed equally. His mind splintered into a thousand shards and reality became abstracted fragments of himself. The world ceased then to exist for him, and he lived in a phantom land, and his ego seized upon icebergs that drifted across the chill sea of thought.

He became noble.

Norma came to consciousness as the car, driven inexpertly by the Senator, rolled toward the airport. Early afternoon sunlight slanted down across the Capitol.

She lay very quiet in the back seat, listening to the hiss of the tires. Her neck was swollen and throbbing. *Don't kill her yet*, her own brother had said, and then, out of the silence of the car, came his own voice again, contradicting what had gone before.

"Dearer to me than all gold," Bud said. "Child of my beloved mother."

"We will take her with us," the starman answered soothingly, reassuringly.

"She's all that's left," Bud said.

Norma lay quiet, unmoving, not daring to open her eyes.

"You can't know what she means to me," Bud said. "You must tell her that. You must promise to tell her."

"I will do it. I promise you."

Bud said intently, "You must promise, I must know."

"I promise."

"Nothing will happen to her? She's all I have left. All. Child of my beloved mother."

Tension accumulated between Bud and the starman. Norma realized that her brother was no longer sane.

The car slowed and stopped. Still Norma did not move. She was too terrified. They came to her door and opened it.

George pulled her roughly from the seat. She moaned but she did not open her eyes. His hard muscles against her were deadly and threatening, and her knees were so weak that, had she wanted to, she could not have supported herself.

She squinted out of one eye and saw that the three spider ships had returned from Arizona. They were directly below one of them. She heard a starman's feet on the steel ladder that descended from the spider ship. She felt herself scooped up and dropped over his shoulder. In the background she heard her brother's voice, "Child of…" The agony of the voice was almost unendurable. "You must tell her what I did to save her."

And she was jolted harshly upon the starman's shoulder as he swung her up the ladder.

George's feet clanged behind her on the steel, and she heard the sharp, laboring hiss of the breath of the man carrying her.

They were at the port. They entered, and the starman dropped her roughly to the floor, and George clanged the door.

"You attended to the other ships?" George asked in the alien tongue of Brionimar.

"Yes," the starman said. "They will both explode shortly after takeoff."

"The others are all aboard? We are the only ones on this one?"

"Yes."

"Good, I will remember this. You have done a good day's work. You follow instructions well. I won't forget."

"Thank you."

"Watch the girl. I'll give the signal to leave."

"What do we do with her?"

"Dump her out as soon as we hit open space."

George's feet went forward. It was over, he was done. The issue lay between Bud and himself and between Bud and Herb, an exciting and dangerous situation that held, in its solution, the Oligarch's (and the Oligarchy's) fate—the fate of two worlds. The stakes were high. The Oligarch, thinking how free he was of the final responsibility, went first to wash the Earth germs from his contaminated hands.

Norma had not understood the conversation that muttered above her. But her terror was replaced by a sense of desperation. She moaned and opened her eyes.

The starman, looking down at her with a cold, impersonal gaze, grunted something unintelligible.

Norma struggled to her feet. He made no move to prevent or assist her. She steadied herself against the wall. Near her hand, in a clip holder, was a short, steel fire-extinguishing rod. When the starman drew back his hand to hit her, she cringed away. Instinctively she found the rod and jerked it loose. Before she was aware of the action with her conscious mind, the starman sank to the floor, and the bar clattered from her nerveless fingers.

Heart racing she turned for the door. A moment later, she was outside, clambering down the ladder.

THERE were no taxis in sight. A jeep, driven by a uniformed messenger, drew to the curb. Herb, holding his breath, crossed to it. The driver cut the motor and got out. When he disappeared in the building across the street, Herb slipped behind the wheel. He was a technician. He began to experiment. Recently acquired knowledge came to his aid.

After what seemed a timeless heat and an endless exposure, he had the motor running.

The CLD man, who had come over on the subway from the House, stepped out into the sunshine. He surveyed the street with a practiced eye.

Herb spun the jeep away from the curb and sent it careening erratically toward the airport. The CLD man—confident of his identification of Herb—fired twice. Herb heard one of the bullets make an explosive pop as it passed near his ear. He hunched over the wheel and gunned the motor.

NORMA stumbled from the ladder and started to run. The spider ships loomed menacingly behind her. An army guard started forward to question her, and a jeep leaped suddenly into sight from around the corner of the Administration Building. A heart heat later the jeep skewed around beside her, and Herb, his face twisted with hate and fury cried, "Where's Bud?"

One of the spider ships behind them became airborne; and then a second leaped away.

CHAPTER TWELVE

GEORGE was at the controls of the ship. As his hand hovered at the firing stud, he heard someone enter behind him. He turned.

It was the starman. His hair was matted with blood. There was a wild, rebellious glint in his eyes. He snarled like an animal.

"She hit me!" he cried. And then he smashed a fist into George's face. George went down and the starman stepped across him to the control panel. His resentment had been accumulating for a lifetime. He had just sabotaged two ships and sent his fellow starmen to death at the orders of the Oligarch; and he must have known (even if he told himself otherwise) that he, too, would not return to Brionimar. That alone of all who had been on the surface of Earth, the Oligarch would survive. But even in this knowledge, he had still remained loyal, caught like Herb, like his whole civilization, by the specter of chaos and held helpless. But now, thinking the destruction of Earth a certainty, his resentment re-channeled, he was able to strike—even kill, if necessary—the Oligarch in order to revenge himself upon the Earth girl who had struck him.

He snapped on the scanner and searched the airport. He saw Norma climb into the jeep. He sent the spider ship lumbering toward her. The jeep began to run.

The spider legs moved faster, and the ship, like a drunk, lurched awkwardly across the runway in pursuit. He was no pilot, but his hands jerked levers and twisted wheels and the ship moved. He sighted the underbelly heat ray.

Just as he depressed the firing lever, the ship stumbled across a transport plane that lay passively interdicting its path. The ship veered sharply to the left, throwing the sighting off target and causing the ray to turn the ground molten short of the speeding car.

The starman struggled to right his vehicle.

George found his weapon. He was numb and horrified. *If Norma were actually killed... if Bud found out...!*

George moved his weapon slowly so as not to attract the starman's attention. He was terribly, desperately frightened and unsure of himself.

The starman reached again for the firing lever. George shot twice. The starman's hand fluttered as if in indecision, and George shot again. The starman fell backwards, and the ship shuddered to a stop.

George rolled to his feet. If Norma were not already dead, he must recapture her.

THE CLD man arrived in time to see the fantastic sight of a red and silver, tri-legged Leviathan from space stumbling after a surplus jeep. He slammed his car to a halt before the army guard station and cried, "Shoot him! Shoot him!" Demonstrating, he fired wildly in the direction of the jeep. "CLD!" he cried. "Shoot, damn it!"

Herb heard the sinister pop of the handgun and, glancing out of the corner of his eye, saw the rifles aligning themselves in his direction. He huddled lower over the wheel and screamed to Norma, "Hold on!"

Norma was transfixed with terror. The huge spider ship seemed almost upon them.

Herb was going too fast for the quick turn he attempted. The steering wheel was wrenched from his hand, and the jeep, like a tripped animal, twisted and threw itself to the ground and rolled over.

At the first bone shattering crash, Norma slammed into Herb and his head cracked the steering wheel solidly.

Far to the west, the sky flashed dull red as the first spider ship exploded in flight. The sky flashed red again. Soldiers were running toward the wreck when the first shock wave rolled in.

In giant strides, George brought his own ship to the overturned jeep. It straddled the wreck like a defiant parent and seemed to challenge the advancing soldiers. George hurried to the port.

He slammed the door back and cried, "Don't shoot! Don't shoot!" The outer ladder fell away at the touch of his hand, and a second later his feet were hurrying down it.

Once on the ground, he was at the jeep in a heart beat. There was no blood, but both figures were very still. "Help me!" he cried to the arriving soldiers.

Two came forward, laid aside their guns, and together, with gentle hands, lifted Norma and then Herb free of the wreckage.

When they were stretched out on the ground, George knelt. Perspiration wetted his upper lip. He poised above Norma, seeking some sign of life, and he was aware of Herb stirring uneasily to his rear. Norma's eyelids fluttered, and a wave of relief and exultation enveloped George.

"She's all right," George said loudly. "Make sure the newspapers carry that. The girl is all right."

"Who is she?"

"She's one of ours," the Oligarch said with nice possessiveness. Bud would know better—that was all that mattered. He would know that the girl was Norma and that the girl was safe. The delicate equation of his decision was once more in balance. "Help me get them aboard the ship."

A small crowd was gathering, and an Army major pushed his way forward. The CLD man, over-awed by the Oligarch's presence, and uncertain of what to do now, held back watching.

"What's this?" the major demanded. "What's this?"

George stood up. "It's our personal problem. This renegade—"

"Is he the one who escaped from you? The nutty one?"

"Yes," George said.

"What about your other two ships? They exploded. They just exploded."

Instantly the surrounding Earthmen rustled suspiciously.

"He—" George said… "It was sabotage. He is responsible. Terrible. Terrible. I'm stunned. We haven't any time to waste. I've got to get this girl back to our big ship out there in space for medical attention."

"We've sent for a doctor," the major said stiffly.

"We have doctors. For God's sake, man, help me get them aboard. There's no time to stand here talking. We have advanced techniques, if I can only get there in time, that may mean the difference between life and death…"

The major hesitated. "All right. You two soldiers—take the girl up the ladder."

"Herb, too," the Oligarch said. "If he survives, he will be tried."

The major grunted at two more soldiers.

GEORGE followed them up the ladder. He greeted the capture of Herb with bitterness. The game was over; he had been denied the excitement of it being played out. And yet there was relief, although he had once more been thrust into a role of player, it was not of his own volition. The conspiracy of events had released him from free choice. It was not his fault that it was necessary to remove Herb prematurely from the arena. He was uncomfortably aware that the major was following him.

Inside the ship, George directed the soldiers to put their burdens in the first compartment to the left. Then he turned to the major. "Your prompt action may well have saved her life." He was tense and frightened. Now that he was sure it would be reported that a girl had been returned to the ship and hurried to medical attention, it was of paramount importance to get the soldiers and the major out of the ship. If Norma were unexpectedly to recover and begin to talk, the major might prove difficult to handle.

The crush of danger hung upon him. An instant, in which he wished to surrender and confess, was transplanted by dedication to victory. The sense of mission returned.

"I don't think I should permit you to leave, sir," the major said politely. "I've thought it over."

"Sir?"

"In view of what happened to the other two ships. How do you know this one hasn't been sabotaged, too? In your understandable anxiousness to get this girl…"

"I'm sure," George said evenly. "I tell you this ship is all right."

"Well, how do you know? Obviously, you knew the other two ships were all right, too; only they weren't…"

The Oligarch restrained an impulse to command. "This is too important a matter to delay with explanations."

The four soldiers clustering around the major seemed ominous.

"Our doctor will be here in a moment. Immediate aid can be given the girl."

George's hands trembled with rage and maddening anxiety. "I am going to takeoff immediately. Explanations can come later when the girl has been treated. I will hold you personally responsible for any—further delay." He went toward the control room.

The major started to follow.

The Oligarch whirled to face him. "You will be responsible for her death. I am going to leave. If necessary, I will take all of you with me. You will have to use force to stop me."

The major stood with his hands clenched into fists at his sides. There was silence. The fists slowly unclenched.

"I would advise you to get off the ship at once," George said. He turned once more. This time he did not look back.

A thrill of uncertainty grew within the major. He swallowed stiffly and then snapped angrily to the waiting soldiers, "All right, get the lead out! Let's go! Let's go, let's go!" He seemed to want to push them physically toward the exit.

THE Oligarch was in the control room by the time they dropped off the ladder to the ground. A flick of the switch, and the ladder retreated. The ship trembled. A savage jab, and the ship became airborne. It was too late now for them to stop him. He had made a successful escape. He was weak with reaction. A few moments more…

He studied the dials. Earth fell away.

He could hurry. He only need save enough fuel for a tie in. He waited impatiently for altitude. Earth shrank. The features of her surface blurred. A cloud occluded her face completely. The air resistance lessened. Gravity weakened. He was able to pour the fuel into the space jets. He fired the first and second banks. Fuel gauges descended. Acceleration pressed against him like, a hand. More jets. He was in a hurry. His mission was accomplished. Within two hours he would be out of the danger area of the Earth explosion. But he was not overly worried about that. He did not expect it until an hour or so after sunrise over Washington.

He locked the ship on automatic. Time enough later to finish computing the trajectory.

He was now free to dispose of Herb and Norma.

The sense of elation increased as he left the control room. He fingered his hand weapon and smiled to himself. Less than a minute later, he stepped into the doorway of the room containing the two people, his gun raised.

CHAPTER THIRTEEN

HERB had regained consciousness.

Herb shot, and flame leaped toward the Oligarch. The room roared with the explosion.

George jerked back, and in mid-motion, something caught him low in his chest, on the left side of his body and slapped him savagely off his feet.

Incredibly, he had been hit!

He shook his head and got one knee under him. His left side was numb. He looked down and saw blood start to color his shirt.

He got to his feet and backed along the corridor. His knees were weak. He covered the door with a trembling hand and prayed for Herb to show himself.

The ship was silent.

He had to sit down. He wanted to be sick.

Perhaps Herb had taken the other door out!

He whirled.

No movement.

He had to have a place to hide. He had to hide, and wait, and when Herb came searching for him—

He staggered back. His side began to throb dully.

The ship was very quiet.

"He's out there," Herb said, knowing that his words would carry over the hidden microphones. "I will manage to kill him before we reach the big ship."

Norma was breathing shallowly, not yet fully recovered from the wreck. "What about Earth?"

"It's too late."

"If we could—if we could destroy the... that ship... if we could ram it—prevent it from setting off the charge..."

"It's too late," Herb said doggedly. But even with the words, he felt the first hesitant flicker of hope. If he could take over this ship, and with it assault the great ship in space, and there capture the remote-control mechanism by which the charge would be detonated, then perhaps Earth could really be saved. First kill the Oligarch. Then...

Norma whimpered to herself, "You stay here," he hissed, too softly, he hoped for the microphones to pick up his voice.

Her eyes widened in protest. "Don't go. He'll..."

"Shhhhhh," he silenced her. Bending, he whispered, "I'll find him first. You'll be all right."

He left her. At the doorway, he looked back. She seemed crumpled and lifeless and defeated.

The Oligarch was somewhere to his left. In the corridor, waiting? Herb could not know. There was only one way to find out. He stepped from the room, gun ready to fire.

The corridor was empty.

Where? In the control room? In the office? In the kitchen? The mess hall?

Herb moved forward silently.

THE Oligarch had backed across the mess hall. One hand clutched at his left side. His breathing was too loud. Herb would surely hear it.

He stood in the far doorway that opened into the short

corridor leading to his office and that extended beyond his office to open into the main corridor. Herb would have to cross before its open face should he come forward. From the doorway, the Oligarch also commanded a view of the main mess hall entrance, should Herb stop to inspect that room first. By ducking either in or out, he could place a protecting wall between himself and his pursuer. The Oligarch knew that Herb would come. His left side was terrifying testimony that the lifetime of conditioning had been stripped away.

It would he so easy to dart to his own office; but the unprotected space between him and it was a barrier more solid than a rock cliff. If Herb should emerge as he was making the exposed crossing, he would be a perfect target. His movements were sluggish. He had to locate Herb in order to know in which direction safety lay. But to be safe in the office, with the door barricaded…

*   *   *

Herb saw the drops of blood drying slowly along the floor of the corridor.

The Oligarch had entered the mess hall. Herb approached cautiously.

Standing just outside, not exposing himself, he could see a clot of blood beyond the main door. Probably the Oligarch had hesitated there, undecided—or resting.

He held the gun more tightly. His heart beat rapidly, and his mouth was dry. But he was not afraid. There was an iciness far down inside of him.

He stepped across the threshold, and just as suddenly, leaped back.

He heard the stumble of the Oligarch's fleeing feet, heard the office door open and slam.

Herb waited, listening—a feint?

No. There was no sound.

Again he stepped into the mess hall. It was empty.

"Herb!" Norma called. "Herb! Are you all right?" She was running down the corridor toward him.

"Get back!" Herb called, but" she came on, and then she was beside him.

"He's in the office. I'm going after him. You stay here."

"No. Leave him there. Prop the door. Keep him in. Take the ship..."

"I'm going in after him," Herb said. "I've got to. It's more than him, more than killing or getting killed. I've got to."

"It's so senseless," she said. "If we could get control of the ship"

He shook his head. "You stay here!"

He walked across the mess hall. He stepped out into the narrow corridor.

"Get away!" the Oligarch cried frantically. His voice was no longer vigorous, and it sounded pathetic and child-like through the door.

Herb, going toward it, said, "I'm coming in!" He tried the door. Locked.

He fired twice at the lock. He stepped back and kicked. The door swung inward.

The Oligarch did not fire. Herb, pressed against the wall, could not see into the room.

"I'm coming in, damn you!"

"Don't," the Oligarch cried weakly. "Please, don't. Don't *now!*"

Herb heard a gun clatter to the floor.

"Don't," the Oligarch moaned. "I've thrown it away. I'm helpless."

Herb balanced on the balls of his feet. Then, taking a deep breath, he stepped into the doorway, his body framed beautifully between the two jambs. He held his gun at ready and then lowered it.

The Oligarch was slumped over his desk.

Herb heard Norma come up behind him…

"He's dying," she said.

Reaction set in, and Herb's knees almost collapsed. His body was trembling and drenched with perspiration.

The Oligarch coughed.

THE Oligarch said something in his own language.

"What?" Herb asked.

"Make him tell us. How we can keep them from setting off the explosion," Norma said.

The Oligarch wanted to talk, and he made a motion—a feeble one—to silence them both. The girl's pathetic conviction that the explosion could be prevented infuriated the Oligarch. There was nothing she could do. The cleverness with which he had executed his mission defied time and eternity.

"It won't be set off in the big ship," the Oligarch said. "I had intended to leave you at the site, Herb, to trigger it personally." He spoke English and was disappointed to see that his vision began to mist. He would have liked to watch the girl's face. "But your later dream forms made me deny you martyrdom. I think I might have done it any way, if you hadn't left. You have the idealism. You were the one I had counted on. And after you, of course, there was only Bud."

Norma choked weakly and her knees half gave way. The sound was satisfying to the Oligarch.

"I told Bud the explosion was planted," the Oligarch said. "Then I…I told him…" He coughed again. "I told him that I had mailed his brother's head along with his confession to…to…Then I gave him a telephone number. He phones long distance, gives the number. At the bombsite, the receiver...lifts automatically... He says, 'Frank Council'... his brother's name... the key... The trigger falls." The Oligarch's hands scrabbled on the desk. "Don't you think he'll do it, in the knowledge of his own personal destruction? ...Oh, he will, yes...And this is the final..." Blood dribbled from the Oligarch's mouth. "I didn't mail his brother's head... I lied to him. Don't you see what a beautiful...what a satisfying lie that was?" He laughed, coughed again, and slumped forward. And the chase ended.

And Herb, looking at death, grabbed Norma by the arm and ran toward the control room.

...And back on Earth, Bud Council sat sick and trembling, his eyes fastened on the telephone beside him...

CHAPTER FOURTEEN

HERB thought first of the bombsite. The chill desert night would be fresh upon it. Overhead, the pale moon would ride toward the terrible apocalypse of dawn—if Bud waited until then to make his phone call.

In a few hours (he thought) he could bring the spider ship down upon the desert. The long dark night beyond would give him time

He visualized the scene as he remembered it from TV— the single sentry shack where an Army guard protected the alien handiwork.

"I'll talk to them when we land. I'll explain about Bud. They'll find him and keep him away from the telephone. They'll tell long distance operators not to place any calls until they can find him. All I need is a few hours to convince someone that Bud, that Bud..."

Norma was in his arms, shaking hysterically. "He...he did that to *Frank*. Bud did that!"

"We've got to hurry," Herb said.

She shivered against him. Gently he disengaged himself.

"In an hour, now…" he said.

His hand rested on the forward firing stud

Rested and withdrew.

"What's wrong?" Norma asked.

"The fuel. I haven't got enough left to brake the ship, to turn it, and then land against Earth gravity."

"No," Norma said. "No! That can't be right!"

Herb re-sorted the information available from the dials, seeking a method to defy the dictates of inertia. Once more he weighed the remaining fuel against that necessary to brake and turn the ship, and still there was none left over to counteract Earth's gravity and the long planetfall. He projected trajectories.

"Maybe I can throw the ship in a long orbit," he said. "If I can kill the speed against the atmosphere…"

"Can you do it?"

Herb's hands eased fuel into the forward port jet and sparked it. "I'm tilting for the orbit."

The gauge dropped alarmingly, and as momentum changed, the center of gravity shifted. The ship nosed up and fell sideways and slipped away to the right.

Norma held her breath, afraid to interrupt even with encouragement.

"It's an ellipse," Herb said. "It's a long fall now, but I'm afraid to make it shorter." He set the controls.

"How long will it take?" Norma asked.

"I'll have to make half a dozen bounces. The first one won't be for nearly six hours… We won't be able to land until sunup."

Norma bit her lip. "But that's"

"We won't have much time. We'll have to try to get to Bud ourselves."

When the time came, he turned to her. "I've got to hit the

atmosphere now. We'll have to strap down."

Numb with tension, she sat in one of the shock-chairs and buckled herself in. Then, in his chair before the panel, Herb adjusted the buckles and waited the few remaining minutes. "This will be the worst," he said.

The ship hit the upper gases—gases, made by speed into an iron curtain; and as the air clawed at the strange shape of the ship, and as the interior cooling system whined into overdrive, he fought against wild, erratic movements, firing precious fuel to brake and stabilize... And then they were free, and shooting away along a shortened and slower ellipse.

Finally they were well into the atmosphere, but they were very high, too high to be more than a speck, so high that the sound spread too thinly to be heard on the surface.

"I'll set down outside Washington," Herb said. "Somewhere outside, where we can get away from the ship before they get there to start asking questions."

He released his blast, and the ship turned nose up. Gravity became heavier. The ship plummeted down.

"Here's the last of the jets," Herb hissed, and he eased them in, slowing the fall, slowing it...

Down the ship came.

The Earth expanded and a fantastically fast painter seemed to be sketching in the details of the landscape.

The sun was cut off by the horizon. A few lights sparkled in slowly waking Washington.

The jets sputtered, and the ship slipped; the jets caught, sputtered, and died.

Herb slammed on the low lift controls. The aerodynamically designed platform-like wings spun and hissed against the air. For a long moment, Herb was afraid they would not brake the fall, but the lifts caught, and the ship jerked, and Herb felt the buoyancy through the ship and through his mind and through his body.

CHAPTER FIFTEEN

LESS than five minutes later, they were stationary. The slowing lifts purred and the landing ladder hissed down.

Herb and Norma were upon it.

"About—five hundred yards," Herb said. "Over that way…the highway…let's go!"

Running at his side, Norma prayed desperately for a car to come soon.

They sprinted the last short distance because of growing headlights from the south. The car was coming fast, and Herb jumped into the roadway, waving his hands.

The car came on, sounding its horn hysterically. Herb waved and brakes squealed, and the car, at almost the last instant, veered away from him. The wind of its passing rustled his hair, and the horn still bleating, it slowly dwindled as the red taillights faded into the darkness.

They waited. Five minutes passed.

"One's got to come!"

Early fire hung over the ocean from the as yet invisible sun. Dew lay on the plowed field behind them. The air was chill.

It seemed that the sun was symbolic fire slowly creeping and coloring the sky, slowly spreading over the world.

"What time is it?" Herb asked.

"Here's a car! Here's a car!"

Both of them leaped into the highway, waving and jumping up and down.

A long way away, the driver set his brakes, and the car coasted slowly, passed them, and finally stopped.

They ran to it. Herb jerked open the door. "You've got to take us to Washington!" Herb said.

Norma, arriving behind him, said, "It's a matter of life and death!"

"Then, get in," the man said.

Overhead a jet thundered in to locate the spider ship.

They were in the car.

"You've got to drive us to an apartment in Georgetown," Norma said.

"Lady, I've been driving all night."

"You've got to!" The urgency in her voice was nearly that of hysteria.

The driver started the car. "If it's that urgent…"

"It is," Herb said.

"Hurry, please hurry. Don't ask us to explain. Just hurry."

The driver stepped down on the gas. The car leaped ahead.

CHAPTER SIXTEEN

THE new buildings pressed against the new sidewalks. The streets were empty except for their car and a turret-like Mobile Sweeper whose gutter broom whispered against the curb. A light here and there in a window heralded the end of sleep. A lone car crossed at an intersection ahead, moving slowly as if fatigued by a nightlong vigil.

The sun seemed reluctant to plunge the world into daylight; it balanced on the horizon in indecision. The moon was high and tiny and rode the growing blueness with a ghostlike pallor.

Herb, leaning forward tensely, thought: *Suppose Bud isn't there? Suppose he's somewhere else?*

"Turn left up here," Norma said. "It's only a few blocks."

The buildings anchored time to the Earth, encapsulating the past in steel and concrete. Morning shadows walked before the onrushing future.

"Here!" Norma cried.

The car braked to a stop.

The driver watched them run wildly, and an uneasiness settled upon him. He glanced to the east. The morning was chill. The excitement their urgency had generated had not vanished with their departure. What the devil? He thought. Whadda you suppose it's all about?

INSIDE, Norma said, "Third floor. He's got guards. I'll take the elevator. You take the stairs. I'll try to get the guards attention."

Herb nodded. He bolted for the stairway. The carpet blanketed his footfalls. He heard the elevator doors click and the cage rattle upward.

First landing.

Silence.

Second landing.

His heart was Loud. His feet became delicate, and he balanced on his toes, moving toward the final encounter.

There.

Norma had the guard. There was only one. She was speaking intently. The guard faced away from Herb.

Herb was in the corridor. He moved like a sigh, and the space between him and the guard shortened.

The guard turned, and Herb sprang. He crashed into the guard before the police automatic was clear of the shiny holster. The impact of his body spun the gun away.

They were down, wrestling viciously. Herb felt his head ring. He stifled a cry. Pain nestled in his groin. He struck out.

The guard smashed an elbow into Herb's nose. He got up and kicked Herb in the face, and Herb jerked his leg savagely. Unbalanced, he went down. Herb was upon him. Breath hissed out, and Herb struck viciously with his gun butt.

Panting, he stood.

"It's locked," he said, testing the door. Norma had recovered the guard's automatic. White-faced she stood.

Bloody nosed, bleeding, Herb threw himself into the panel. There was a great, kettledrum boom and the panel held. Again he slammed into it. It splintered away. He fought through the shards of maple, and was halfway into the room when Bud, looking up from the telephone, fired. Herb sighed and fell to the left and his gun slipped from his hand.

CHAPTER SEVENTEEN

BUD, drained of color, cried, "Hurry that call, operator!"

His gun was on the door when Norma filled it. "Stop, Bud!"

His eyes dulled. Conflicting emotions ran jagged edges over his face. One hand held the phone, the other the gun. Norma was afraid to fire for fear she would miss. "I'll kill you if you try to stop me!" he screamed. He could not place the person in the doorway. And then he realized that it was the Devil cleverly disguised as his sister.

Norma stepped into the room, drawing closer. Her hand trembled violently. Bud was perspiring.

"Bud," she said. Her voice choked. "He didn't mail...he didn't mail the...package...the...the package." Tears ran down her cheeks.

"Get away! *Get away!*"

"He didn't mail it! No one need know...you're safe...your secret... Put down the phone, Bud. Please, now. *Put down the Phone!*"

Very clever nonsense, Bud thought, not believing it for a moment. What package? There was no... He must shoot this creature, now, before she...

The operator said in his ear: "Here is your number, sir."

"Put me on!"

The Devil was nearer. It was too late, he thought. Norma thought: Now, now, *now*.

Bud's hand whitened at the knuckles. His throat was dry. He was ready to scream the Name. He did not see Herb's hand close on the weapon, nor see the muzzle elevate.

"Bud, Bud, Bud, please, please, Bud!" Norma said. The trigger of her gun would not respond.

"Get away," Bud said. He opened his mouth. "Frank C—"

And Herb fired until the weapon was empty.

There was echoing silence, and then Bud fell.

Norma was upon the telephone, ripping it free from the wall.

Herb staggered erect. Blood covered his suit. It hurt to move. A broken collarbone, he thought. Too high for the lungs.

He found Norma weeping hysterically in his arm. The other arm hung limp, and he winced with pain as he drew her tight.

He choked and bent to her ear and said, "Yes, yes," and suddenly he bent to kiss her tear stained lips, and he wanted to brush away the hair from her face, but that arm refused to move. She trembled against him, and he whispered, "Yes."

The sunlight came in the broad windows and slanted across Bud's face, boyish and petulant still in death; the sun, moving toward noon, bathed the whole awakening world with light, and far beyond it, in space but not in time, lay other stars.

And Herb felt free. For the first time in his life. Here, on Earth...

It was a wonderful feeling.

THE END

If you've enjoyed this book, you will not want to miss these terrific titles…

ARMCHAIR SCI-FI & HORROR DOUBLE NOVELS, $12.95 each

D-11 **PERIL OF THE STARMEN** by Kris Neville
THE FORGOTTEN PLANET by Murray Leinster

D-12 **THE STAR LORD** by Boyd Ellanby
CAPTIVES OF THE FLAME by Samuel R. Delany

D-13 **MEN OF THE MORNING STAR** by Edmond Hamilton
PLANET FOR PLUNDER by Hal Clement and Sam Merwin, Jr.

D-14 **ICE CITY OF THE GORGON** by Chester S. Geier and Richard Shaver
WHEN THE WORLD TOTTERED by Lester del Rey

D-15 **WORLDS WITHOUT END** by Clifford D. Simak
THE LAVENDER VINE OF DEATH by Don Wilcox

D-16 **SHADOW ON THE MOON** by Joe Gibson
ARMAGEDDON EARTH by Geoff St. Reynard

D-17 **THE GIRL WHO LOVED DEATH** by Paul W. Fairman
SLAVE PLANET by Laurence M. Janifer

D-18 **SECOND CHANCE** by J. F. Bone
MISSION TO A DISTANT STAR by Frank Belknap Long

D-19 **THE SYNDIC** by C. M. Kornbluth
FLIGHT TO FOREVER by Poul Anderson

D-20 **SOMEWHERE I'LL FIND YOU** by Milton Lesser
THE TIME ARMADA by Fox B. Holden

ARMCHAIR SCIENCE FICTION CLASSICS, $12.95 each

C-4 **CORPUS EARTHLING**
by Louis Charbonneau

C-5 **THE TIME DISSOLVER**
by Jerry Sohl

C-6 **WEST OF THE SUN**
by Edgar Pangborn

ARMCHAIR SCI-FI & HORROR GEMS SERIES, $12.95 each

G-1 **SCIENCE FICTION GEMS, Vol. One**
Isaac Asimov and others

G-2 **HORROR GEMS, Vol. One**
Carl Jacobi and others

NATURE'S MISLEAD MADHOUSE!

Beneath dense gray clouds through which no sun shone lay a forgotten planet. It was a nightmare world of grotesque and terrifying animal-plant life. Gigantic beetles, spiders, bugs and ants filled the putrid, musty earth—ready to kill and devour anything in sight. There were men amidst this horror— men who cringed and ran from the ravening monsters and huddled in the mushroom forests at night.

Burl was one of these creatures. But one day inspiration hit Burl. He would find a weapon—he would fight back.

And with this idea the first step was taken in man's most desperate flight for freedom in this most horrible of all worlds. But it was only a first step.

ABOUT THE CHARACTERS IN THIS BOOK:

This is something of an oddity among fiction stories, because some of its characters may be met in person if you wish. Down at the nearest weed-patch or thicket you are quite likely to see a large and unusually perfect spider-web with a zig-zag silk ribbon woven into its center. Its engineer is the yellow-banded garden spider (*Epeira Fasciata*) whose abdomen may be as big as your thumb. I do not name it to impress you, but to suggest a sort of science-fiction experience.

Take a bit of straw and disturb the web. Don't break the cables. Simply tap them a bit. The spider will know by the feel of things that you aren't prey and that it can't eat you. So it will set out frightening you away. It will run nimbly to the center of the web and shake itself violently. The whole web will vibrate, so that presently the spider may be swinging through an arc inches in length, and blurred by the speed of its swing. You are supposed to be scared. When you are alarmed enough, the spider will stop.

That spider, very much magnified, is in this book with crickets and grasshoppers and divers beetles you may not know personally. But this is not an insect book, but science-fiction. If the habits of the creatures in it are authentic, it is because they are much more dramatic and interesting than things one can invent.

THE
FORGOTTEN
PLANET

By
MURRAY LEINSTER

ARMCHAIR FICTION
PO Box 4369, Medford, Oregon 97504

To Joan Patricia Jenkins

For more information about Armchair Books and products, visit our website at...

www.armchairfiction.com

Or email us at...

armchairfiction@yahoo.com

PROLOGUE

The Survey-Ship *Tethys* made the first landing on the planet, which had no name. It was an admirable planet in many ways. It had an ample atmosphere and many seas, which the nearby sun warmed so lavishly that a perpetual cloud-bank hid them and most of the solid ground from view. It had mountains and continents and islands and high plateaus. It had day and night and wind and rain, and its mean temperature was within the range to which human beings could readily accommodate. It was rather on the tropic side, but not unpleasant.

But there was no life on it.

No animals roamed its continents. No vegetation grew from its rocks. Not even bacteria struggled with its stones to turn them into soil. So there was no soil. Rock and stones and gravel and even sand—yes. But no soil in which any vegetation could grow. No living thing, however small, swam in its oceans, so there was not even mud on its ocean-bottoms. It was one of that disappointing vast majority of worlds which turned up when the Galaxy was first explored. People couldn't live on it because nothing had lived there before.

Its water was fresh and its oceans were harmless. Its air was germ-free and breathable. But it was of no use whatever for men. The only possible purpose it could serve would have been as a biological laboratory for experiments involving things growing in a germ-free environment. But there were too many planets like that already. When men first traveled to the stars they made the journey because it was starkly necessary to find new worlds for men to live on. Earth was over-crowded—terribly so. So men looked for new worlds to move to. They found plenty of new worlds, but presently they were searching desperately for new worlds where life had preceded them. It didn't matter whether the life was meek and harmless, or ferocious and deadly. If life of any sort were present, human beings could move in. But highly organized beings like men could not live where there was no other life.

So the Survey-Ship *Tethys* made sure that the world had no life upon it. Then it made routine measurements of the gravitational

The MAD PLANET
By Murray Leinster
Author of "The Runaway Skyscraper."

Burl screamed again, and thrust out his arms to ward off the impact of the tarantula's leap. The spear-point shot out and the tarantula fell upon it. Nearly a quarter of the spear entered the body of the ferocious thing.

constant and the magnetic field and the temperature gradient; it took samples of the air and water. But that was all. The rocks were familiar enough. No novelties there! But the planet was simply useless. The survey-ship put its findings on a punched card, six inches by eight, and went hastily on in search of something better. The ship did not even open one of its ports while on the planet. There were no consequences of the *Tethys'* visit except that card. None whatever.

No other ship came near the planet for eight hundred years.

Nearly a millenium later, however, the Seed-Ship *Orana* arrived. By that time humanity had spread very widely and very far. There were colonies not less than a quarter of the way to the Galaxy's rim, and Earth was no longer over-crowded. There was still emigration, but it was now a trickle instead of the swarming flood of centuries before. Some of the first-colonized worlds had emigrants, now. Mankind did not want to crowd itself together again! Men now considered that there was no excuse for such monstrous slums as overcrowding produced.

Now, too, the star-ships were faster. A hundred light-years was a short journey. A thousand was not impractical. Explorers had gone many times farther, and reported worlds still waiting for mankind on beyond. But still the great majority of discovered planets did not contain life. Whole solar systems floated in space with no single living cell on any of their members.

So the Seed-Ships came into being. Theirs was not a glamorous service. They merely methodically contaminated the sterile worlds with life. The Seed-Ship *Orana* landed on this planet—which still had no name. It carefully infected it. It circled endlessly above the clouds, dribbling out a fine dust,—the spores of every conceivable microörganism which could break down rock to powder, and turn that dust to soil. It was also a seeding of moulds and fungi and lichens, and everything which could turn powdery primitive soil into stuff on which higher forms of life could grow. The *Orana* polluted the seas with plankton. Then it, too, went away.

More centuries passed. Human ships again improved. A thousand light-years became a short journey. Explorers reached the Galaxy's very edge, and looked estimatingly across the emptiness toward other island universes. There were colonies in the Milky Way. There were freight-lines between star-clusters, and the commercial center of human affairs shifted some hundreds of parsecs toward the Rim. There were many worlds where the schools painstakingly taught the children what Earth was, and where, and that all other worlds had been populated from it. And the schools repeated, too, the one lesson that humankind seemed genuinely to have learned. That the secret of peace is freedom, and the secret of freedom is to be able to move away from people with whom you do not agree. There were no crowded worlds any more. But human beings love children, and they have them. And children grow up and need room. So more worlds had to be looked out for. They weren't urgently needed yet, but they would be.

Therefore, nearly a thousand years after the *Orana*, the Ecology-Ship *Ludred* swam to the planet from space and landed on it. It was a gigantic ship of highly improbable purpose. First of all, it checked on the consequences of the *Orana's* visit.

They were highly satisfactory, from a technical point of view. Now there was soil which swarmed with minute living things. There were fungi which throve monstrously. The seas stank of minuscule life-forms. There were even some novelties, developed by the strictly local conditions. There were, for example, paramoecia as big as grapes, and yeasts had increased in size until they bore flowers visible to the naked eye. The life on the planet was not aboriginal, though. All of it was descended and adapted and modified from the microörganisms planted by the seed-ship whose hulk was long since rust, and whose crew were merely names in genealogies—if that.

The *Ludred* stayed on the planet a considerably longer time than either of the ships that had visited it before. It dropped the seeds of plants. It broadcast innumerable varieties of things which should take root and grow. In some places it deliberately seeded the stinking soil. It put marine plants in the oceans. It put alpine plants on the high ground. And when all its stable varieties were set out it added plants which were genetically unstable. For generations to come they would throw sports, some of which should be especially suited to this planetary environment.

Before it left, the *Ludred* dumped finny fish into the seas. At first they would live on the plankton which made the oceans almost broth. There were many varieties of fish. Some would multiply swiftly while small; others would grow and feed on the smaller varieties. And as a last activity, the *Ludred* set up refrigeration-units loaded with insect-eggs. Some would release their contents as soon as plants had grown enough to furnish them with food. Others would allow their contents to hatch only after certain other varieties had multiplied—to be their food-supply.

When the Ecology-Ship left, it had done a very painstaking job. It had treated the planet to a sort of Russell's Mixture of life-forms. The real Russell's Mixture is that blend of the simple elements in the proportions found in suns. This was a blend of life-forms in which some should survive by consuming the now-habituated flora, others by preying on the former. The planet was stocked, in effect, with everything that it could be hoped would live there.

But only certain things could have that hope. Nothing which needed parental care had any chance of survival. The creatures seeded at this time had to be those which could care for themselves from the instant they burst their eggs. So there were no birds or mammals. Trees and plants of many kinds, fish and crustaceans and tadpoles, and all kinds of insects could be planted. But nothing else.

The *Ludred* swam away through emptiness.

There should have been another planting centuries later. There should have been a ship from the Zoölogical Branch of the Ecological Service. It should have landed birds and beasts and reptiles. It should have added pelagic mammals to the seas. There should have been herbivorous animals to live on the grasses and plants which would have thriven, and carnivorous animals to live on them in turn. There should have been careful stocking of the planet with animal life, and repeated visits at intervals of a century or so to make sure that a true ecological balance had been established. And then when the balance was fixed men would come and destroy it for their own benefit.

But there was an accident.

Ships had improved again. Even small private space-craft now journeyed tens of light-years on holiday journeys. Personal cruisers traveled hundreds. Liners ran matter-of-factly on ship-lines tens of thousands of light-years long. An exploring-ship was on its way to a second island universe. (It did not come back.) The inhabited planets were all members of a tenuous organization which limited itself to affairs of space, without attempting to interfere in surface matters. That tenuous organization moved the Ecological Preparation Service files to Algol IV as a matter of convenience. In the moving, a card-file was upset. The cards it contained were picked up and replaced, but one was missed. It was not picked up. It was left behind.

So the planet which had no name was forgotten. No other ship came to prepare it for ultimate human occupancy. It circled its sun, unheeded and unthought-of. Cloud-banks covered it from pole to pole. There were hazy markings in some places, where high plateaus penetrated its clouds. But that was all. From space the planet was essentially featureless. Seen from afar it was merely a round white ball—white from its cloud-banks—and nothing else.

But on its surface, on its lowlands, it was pure nightmare. But this fact did not matter for a very long time.

Ultimately, it mattered a great deal—to the crew of the space-liner *Icarus*. The *Icarus* was a splendid ship of its time. It bore passengers headed for one of the Galaxy's spiral arms, and it cut across the normal lanes and headed through charted but unvisited parts of the Galaxy toward its destination. And it had one of the very, very, very few accidents known to happen to space-craft licensed for travel off the normal space-lanes. It suffered shipwreck in space, and its passengers and crew were forced to take to the life-craft.

The lifeboats' range was limited. They landed on the planet that the *Tethys* had first examined, that the *Orana* and the *Ludred* had seeded, and of which there was no longer any record in the card-files of the Ecological Service. Their fuel was exhausted. They could not leave. They could not signal for help. They had to stay there. And the planet was a place of nightmares.

After a time the few people—some few thousands—who knew that there was a space-liner named *Icarus*, gave it up for lost. They forgot about it. Everybody forgot. Even the passengers and crew of the ship forgot it. Not immediately, of course. For the first few generations their descendants cherished hopes of rescue. But the planet which had no name—the forgotten planet—did not encourage the cherishing of hope.

After forty-odd generations, nobody remembered the *Icarus* anywhere. The wreckage of the lifeboats was long since hidden under the seething, furiously striving fungi of the soil. The human beings had forgotten not only their ancestors' ship, but very nearly everything their ancestors had brought to this world: the use of metals, the existence of fire, and even the fact that there was such a thing as sunshine. They lived in the lowlands, deep under the cloud-bank, amid surroundings which were riotous, swarming, frenzied horror. They had become savages.

They were less than savages, because they had forgotten their destiny as men.

CHAPTER ONE
The Mad Planet

In all his lifetime of perhaps twenty years, it had never occurred to Burl to wonder what his grandfather had thought about his surroundings. The grandfather had come to an untimely end in a fashion which Burl remembered as a succession of screams coming more and more faintly to his ears, while he was being carried away at the topmost speed of which his mother was capable.

Burl had rarely or never thought of his grandfather since. Surely he had never wondered what his great-grandfather had thought, and most surely of all he never speculated upon what his many-times-removed great-grandfather had thought when his lifeboat landed from the *Icarus*. Burl had never heard of the *Icarus*. He had done very little thinking of any sort. When he did think, it was mostly agonized effort to contrive a way to escape some immediate and paralyzing danger. When horror did not press upon him, it was better not to think, because there wasn't much but horror to think about.

At the moment, he was treading cautiously over a brownish carpet of fungus, creeping furtively toward the stream which he knew only by the generic name of "water." It was the only water he knew. Towering far above his head, three man-heights high, great toadstools hid the gray sky from his sight. Clinging to the yard-thick stalks of the toadstools were still other fungi, parasites upon the growths that once had been parasites themselves.

Burl appeared a fairly representative specimen of the descendants of the long-forgotten *Icarus* crew. He wore a single garment twisted about his middle, made from the wing-fabric of a great moth which the members of his tribe had slain as it emerged from its cocoon. His skin was fair without a trace of sunburn. In all his lifetime he had never seen the sun, though he surely had seen the sky often enough. It was rarely hidden from him save by giant fungi, like those about him now, and sometimes by the gigantic cabbages which were nearly the only green growths he knew. To him normal landscape contained only fantastic pallid mosses, and misshapen fungus growths, and colossal moulds and yeasts.

He moved onward. Despite his caution, his shoulder once touched a cream-colored toadstool stalk, giving the whole fungus a tiny shock. Instantly a fine and impalpable powder fell upon him from the umbrella like top above. It was the season when the toadstools sent out their spores. He paused to brush them from his head and shoulders. They were, of course, deadly poison.

Burl knew such matters with an immediate and specific and detailed certainty. He knew practically nothing else. He was ignorant of the use of fire, of metals, and even of the uses of stone and wood. His language was a scanty group of a few hundred labial sounds, conveying no abstractions and few concrete ideas. He knew nothing of wood, because there was no wood in the territory furtively inhabited by his tribe. This was the lowlands. Trees did not thrive here. Not even grasses and tree-ferns could compete with mushrooms and toadstools and their kin. Here was a soil of rusts and yeasts. Here were toadstool forests and fungus jungles. They grew with feverish intensity beneath a cloud-hidden sky, while above them fluttered butterflies no less enlarged than they, moths as much magnified, and other creatures which could thrive on their corruption.

The only creatures on the planet which crawled or ran or flew—save only Burl's fugitive kind—were insects. They had been here before men came, and they had adapted to the planet's extraordinary ways. With a world made ready before their first progenitors arrived, insects had thriven incredibly. With unlimited food-supplies, they had grown large. With increased size had come increased opportunity for survival, and enlargement became hereditary. Other than fungoid growths, the solitary vegetables were the sports of unstable varieties of the plants left behind by the *Ludred.* There were enormous cabbages, with leaves the size of ship-sails, on which stolid grubs and caterpillars ate themselves to maturity, and then swung below in strong cocoons to sleep the sleep of metamorphosis. The tiniest butterflies of Earth had increased their size here until their wings spread feet across, and some—like the emperor moths—stretched out purple wings which were yards in span. Burl himself would have been dwarfed beneath a great moth's wing.

But he wore a gaudy fabric made of one. The moths and giant butterflies were harmless to men. Burl's fellow tribesmen sometimes came upon a cocoon when it was just about to open, and if they dared they waited timorously beside it until the creature inside broke through its sleeping-shell and came out into the light.

Then, before it gathered energy from the air and before its wings swelled to strength and firmness, the tribesmen fell upon it. They tore the delicate wings from its body and the still-flaccid limbs from their places. And when it lay helpless before them they fled away to feast on its juicy meat-filled limbs.

They dared not linger, of course. They left their prey helpless—staring strangely at the world about it through its many-faceted eyes—before the scavengers came to contest its ownership. If nothing more deadly appeared, surely the ants would come. Some of them were only inches long, but others were the size of fox-terriers. All of them had to be avoided by men. They would carry the moth-carcass away to their underground cities, triumphantly, in shreds and morsels.

But most of the insect world was neither so helpless nor so unthreatening. Burl knew of wasps almost the length of his own body, with stings that were instantly fatal. To every species of wasp, however, some other insect is predestined prey. Wasps need not be dreaded too much. And bees were similarly aloof. They were hard put to it for existence, those bees. Since few flowers bloomed, they were reduced to expedients that once were considered signs of degeneracy in their race: bubbling yeasts and fouler things, or occasionally the nectarless blooms of the rank giant cabbages. Burl knew the bees. They droned overhead, nearly as large as he was, their bulging eyes gazing at him and everything else in abstracted preoccupation.

There were crickets, and beetles, and spiders... Burl knew spiders! His grandfather had been the prey of a hunting tarantula which had leaped with incredible ferocity from its tunnel in the ground. A vertical pit, a yard in diameter, went down for twenty feet. At the bottom of the lair the monster waited for the tiny sounds that would warn him of prey approaching his hiding-place.

Burl's grandfather had been careless. The terrible shrieks he uttered as he was seized still lingered vaguely in Burl's mind. And he had seen, too, the webs of another species of spider—inch-thick cables of dirty silk—and watched from a safe distance as the misshapen monster sucked the juices from a three-foot cricket its trap had caught. He remembered the stripes of yellow and black and silver that crossed upon its abdomen. He had been fascinated and horrified by the blind struggling of the cricket, tangled in hopeless coils of gummy cord, before the spider began its feast.

Burl knew these dangers. They were part of his life. It was this knowledge that made life possible. He knew the ways to evade these dangers. But if he yielded to carelessness for one moment, or if he relaxed his caution for one instant, he would be one with his ancestors. They were the long-forgotten meals of inhuman monsters.

Now, to be sure, Burl moved upon an errand that probably no other of his tribe would have imagined. The day before, he had crouched behind a shapeless mound of inter-tangled growths and watched a duel between two huge horned beetles. Their bodies were feet long. Their carapaces were waist-high to Burl when they crawled. Their mandibles, gaping laterally, clicked and clashed upon each other's impenetrable armor. Their legs crashed like so many cymbals as they struck against each other. They fought over some particularly attractive bit of carrion.

Burl had watched with wide eyes until a gaping hole appeared in the armor of the smaller one. It uttered a grating outcry—or seemed to. The noise was actually the tearing of its shell between the mandibles of the victor.

The wounded creature struggled more and more feebly. When it ceased to offer battle, the conqueror placidly began to dine before its prey had ceased to live. But this was the custom of creatures on this planet.

Burl watched, timorous but hopeful. When the meal was finished, he darted in quickly as the diner lumbered away. He was almost too late, even then. An ant—the forerunner of many—already inspected the fragments with excitedly vibrating antennae.

Burl needed to move quickly and he did. Ants were stupid and short-sighted insects; few of them were hunters. Save when offered battle, most of them were scavengers only. They hunted the scenes of nightmare for the dead and dying only, but fought viciously if their prey were questioned. And always there were others on the way.

Some were arriving now. Hearing the tiny clickings of their approach, Burl was hasty. Over-hasty. He seized a loosened fragment and fled. It was merely the horn, the snout of the dead and eaten creature. But it was loose and easily carried. He ran.

Later he inspected his find with disappointment. There was little meat clinging to it. It was merely the horn of a Minotaur beetle, shaped like the horn of a rhinoceros. Plucking out the shreds left by its murderer, he pricked his hand. Pettishly, he flung it aside. The time of darkness was near, so he crept to the hiding place of his tribe to huddle with them until light came again.

There were only twenty of them; four or five men and six or seven women. The rest were girls or children. Burl had been wondering at the strange feelings that came over him when he looked at one of the girls. She was younger than Burl—perhaps eighteen—and fleeter of foot. They talked together sometimes and, once or twice, Burl shared an especially succulent find of foodstuffs with her.

He could share nothing with her now. She stared at him in the deepening night when he crept to the labyrinthine hiding place the tribe now used in a mushroom forest. He considered that she looked hungry and hoped that he would have food to share. And he was bitterly ashamed that he could offer nothing. He held himself a little apart from the rest, because of his shame. Since he too was hungry, it was some time before he slept. Then he dreamed.

Next morning he found the horn where he had thrown it disgustedly the day before. It was sticking in the flabby trunk of a toadstool. He pulled it out. In his dream he had used it...

Presently he tried to use it. Sometimes—not often—the men of the tribe used the saw-toothed edge of a cricket-leg, or the leg of a grasshopper, to sever tough portions of an edible mushroom. The horn had no cutting edge, but Burl had used it in his dream. He was not quite capable of distinguishing clearly between reality and dreams; so he tried to duplicate what happened in the dream. Remembering that it had stuck into the mushroom-stalk, he thrust it. It stabbed. He remembered distinctly how the larger beetle had used its horn as a weapon. It had stabbed, too.

He considered absorbedly. He could not imagine himself fighting one of the dangerous insects, of course. Men did not fight, on the forgotten planet. They ran away. They hid. But somehow Burl formed a fantastic picture of himself stabbing food with this horn, as he had stabbed a mushroom. It was longer than his arm and though naturally clumsy in his hand, it would have been a deadly weapon in the grip of a man prepared to do battle.

Battle did not occur to Burl. But the idea of stabbing food with it was clear. There could be food that would not fight back. Presently he had an inspiration. His face brightened. He began to make his way toward the tiny river that ran across the plain in which the tribe of humans lived by foraging in competition with the ants. Yellow-bellied newts—big enough to be lusted for—swam in its waters. The swimming larvae of a thousand kinds of creatures floated on the sluggish surface or crawled over the bottom.

There were deadly things there, too. Giant crayfish snapped their claws at the unwary. One of them could sever Burl's arm with ease. Mosquitoes sometimes hummed high above the river. Mosquitoes had a four-inch wing-spread, now, though they were dying out for lack of plant-juices on which the males of their species fed. But they were formidable. Burl had learned to crush them between fragments of fungus.

He crept slowly through the forest of toadstools. What should have been grass underfoot was brownish rust. Orange and red and purple moulds clustered about the bases of the creamy mushroom-trunks. Once, Burl paused to run his weapon through a fleshy column and reassure himself that what he planned was possible.

He made his way furtively through the bulbous growths. Once he heard clickings and froze to stillness. Four or five ants, minims only eight inches long, were returning by an habitual pathway to their city. They moved sturdily along, heavily laden, over the route marked by the scent of formic acid left by their fellow-townsmen. Burl waited until they had passed, then went on.

He came to the bank of the river. It flowed slowly, green scum covering a great deal of its surface in the backwaters, occasionally broken by a slowly enlarging bubble released from decomposing matter on the bottom. In the center of the stream the current ran a little more swiftly and the water itself seemed clear. Over it ran many water-spiders. They had not shared in the general increase of size in the insect world. Depending as they did on the surface tension of the water for support, to have grown larger and heavier would have destroyed them.

Burl surveyed the scene. His search was four parts for danger and only one part for a way to test his brilliant notion, but that was natural. Where he stood, the green scum covered the stream for many yards. Down-river a little, though, the current came closer to the bank. Here he could not see whatever swam or crawled or wriggled underwater; there he might.

There was an outcropping rock forming a support for crawling stuff, which in turn supported shelf-fungi making wide steps almost down to the water's edge. Burl was making his way cautiously toward them when he saw one of the edible mushrooms which formed so large a part of his diet. He paused to break off a flabby white piece large enough to feed him for many days. It was the custom of his people, when they found a store of food, to hide with it and not venture out again to danger until it was all eaten. Burl was tempted to do just that with his booty. He could give Saya of this food and they would eat together. They might hide together until it was all consumed.

But there was a swirling in the water under the descending platforms of shelf-fungi. A very remarkable sensation came to Burl. He may have been the only man in many generations to be aware of the high ambition to stab something to eat. He may have been a throw-back to ancestors who had known bravery, which had no survival-value here. But Burl had imagined carrying Saya food which he had stabbed with the spear of a Minotaur beetle. It was an extraordinary idea.

It was new, too. Not too long ago, when he was younger, Burl would have thought of the tribe instead. He'd have thought of old Jon, bald-headed and wheezing and timorous, and how that patriarch would pat his arm exuberantly when handed food; or old Tama, wrinkled and querulous, whose look of settled dissatisfaction would vanish at sight of a tidbit; of Dik and Tet, the tribe-members next younger, who would squabble zestfully over the fragments allotted them.

But now he imagined Saya looking astonished and glad when he grandly handed her more food than she could possibly eat. She would admire him enormously!

Of course he did not imagine himself fighting to get food for Saya. He meant only to stab something edible in the water. Things in the water did not fight things on land. Since he would not be in the water, he would not be in a fight. It was a completely delectable idea, which no man within memory had ever entertained before. If Burl accomplished it, his tribe would admire him. Saya would admire him. Everybody, observing that he had found a new source of food, would even envy him until he showed them how to do it too. Burl's fellow-humans were preoccupied with the filling of their stomachs. The preservation of their lives came second. The perpetuation of the race came a bad third in their consideration. They were herded together in a leaderless group, coming to the same hiding-place nightly only that they might share the finds of the lucky and gather comfort from their numbers. They had no weapons. Even Burl did not consider his spear a weapon. It was a tool for stabbing something to eat only. Yet he did not think of it in that way exactly. His tribe did not even consciously use tools. Sometimes they used stones to crack open the limbs of great insects they found incompletely devoured. They did not even carry rocks about with them for that purpose. Only Burl had a vague idea of taking something to some place to do something with it. It was unprecedented. Burl was at least an atavar. He may have been a genius.

But he was not a high-grade genius. Certainly not yet.

He reached a spot from which he could look down into the water. He looked behind and all about, listening, then lay down to stare into the shallow depths. Once, a huge crayfish, a good eight feet long, moved leisurely across his vision. Small fishes and even huge newts fled before it.

After a long time the normal course of underwater life resumed. The wriggling caddis-flies in their quaintly ambitious houses reappeared. Little flecks of silver swam into view—a school of tiny fish. Then a larger fish appeared, moving slowly in the stream.

Burl's eyes glistened; his mouth watered. He reached down with his long weapon. It barely broke through the still surface of the water below. Disappointment filled him, yet the nearness and apparent probability of success spurred him on.

He examined the shelf-fungi beneath him. Rising, he moved to a point above them and tested one with his spear. It resisted. Burl felt about tentatively with his foot, then dared to put his whole weight on the topmost. It held firmly. He clambered down upon the lower ones, then lay flat and peered over the edge.

The large fish, fully as long as Burl's arm, swam slowly to and fro beneath him. Burl had seen the former owner of this spear strive to thrust it into his adversary. The beetle had been killed by the more successful stab of a similar weapon. Burl had tried this upon toadstools, practising with it. When the silver fish drifted close by again, he thrust sharply downward.

The spear seemed to bend when it entered the water. It missed its mark by inches, much to Burl's astonishment. He tried again. Once more the spear seemed diverted by the water. He grew angry with the fish for eluding his efforts to kill it.

This anger was as much the reaction of a throw-back to a less fearful time as the idea of killing itself. But Burl scowled at the fish. Repeated strokes had left it untouched. It was unwary. It did not even swim away.

Then it came to rest directly beneath his hand. He thrust directly downward, with all his strength. This time the spear, entering vertically, did not appear to bend, but went straight down. Its point penetrated the scales of the swimming fish, transfixing the creature completely.

An uproar began with the fish wriggling desperately as Burl tried to draw it up to his perch. In his excitement he did not notice a tiny ripple a little distance away. The monster crayfish, attracted by the disturbance, was coming back.

The unequal combat continued. Burl hung on desperately to the end of his spear. Then there was a tremor in the shelf-fungus on which he lay. It yielded, collapsed, and fell into the stream with a mighty splash. Burl went under, his eyes wide open, facing death. As he sank he saw the gaping, horrible claws of the crustacean, huge enough to sever any of Burl's limbs with a single snap.

He opened his mouth to scream, but no sound came out. Only bubbles floated up to the surface. He beat the unresisting fluid in a frenzy of horror with his hands and feet as the colossal crayfish leisurely approached.

His arms struck a solid object. He clutched it convulsively. A second later he had swung it between himself and the crustacean. He felt the shock as the claws closed upon the cork-like fungus. Then he felt himself drawn upward as the crayfish disgustedly released its hold and the shelf-fungus floated slowly upward. Having given way beneath him, it had been pushed below when he fell, only to rise within his reach just when most needed.

Burl's head popped above-water and he saw a larger bit of the fungus floating nearby. Even less securely anchored to the river-bank than the shelf to which he had trusted himself, it had broken away when he fell. It was larger and floated higher.

He seized it, crazily trying to climb up. It tilted under his weight and very nearly overturned. He paid no heed. With desperate haste he clawed and kicked until he could draw himself clear of the water.

As he pulled himself up on the furry, orange-brown surface, a sharp blow struck his foot. The crayfish, disappointed at finding nothing tasty in the shelf-fungus, had made a languid stroke at

Burl's foot wriggling in the water. Failing to grasp the fleshy member, it went annoyedly away.

Burl floated downstream, perched weaponless and alone upon a flimsy raft of degenerate fungus; floated slowly down a stagnant river in which death swam, between banks of sheer peril, past long reaches above which death floated on golden wings.

It was a long while before he recovered his self-possession. Then—and this was an action individual in Burl: none of his tribesmen would have thought of it—he looked for his spear.

It was floating in the water, still transfixing the fish whose capture had brought him to this present predicament. That silvery shape, so violent before, now floated belly-up, all life gone.

Burl's mouth watered as he gazed at the fish. He kept it in view constantly while the unsteady craft spun slowly downstream in the current. Lying flat he tried to reach out and grasp the end of the spear when it circled toward him.

The raft tilted, nearly capsizing. A little later he discovered that it sank more readily on one side than the other. This was due, of course, to the greater thickness of one side. The part next to the river-bank had been thicker and was, therefore, more buoyant.

He lay with his head above that side of the raft. It did not sink into the water. Wriggling as far to the edge as he dared, he reached out and out. He waited impatiently for the slower rotation of his float to coincide with the faster motion of the speared fish. The spear-end came closer, and closer... He reached out—and the raft dipped dangerously. But his fingers touched the spear-end. He got a precarious hold, pulled it toward him.

Seconds later he was tearing strips of scaly flesh from the side of the fish and cramming the greasy stuff into his mouth with vast enjoyment. He had lost the edible mushroom. It floated several yards away. He ate contentedly none-the-less.

He thought of the tribesfolk as he ate. This was more than he could finish alone. Old Tama would coax him avidly for more than her share. She had a few teeth left. She would remind him anxiously of her gifts of food to him when he was younger. Dik and Tet—being boys—would clamorously demand of him where he'd gotten it. How? He would give some to Cori, who had younger children, and she would give them most of the gift. And Saya—.

Burl gloated especially over Saya's certain reaction.

Then he realized that with every second he was being carried further away from her. The nearer river-bank moved past him. He could tell by the motion of the vividly colored growths upon the shore.

Overhead, the sun was merely a brighter patch in the haze-filled sky. In the pinkish light all about, Burl looked for the familiar and did not find it, and dolefully knew that he was remote from Saya and going farther all the time.

There were a multitude of flying objects to be seen in the miasmatic air. In the daytime a thin mist always hung above the lowlands. Burl had never seen any object as much as three miles distant. The air was never clear enough to permit it. But there was much to be seen even within the limiting mist.

Now and then a cricket or a grasshopper made its bullet-like flight from one spot to another. Huge butterflies fluttered gaily above the silent, loathesome ground. Bees lumbered anxiously about, seeking the cross-shaped flowers of the giant cabbages which grew so rarely. Occasionally a slender-waisted, yellow-bellied wasp flashed swiftly by.

But Burl did not heed any of them. Sitting dismally upon his fungus raft, floating in midstream, an incongruous figure of pink skin and luridly-tinted loin-cloth, with a greasy dead fish beside him, he was filled with a panicky anguish because the river carried him away from the one girl of his tiny tribe whose glances roused a commotion in his breast.

The day wore on. Once, he saw a band of large amazon ants moving briskly over a carpet of blue-green mould to raid the city of a species of black ants. The eggs they would carry away from the city would hatch and the small black creatures would become the slaves of the brigands who had stolen them.

Later, strangely-shaped, swollen branches drifted slowly into view. They were outlined sharply against the steaming mist behind them. He knew what they were: a hard-rinded fungus growing upon itself in peculiar mockery of the trees which Burl had never seen because no trees could survive the conditions of the lowland.

Much later, as the day drew to an end, Burl ate again of the oily fish. The taste was pleasant compared to the insipid mushrooms he usually ate. Even though he stuffed himself, the fish was so large that the greater part remained still uneaten.

The spear was beside him. Although it had brought him trouble, he still associated it with the food it had secured rather than the difficulty into which it had led him. When he had eaten his fill, he picked it up to examine again. The oil-covered point remained as sharp as before.

Not daring to use it again from so unsteady a raft, he set it aside as he stripped a sinew from his loin-cloth to hang the fish around his neck. This would leave his arms free. Then he sat cross-legged, fumbling with the spear as he watched the shores go past.

CHAPTER TWO
A Man Escapes

It was near to sunset. Burl had never seen the sun, so it did not occur to him to think of the coming of night as the setting of anything. To him it was the letting down of darkness from the sky.

The process was invariable. Overhead there was always a thick and unbroken bank of vapor which seemed featureless until sunset. Then, toward the west, the brightness overhead turned orange and then pink, while to the east it simply faded to a deeper gray. As nightfall progressed, the red colorings grew deeper, moving toward mid-sky. Ultimately, scattered blotches of darkness began to spot that reddening sky as it grew darker in tone, going down toward that impossible redness which is indistinguishable from black. It was slowly achieving that redness.

Today Burl watched as never before. On the oily surface of the river the colors and shadings of dusk were reflected with incredible faithfulness. The round tops of toadstools along the shore glowed pink. Dragonflies glinted in swift and angular flight, the metallic sheen of their bodies flashing in the redness. Great, yellow butterflies sailed lightly above the stream. In every direction upon the water appeared the scrap-formed boats of a thousand caddis-flies, floating at the surface while they might. Burl could have thrust his hand down into their cavities to seize the white worms nesting there.

The bulk of a tardy bee droned heavily overhead. He saw the long proboscis and the hairy hind-legs with their scanty load of pollen. The great, multi-faceted eyes held an expression of stupid preoccupation.

The crimson radiance grew dim and the color overhead faded toward black. Now the stalks of ten thousand domed mushrooms lined the river-bank. Beneath them spread fungi of all colors, from the rawest red to palest blue, now all fading slowly to a monochromatic background as the darkness deepened.

The buzzing and fluttering and flapping of the insects of the day died down. From a million hiding places there crept out—into the night—the soft and furry bodies of great moths who preened themselves and smoothed their feathery antennae before taking to the air. The strong-limbed crickets set up their thunderous noise, grown gravely bass with the increasing size of the noise-making organs. Then there began to gather on the water those slender spirals of deeper mist which would presently blanket the stream in fog.

Night arrived. The clouds above grew wholly black. Gradually the languid fall of large, warm raindrops—they would fall all through the night—began. The edge of the stream became a place where disks of cold blue flame appeared.

The mushrooms on the river bank were faintly phosphorescent, shedding a ghostly light over the ground below them. Here and there, lambent chilly flames appeared in mid-air, drifting idly above the festering earth. On other planets men call them "Will-o'-the-wisps," but on this planet mankind had no name for them at all.

Then huge, pulsating glows appeared in the blackness: fireflies that Burl knew to be as long as his spear. They glided slowly through the darkness over the stream, shedding intermittent light over Burl crouched on his drifting raft. On the shore, too, tiny paired lights glowed eagerly upward as the wingless females of the species crawled to where their signals could be seen. And there were other glowing things. Fox-fire burned in the night, consuming nothing. Even the water of the river glowed with marine organisms—adapted to fresh water here—contributing their mites of brilliance.

The air was full of flying creatures. The beat of invisible wings came through the night. Above, about, on every side the swarming, feverish life of the insect world went on ceaselessly, while Burl rocked back and forth upon his unstable raft, wanting to weep because he was being carried farther away from Saya whom he could picture looking for him, now, among the hidden, furtive members of the tribe. About him sounded the discordant, machine-like mating cries of creatures trying to serve life in the midst of death and the horrible noises of those who met death and were devoured in the dark.

Burl was accustomed to such tumult. But he was not accustomed to such despair as he felt at being lost from Saya of the swift feet and white teeth and shy smile. He lay disconsolate on his bobbing craft for the greater part of the night. It was long past midnight when the raft struck gently, swung, and then remained grounded upon a shallow in the stream.

When light came back in the morning, Burl gazed about him fearfully. He was some twenty yards from the shore and thick greenish scum surrounded his disintegrating vessel. The river had widened greatly until the opposite bank was hidden in the morning mist, but the nearer shore seemed firm and no more full of dangers than the territory inhabited by Burl's tribe.

He tested the depth of the water with his spear, struck by the multiple usefulness of the weapon. The water was no more than ankle-deep.

Shivering a little, Burl stepped down into the green scum and made for the shore at top speed. He felt something soft clinging to his bare foot. With a frantic rush he ran even faster and stumbled upon the shore with horror not at his heels but on one. He stared down at his foot. A shapeless, flesh-colored pad clung to the skin. As he watched, it swelled visibly, the pink folds becoming a deeper shade.

It was no more than a leech, the size of his palm, sharing in the enlargement nearly all the insect and fungoid world had undergone, but Burl did not know that. He thrust at it with the edge of his spear, scraping it frantically away. As it fell off Burl stared in horror, first at the blotch of blood on his foot, then at the thing writhing and pulsating on the ground. He fled.

A short while later he stumbled into one of the familiar toadstool forests and paused, uncertainly. The towering toadstools were not strange to Burl. He fell to eating. The sight of food always produced hunger in him—a provision of nature to make up for the lack of any instinct to store food away. In human beings the storage of food has to be dictated by intellect. The lower orders of creatures are not required to think.

Even eating, though, Burl's heart was small within him. He was far from his tribe and Saya. By the measurements of his remotest ancestors, no more than forty miles separated them. But Burl did not think in such terms. He'd never had occasion to do so. He'd come down the river to a far land filled with unknown dangers. And he was alone.

All about him was food, an excellent reason for gladness. But being solitary was reason enough for distress. Although Burl was a creature to whom reflection was normally of no especial value and, therefore, not practiced in thought, this was a situation providing an emotional paradox. A good fourth of the mushrooms in this particular forest were edible. Burl should have gloated over this vast stock of food. But he was isolated, alone; in particular, he was far away from Saya, therefore, he should have wept. But he could not gloat because he was away from Saya and he could not mourn because he was surrounded by food.

He was subject to a stimulus to which apparently only humankind can respond: an emotional dilemma. Other creatures can respond to objective situations where there is the need to choose a course of action: flight or fighting, hiding or pursuit. But only man can be disturbed by not knowing which of two emotions to feel. Burl had reason to feel two entirely different emotional states at the same time. He had to resolve the paradox. The problem was inside him, not out. So he thought.

He would bring Saya here! He would bring her and the tribe to this place where there was food in vast quantity!

Instantly pictures flooded into his mind. He could actually see old Jon, his bald head naked as a mushroom itself, stuffing his belly with the food which was so plentiful here. He imagined Cori feeding her children. Tama's complaints stilled by mouthfuls of food. Tet and Dik, stuffed to repletion, throwing scraps of foodstuff at each other. He pictured the tribe zestfully feasting.— And Saya would be very glad.

It was remarkable that Burl was able to think of his feelings instead of his sensations. His tribesmen were closer to it than equally primitive folk had been back on Earth, but they did not often engage in thought. Their waking lives were filled with nerve-racked physical responses to physical phenomena. They were hungry and they saw or smelled food: they were alive and they perceived the presence of death. In the one case they moved toward the sensory stimulus of food; in the other they fled from the detected stimulus of danger. They responded immediately to the world about them. Burl, for the first significant time in his life, had responded to inner feelings. He had resolved conflicting emotions by devising a purpose that would end their conflict. He determined to do something because he wanted to and not because he had to.

It was the most important event upon the planet in generations.

With the directness of a child, or a savage, Burl moved to carry out his purpose. The fish still slung about his neck scraped against his chest. Fingering it tentatively, he got himself thoroughly greasy in the process, but could not eat. Although he was not hungry now, perhaps Saya was. He would give it to her. He imagined her eager delight, the image reinforcing his resolve. He had come to this far place down the river flowing sluggishly past this riotously-colored bank. To return to the tribe he would go back up that bank, staying close to the stream.

He was remarkably exultant as he forced a way through the awkward aisles of the mushroom-forest, but his eyes and ears were still open for any possible danger. Several times he heard the omnipresent clicking of ants scavenging in the mushroom-glades, but they could be ignored. At best they were short-sighted. If he dropped his fish, they would become absorbed in it. There was only one kind of ant he needed to fear—the army ant, which sometimes traveled in hordes of millions, eating everything in their path.

But there was nothing of the sort here. The mushroom forest came to an end. A cheerful grasshopper munched delicately at some dainty it had found—the barrel-sized young shoot of a cabbage-plant. Its hind legs were bunched beneath it in perpetual readiness for flight. A monster wasp appeared a hundred feet overhead, checked in its flight, and plunged upon the luckless banqueter.

There was a struggle, but it was brief. The grasshopper strained terribly in the grip of the wasp's six barbed legs. The wasp's flexible abdomen curved delicately. Its sting entered the jointed armor of its prey just beneath the head with all the deliberate precision of a surgeon's scalpel. A ganglion lay there; the wasp-poison entered it. The grasshopper went limp. It was not dead, of course, simply paralyzed. Permanently paralyzed. The wasp preened itself, then matter-of-factly grasped its victim and flew away. The grasshopper would be incubator and food-supply for an egg to be laid. Presently, in a huge mud castle, a small white worm would feed upon the living, motionless victim of its mother—who would never see it, or care, or remember...

Burl went on.

The ground grew rougher; progress became painful. He clambered arduously up steep slopes—all of forty or fifty feet high—and made his way cautiously down to the farther sides. Once he climbed through a tangled mass of mushrooms so closely placed and so small that he had to break them apart with blows of his spear in order to pass. As they crumbled, torrents of a fiery-red liquid showered down upon him, rolling off his greasy breast and sinking into the ground.

A strange self-confidence now took possession of Burl. He walked less cautiously and more boldly. He had thought and he had struck something, feeling the vainglorious self-satisfaction of a child. He pictured himself leading his tribe to this place of very much food—he had no real idea of the distance—and he strutted all alone amid the nightmare-growths of the planet that had been forgotten.

Presently he could see the river. He had climbed to the top of a red-clay mound perhaps a hundred feet high. One side was crumbled where the river overflowed. At some past flood-time the water had lapped at the base of the cliff along which Burl was strutting. But now there was a quarter-mile of space between himself and the water. And there was something else in mid-air.

The cliffside was thickly coated with fungi in a riotous confusion of white and yellow and orange and green. From a point halfway up the cliff the inch-thick cable of a spider-web stretched down to anchorage on the ground below. There were other cables beyond this one and circling about their radial pattern the snare-cords of the web formed a perfect logarithmic spiral.

Somewhere among the fungi of the cliffside the huge spider who had built this web awaited the entrapment of prey. When some unfortunate creature struggled frenziedly in its snare it would emerge. Until then it waited in a motionless, implacable patience; utterly certain of victims, utterly merciless to them.

Burl strutted on the edge of the cliff, a rather foolish pink-skinned creature with an oily fish slung about his neck and the draggled fragment of moth's wing draping his middle. He waved the long shard of beetle armor exultantly above his head.

The activity was not very sensible. It served no purpose. But if Burl was a genius among his fellows, then he still had a great deal to learn before his genius would be effective. Now he looked down scornfully upon the shining white trap below. He had struck a fish, killing it. When he hit mushrooms they fell into pieces before him. Nothing could frighten him! He would go to Saya and bring her to this land where food grew in abundance.

Sixty paces away from Burl, near the edge of the cliff, a shaft sank vertically into the soil of the clay-mound. It was carefully rounded and lined with silk. Thirty feet down, it enlarged itself into a chamber where the engineer and proprietor of the shaft might rest. The top of the hole was closed by a trap-door, stained with mud and earth to imitate the surrounding soil. A sharp eye would have been needed to detect the opening. But a keener eye now peered out from the crack at its edge.

That eye belonged to the proprietor.

Eight hairy legs surrounded the body of the monster hanging motionless at the top of the silk-lined shaft. Its belly was a huge misshapen globe colored a dirty brown. Two pairs of mandibles stretched before its mouth-parts; two eyes glittered in the semi-darkness of the burrow. Over the whole body spread a rough and mangy fur.

It was a thing of implacable malignance, of incredible ferocity. It was the brown hunting spider, the American tarantula, enlarged here upon the forgotten planet so that its body was two feet and more in diameter. Its legs, outstretched, would cover a circle three yards across. The glittering eyes followed as Burl strutted forward on the edge of the cliff, puffed up with a sense of his own importance.

Spread out below, the white snare of the spinning-spider impressed Burl as amusing. He knew the spider wouldn't leave its web to attack him. Reaching down, he broke off a bit of fungus growing at his feet. Where he broke it away oozed a soupy liquid full of tiny maggots in a delirium of feasting. Burl flung it down into the web, laughing as the black bulk of the watchful spider swung down from its hiding place to investigate.

The tarantula, peering from its burrow, quivered with impatience. Burl drew nearer, gleefully using his spear as a lever to pry off bits of trash to fall down the cliffside into the giant web. The spider below moved leisurely from one spot to another, investigating each new missile with its palpi and then ignoring it as lifeless and undesirable prey.

Burl leaped and laughed aloud as a particularly large lump of putrid fungus narrowly missed the black-and-silver shape below. Then—

The trap-door fell into place with a faint sound. Burl whirled about, his laughter transformed instantly into a scream. Moving toward him furiously, its eight legs scrambling, was the monster tarantula. Its mandibles gaped wide; the poison fangs were unsheathed. It was thirty paces away—twenty paces—ten.

Eyes glittering, it leaped, all eight legs extended to seize the prey.

Burl screamed again and thrust out his arms to ward off the creature. It was pure blind horror. There was no genius in that gesture. Because of sheer terror his grip upon the spear had become agonized. The spear-point shot out and the tarantula fell upon it. Nearly a quarter of the spear entered the body of the ferocious thing.

Stuck upon the spear the spider writhed horribly, still striving to reach the paralytically frozen Burl. The great mandibles clashed. Furious bubbling noises came from it. The hairy legs clutched at his arm. He cried out hoarsely in ultimate fear and staggered backward—and the edge of the cliff gave way beneath him.

He hurtled downward, still clutching the spear, incapable of letting go. Even while falling the writhing thing still struggled maniacally to reach him. Down through emptiness they fell together, Burl glassy-eyed with panic. Then there was a strangely elastic crash and crackling. They had fallen into the web at which Burl had been laughing so scornfully only a little while before.

Burl couldn't think. He only struggled insanely in the gummy coils of the web. But the snare-cords were spiral threads, enormously elastic, exuding impossibly sticky stuff, like bird-lime, from between twisted constituent fibres. Near him—not two yards away—the creature he had wounded thrashed and fought to reach him, even while shuddering in anguish.

Burl had reached the absolute limit of panic. His arms and breast were greasy from the oily fish; the sticky web did not adhere to them. But his legs and body were inextricably tangled by his own frantic struggling in the gummy and adhesive elastic threads. They had been spread for prey. He was prey.

He paused in his blind struggle, gasping from pure exhaustion. Then he saw, not five yards away, the silvery-and-black monster he had mocked so recently now patiently waiting for him to cease his struggles. The tarantula and the man were one to its eyes—one struggling thing that had fallen opportunely into its trap. They were moving but feebly, now. The web-spider advanced delicately, swinging its huge bulk nimbly, paying out a silken cable behind it as it approached.

Burl's arms were free; he waved them wildly, shrieking at the monster. The spider paused. Burl's moving arms suggested mandibles that might wound.

Spiders take few chances. This one drew near cautiously, then stopped. Its spinnerets became busy and with one of its eight legs, used like an arm, it flung a sheet of gummy silk impartially over the tarantula and the man.

Burl fought against the descending shroud. He strove to thrust it away, futilely. Within minutes he was completely covered in a coarse silken fabric that hid even the light from his eyes. He and his enemy, the monstrous tarantula, were beneath the same covering. The tarantula moved feebly.

The shower ceased. The web-spider had decided they were helpless. Then Burl felt the cables of the web give slightly as the spider approached to sting and suck the juices from its prey.

The web yielded gently. Burl froze in an ecstasy of horror. But the tarantula still writhed in agony upon the spear piercing it. It clashed its jaws, shuddering upon the horny shaft.

Burl waited for the poison-fangs to be thrust into him. He knew the process. He had seen the leisurely fashion in which the web-spider delicately stung its victim, then withdrew to wait with horrible patience for the poison to take effect. When the victim no longer struggled, it drew near again to suck out the juices first from one joint or limb and then from another, leaving a creature once vibrant with life a shrunken, withered husk, to be flung from the web at nightfall.

The bloated monstrosity now moved meditatively about the double object swathed in silk. Only the tarantula stirred. Its bulbous abdomen stirred the concealing shroud. It throbbed faintly as it still struggled with the spear in its vitals. The irregularly rounded projection was an obvious target for the web-spider. It moved quickly forward. With fine, merciless precision, it stung.

The tarantula seemed to go mad with pain. Its legs struck out purposelessly, in horrible gestures of delirious suffering. Burl screamed as a leg touched him. He struggled no less wildly.

His arms and head were enclosed by the folds of silk, but not glued to it because of the grease. Clutching at the cords he tried desperately to draw himself away from his deadly neighbor. The threads wouldn't break, but they did separate. A tiny opening appeared.

One of the tarantula's horribly writhing legs touched him again. With a strength born of utter panic he hauled himself away and the opening enlarged. Another lunge and Burl's head emerged into the open air. He was suspended twenty feet above the ground, which was almost carpeted with the chitinous remains of past victims of this same web.

Burl's head and breast and arms were free. The fish slung over his shoulder had shed its oil upon him impartially. But the lower part of his body was held firm by the viscous gumminess of the web-spider's cord. It was vastly more adhesive than any bird-lime ever made by men.

He hung in the little window for a moment, despairing. Then he saw the bulk of his captor a little distance away, waiting patiently for its poison to work and its prey to cease struggling. The tarantula was no more than shuddering now. Soon it would be quite still and the black-bellied creature would approach for its meal.

Burl withdrew his head and thrust desperately at the sticky stuff about his loins and legs. The oil upon his hands kept them free. The silk shroud gave a little. Burl grasped at the thought as at a straw. He grasped the fish and tore it, pushing frantically at his own body with the now-rancid, scaly, odorous mass. He scraped gum from his legs with the fish, smearing the rancid oils all over them in the process.

He felt the web tremble again. To the spider Burl's movements meant that its poison had not taken full effect. Another sting seemed to be necessary. This time it would not insert its sting into the quiescent tarantula, but where there was still life. It would send its venom into Burl.

He gasped and drew himself toward his window as if he would have pulled his legs from his body. His head emerged. His shoulders—half his body was out of the hole.

The great spider surveyed him and made ready to cast more of its silken stuff upon him. The spinnerets became active. A leg gathered it up—

The sticky stuff about Burl's feet gave way.

He shot out of the opening and fell heavily, sprawling upon the earth below and crashing into the shrunken shell of a flying beetle that had blundered into the snare and not escaped as he had done.

Burl rolled over and over and then sat up. An angry, foot-long ant stood before him, its mandibles extended threateningly, while a shrill stridulation filled the air.

In ages past, back on Earth—where most ants were to be measured in fractions of an inch—the scientists had debated gravely whether their tribe possessed a cry. They believed that certain grooves upon the body of the insect, like those upon the great legs of the cricket, might be the means of making a sound too shrill for human ears to catch. It was greatly debated, but evidence was hard to obtain.

Burl did not need evidence. He knew that the stridulation was caused by the insect before him, though he had never wondered how it was produced. The cry was emitted to summon other ants from its city to help it in difficulty or good fortune.

Harsh clickings sounded fifty or sixty feet away; comrades were coming. And while only army ants were normally dangerous, any tribe of ants could be formidable when aroused. It was overwhelming enough to pull down and tear a man to shreds as a pack of infuriated fox-terriers might do on Earth.

Burl fled without further delay, nearly colliding with one of the web's anchor-cables. Then he heard the shrill outcry subside. The ant, short-sighted as all its kind, no longer felt threatened. It went peacefully about the business Burl had interrupted. Presently it found some edible carrion among the debris from the spider-web and started triumphantly back to its city.

Burl sped on for a few hundred yards and then stopped. He was shaken and dazed. For the moment, he was as timid and fearful as any other man in his tribe. Presently he would realize the full meaning of the unparalleled feat he had performed in escaping from the giant spider web while cloaked with folds of gummy silk. It was not only unheard-of; it was unimaginable! But Burl was too shaken to think of it now.

Rather quaintly, the first sensation that forced itself into his consciousness was that his feet hurt. The gluey stuff from the web still stuck to his soles, picking up small objects as he went along. Old, ant-gnawed fragments of insect armor pricked him so persistently, even through his toughened foot-soles, that he paused to scrape them away, staring fearfully about all the while. After a dozen steps more he was forced to stop again.

It was this nagging discomfort, rather than vanity or an emergency which caused Burl to discover—imagine—blunder into a new activity as epoch-making as anything else he had done. His brain had been uncommonly stimulated in the past twenty-some hours. It had plunged him into at least one predicament because of his conceiving the idea of stabbing something, but it had also allowed him escape from another even more terrifying one just now. In between it had led to the devising of a purpose—the bringing of Saya here—though that decision was not so firmly fixed as it had been before the encounter with the web-spider. Still, it had surely been reasoning of a sort that told him to grease his body with the fish. Otherwise he would now be following the tarantula as a second course for the occupant of the web.

Burl looked cautiously all about him. It seemed to be quite safe. Then, quite deliberately, he sat down to think. It was the first time in his life that he had ever deliberately contemplated a problem with the idea of finding an answer to it. And the notion of doing such a thing was epoch-making—on this planet!

He examined his foot. The sharp edges of pebbles and the remnants of insect-armor hurt his feet when he walked. They had done so ever since he had been born, but never before had his feet been sticky, so that the irritation from one object persisted for more than a step. He carefully picked away each sharp-pointed fragment, one by one. Partly coated with the half-liquid gum, they even tended to cling to his fingers, except where the oil was thick.

Burl's reasoning had been of the simplest sort. He had contemplated a situation—not deliberately but because he had to—and presently his mind showed him a way out of it. It was a way specifically suited to the situation. Here he faced something different. Presently he applied the answer of one problem to a second problem. Oil on his body had let him go free of things that would stick to him. Here things stuck to his feet; so he oiled them.

And it worked. Burl strode away, almost—but not completely—untroubled by the bothersome pebbles and bits of discarded armor. Then he halted to regard himself with astonished appreciation. He was still thirty-five miles from his tribe; he was naked and unarmed, utterly ignorant of wood and fire and weapons other than the one he had lost. But he paused to observe with some awe that he was very wonderful indeed.

He wanted to display himself. But his spear was gone. So Burl found it necessary to think again. And the remarkable thing about it was that he succeeded.

In a surprisingly brief time he had come up with a list of answers. He was naked, so he would find garments for himself. He was weaponless: he would find himself a spear. He was hungry and he would seek food. Since he was far from his tribe, he would go to them. And this was, in a fashion, quite obviously thought; but it was not oblivious on the forgotten planet because it had been futile—up to now. The importance of such thought in the scheme of things was that men had not been thinking even so simply as this, living only from minute to minute. Burl was fumbling his way into a habit of thinking from problem to problem. And that was very important indeed.

Even in the advanced civilization of other planets, few men really used their minds. The great majority of people depended on machines not only for computations but decisions as well. Any decisions not made by machines most men left to their leaders. Burl's tribesfolk thought principally with their stomachs, making few if any decisions on any other basis—though they did act, very often, under the spur of fear. Fear-inspired actions, however, were not thought out. Burl was thinking out his actions.

There would be consequences.

He faced upstream and began to move again, slowly and warily, his eyes keenly searching out the way ahead, ears alert for the slightest sound of danger. Gigantic butterflies, riotous in coloring, fluttered overhead through the hazy air. Sometimes a grasshopper hurtled from one place to another like a projectile, its transparent wings beating frantically. Now and then a wasp sped by, intent upon its hunting, or a bee droned heavily alone, anxious and worried, striving to gather pollen in a nearly flowerless world.

Burl marched on. From somewhere far behind him came a very faint sound. It was a shrill noise, but very distant indeed. Absorbed in immediate and nearby matters, Burl took no heed. He had the limited local viewpoint of a child. What was near was important and what was distant could be ignored. Anything not imminent still seemed to him insignificant—and he was preoccupied.

The source of this sound was important, however. Its origin was a myriad of clickings compounded into a single noise. It was, in fact, the far-away but yet perceptible sound of army ants on the march. The locusts of Earth were very trivial nuisances compared to the army ants of this planet.

Locusts, in past ages on Earth, had eaten all green things. Here in the lowlands were only giant cabbages and a few rank, tenacious growths. Grasshoppers were numerous here, but could never be thought of as a plague; they were incapable of multiplying to the size of locust hordes. Army ants, however…

But Burl did not notice the sound. He moved forward briskly though cautiously, searching the fungus-landscape for any sign of garments, food, and weapons. He confidently expected to find all of them within a short distance. Indeed, he did find food very soon. No more than a half mile ahead he found a small cluster of edible fungi.

With no special elation, Burl broke off a food supply from the largest of them. Naturally, he took more than he could possibly eat at one time. He went on, nibbling at a big piece of mushroom abstractedly, past a broad plain, more than a mile across and broken into odd little hillocks by gradually ripening mushrooms which were unfamiliar to him. In several places the ground had been pushed aside by rounded objects, only the tips showing. Blood-red hemispheres seemed to be forcing themselves through the soil, so they might reach the outer air. Careful not to touch any of them, Burl examined the hillocks curiously as he entered the plain. They were strange, and to Burl most strange things meant danger. In any event, he had two conscious purposes now. He wanted garments and weapons.

Above the plain a wasp hovered, dangling a heavy object beneath its black belly across which ran a single red band. It was the gigantic descendant of the hairy sand-wasp, differing only in size from its far-away, remote ancestors on Earth. It was taking a paralyzed gray caterpillar to its burrow. Burl watched it drop down with the speed and sureness of an arrow, pull aside a heavy, flat stone, and descend into the burrow with its caterpillar-prey momentarily laid aside.

It vanished underground into a vertical shaft dug down forty feet or more. It evidently inspected the refuge. Reappearing, it vanished into the hole again, dragging the gray worm after it. Burl, marching on over the broad plain spotted with some eruptive disease, did not know what passed below. But he did observe the wasp emerge again to scratch dirt and stones previously excavated laboriously back into the shaft until it was full.

The wasp had paralyzed a caterpillar, taken it into the ready-prepared burrow, laid an egg upon it, and sealed up the entrance. In time the egg would hatch into a grub barely the size of Burl's forefinger. And the grub, deep underground, would feed upon the living but helpless caterpillar until it waxed large and fat. Then it would weave itself a cocoon and sleep a long sleep, only to wake as a wasp and dig its way out to the open air.

Reaching the farther side of the plain, Burl found himself threading the aisles of a fungus forest in which the growths were misshapen travesties of the trees which could not live here. Bloated yellow limbs branched off from rounded swollen trunks. Here and there a pear-shaped puffball, Burl's height and half his height again, waited until a chance touch should cause it to shoot upward a curling puff of infinitely fine dust.

He continued to move with caution. There were dangers here, but he went forward steadily. He still held a great mass of edible mushroom under one arm and from time to time broke off a fragment, chewing it meditatively. But always his eyes searched here and there for threats of harm.

Behind him the faint, shrill outcry had risen only slightly in volume. It was still too far away to attract his notice. Army ants, however, were working havoc in the distance. By thousands and millions, myriads of them advanced across the fungoid soil. They clambered over every eminence. They descended into every depression. Their antennae waved restlessly. Their mandibles were extended threateningly. The ground was black with them, each one more than ten inches long.

A single such creature, armored and fearless as it was, could be formidable enough to an unarmed and naked man like Burl. The better part of discretion would be avoidance. But numbering in the thousands and millions, they were something which could not be avoided. They advanced steadily and rapidly; the chorus of shrill stridulations and clickings marking their progress.

Great, inoffensive caterpillars crawling over the huge cabbages heard the sound of their coming, but were too stupid to flee. The black multitudes blanketed the rank vegetables. Tiny, voracious jaws tore at the flaccid masses of greasy flesh.

The caterpillars strove to throw off their assailants by writhings and contortions—uselessly. The bees fought their entrance into the monster hives with stings and wing-beats. Moths took to the air in daylight with dazzled, blinded eyes. But nothing could withstand the relentless hordes of small black things that reeked of formic acid and left the ground behind them empty of life.

Before the horde was a world of teeming life, where mushrooms and other fungi fought with thinning numbers of cabbages and mutant earth-weeds for a foothold. Behind the black multitude was—nothing. Mushrooms, cabbages, bees, wasps, crickets, grubs—every living thing that could not flee before the creeping black tide reached it was lost, torn to bits by tiny mandibles.

Even the hunting spiders and tarantulas fell before the black host. They killed many in their desperate self-defense, but the army ants could overwhelm anything—anything at all—by sheer numbers and ferocity. Killed or wounded ants served as food for their sound comrades. Only the web spiders sat unmoved and immovable in their collossal snares, secure in the knowledge that their gummy webs could not be invaded along the slender supporting cables.

CHAPTER THREE
The Purple Hills

The army ants flowed over the ground like a surging, monstrous, inky tide. Their vanguard reached the river and recoiled. Burl was perhaps five miles away when they changed their course. The change was made without confusion, the leaders somehow communicating the altered line of march to those behind them.

Back on Earth, scientists had gravely debated the question of how ants conveyed ideas to each other. Honeybees, it was said, performed elaborate ritual dances to exchange information. Ants, it had been observed, had something less eccentric. A single ant, finding a bit of booty too big for it to manage alone, would return to its city to secure the help of others. From that fact men had deduced that a language of gestures made with crossed antennae must exist.

Burl had no theories. He merely knew facts, but he did know that ants could and did pass information to one another. Now, however, he moved cautiously along toward the sleeping-place of his tribe in complete ignorance of the black blanket of living creatures spreading over the ground behind him.

A million tragedies marked the progress of the insect army. There was a tiny colony of mining bees, their habits unchanged despite their greater size, here on the forgotten planet. A single mother, four feet long, had dug a huge gallery with some ten offshooting cells, in which she had laid her eggs and fed her grubs with hard-gathered pollen. The grubs had waxed fat and large, become bees, and laid eggs in their turn within the same gallery their mother had dug out for them.

Ten bulky insects now foraged busily to feed their grubs within the ancestral home, while the founder of the colony had grown draggled and wingless with the passing of time. Unable to bring in food, herself, the old bee became the guardian of the hive. She closed the opening with her head, making a living barrier within the entrance. She withdrew only to grant admission or exit to the duly authorized members,—her daughters.

The ancient concierge of the underground dwelling was at her post when the wave of army ants swept over. Tiny, evil-smelling feet trampled upon her and she emerged to fight with mandible and sting for the sanctity of her brood. Within moments she was a shaggy mass of biting ants. They rent and tore at her chitinous armor. But she fought on madly, sounding a buzzing alarm to the colonists yet within.

They came out, fighting as they came: ten huge bees, each four to five feet long and fighting with legs and jaws, with wing and mandible, and with all the ferocity of so many tigers. But the small ants covered them, snapping at their multiple eyes, biting at the tender joints in their armour,—and sometimes releasing the larger prey to leap upon an injured comrade, wounded by the monster they battled together.

Such a fight, however, could have but one end. Struggle as the bees might, they were powerless against their un-numbered assailants. They were being devoured even as they fought. And before the last of the ten was down the underground gallery had been gutted both of the stored food brought by the adult defenders and the last morsels of what had been young grubs, too unformed to do more than twitch helplessly, inoffensively, as they were torn to shreds.

When the army ants went on there were merely an empty tunnel and a few fragments of tough armor, unappetizing even to the ants.

Burl heard them as he meditatively inspected the scene of a tragedy of not long before. The rent and scraped fragments of a great beetle's shiny casing lay upon the ground. A greater beetle had come upon the first and slain him. Burl regarded the remains of the meal.

Three or four minims, little ants barely six inches long, foraged industriously among the bits. A new ant-city was to be formed and the queen lay hidden half a mile away. These were the first hatchlings. They would feed their younger kindred until they grew large enough to take over the great work of the ant-city. Burl ignored the minims. He searched for a weapon of some sort. Behind him the clicking, high-pitched roar of the horde of army ants increased in volume.

He turned away disgustedly. The best thing he could find in the way of a weapon was a fiercely-toothed hind-leg. When he picked it up an angry whine rose from the ground. One of the minims had been struggling to detach a morsel of flesh from the leg-joint. Burl had snatched the tidbit from him.

The little creature was surely no more than half a foot long, but it advanced angrily upon Burl, shrilling a challenge. He struck with the beetle's leg and crushed the ant. Two of the other minims appeared, attracted by the noise the first had made. They discovered the crushed body of their fellow, unceremoniously dismembered it, and bore it away in triumph.

Burl went on, swinging the toothed limb in his hand. The sound behind him became a distant whispering, high-pitched and growing steadily nearer. The army ants swept into a mushroom forest and the yellow, umbrella-like growths soon swarmed with the black creatures.

A great bluebottle fly, shining with a metallic lustre, stood beneath a mushroom on the ground. The mushroom was infected with maggots which exuded a solvent pepsin that liquefied the firm white meat. They swam ecstatically in the liquid gruel, some of which dripped and dripped to the ground. The bluebottle was sipping the dark-colored liquid through its long proboscis, quivering with delight as it fed on the noisomeness.

Burl drew near and struck. The fly collapsed in a quivering heap. Burl stood over it for an instant and pondered.

The army ants were nearer, now. They swarmed down into a tiny valley, rushing into and through a little brook over which Burl had leaped. Since ants can remain underwater for a long time without drowning, the small stream was not even dangerous. Its current did sweep some of them away. A great many of them, however, clung together until they chocked its flow by the mass of their bodies, the main force marching across the bridge they constituted.

The ants reached a place about a quarter of a mile to the left of Burl's line of march, perhaps a mile from the spot where he stood over the dead bluebottle. There was an expanse of some acres in which the giant, rank cabbages had so far succeeded in their competition with the world of fungi. The pale, cross-shaped flowers of the cabbages formed food for many bees. The leaves fed numberless grubs and worms. Under the fallen-away dead foliage—single leaves were twenty feet across at their largest—crickets hid and fed.

The ant-army flowed into this space, devouring every living thing it encountered. A terrible din arose. The crickets hurtled away in erratic leapings. They shot aimlessly in any direction. More than half of them landed blindly in the carpeting of clicking black bodies which were the ants from whose vanguard they had fled. Their blind flight had no effect save to give different individuals the opportunity to seize them as they fell and instantly begin to devour them. As they were torn to fragments, horrible screamings reached Burl's ears.

A single such cry of agony would not have attracted Burl's attention. He lived in a world of nightmare horror. But a chorus of creatures in torment made him look up. This was no minor horror. Something wholesale was in progress. He jerked his head about to see what it was.

A wild stretch of sickly yellow fungus was interspersed here and there with a squat toadstool, or a splash of vivid color where one of the many rusts had found a foothold. To the left a group of branched fungoids clustered in silent mockery of a true forest. Burl saw the faded green of the cabbages.

With the sun never shining on the huge leaves save through the cloud-bank overhead, the cabbages were not vivid. There were even some mouldy yeasts of a brighter green and slime much more luridly tinted. Even so, the cabbages were the largest form of true vegetation Burl had ever seen. The nodding white cruciform flowers stood out plainly against the yellowish, pallid green of the leaves. But as Burl gazed at them, the green slowly became black.

Three great grubs, in lazy contentment, were eating ceaselessly of the cabbages on which they rested. Suddenly first one and then another began to jerk spasmodically. Burl saw that around each of them a rim of black had formed. Then black motes milled all over them.

The grubs became black—covered with biting, devouring ants. The cabbages became black. The frenzied contortions of the grubs told of the agonies they underwent as they were literally devoured alive. And then Burl saw a black wave appear at the nearer edge of the stretch of yellow fungus. A glistening, living flood flowed forward over the ground with a roar of clickings and a persistent overtone of shrill stridulations.

Burl's scalp crawled. He knew what this meant. And he did not pause to think. With a gasp of pure panic he turned and fled, all intellectual preoccupations forgotten.

The black tide came on after him.

He flung away the edible mushroom he had carried under his arm. Somehow, though, he clung to the sharp-toothed club as he darted between tangled masses of fungus, ignoring now the dangers that ordinarily called for vast caution.

Huge flies appeared. They buzzed about him loudly. Once he was struck on the shoulder by one of them—at least as large as his hand—and his skin torn by its swiftly vibrating wings.

He brushed it away and sped on. But the oil with which he was partly covered had turned rancid, now, and the fetid odor attracted them. There were half a dozen—then a dozen creatures the size of pheasants, droning and booming as they kept pace with his wild flight.

A weight pressed onto his head. It doubled. Two of the disgusting creatures had settled upon his oily hair to sip the stuff through their hairy feeding-tubes. Burl shook them off with his hand and raced madly on, his ears attuned to the sounds of the ants behind him.

That clicking roar continued, but in Burl's ears it was almost drowned out by the noise made by the halo of flies accompanying him. Their buzzing had deepened in pitch with the increase in size of all their race. It was now the note close to the deepest bass tone of an organ. Yet flies—though greatly enlarged on the forgotten planet—had not become magnified as much as some of the other creatures. There were no great heaps of putrid matter for them to lay their eggs in. The ants were busy scavengers, carting away the debris of tragedies in the insect world long before it could acquire the gamey flavor beloved of fly-maggots. Only in isolated spots were the flies really numerous. In such places they clustered in clouds.

Such a cloud began to form about Burl as he fled. It seemed as though a miniature whirlwind kept pace with him—a whirlwind composed of furry, revolting bodies and multi-faceted eyes. Fleeing, Burl had to swing his club before him to clear the way. Almost every stroke was interrupted by an impact against some thinly-armored body which collapsed with the spurting of reddish liquid.

Then an anguish as of red-hot iron struck upon Burl's back. One of the stinging flies had thrust its sharp-tipped proboscis into his flesh to suck the blood. Burl uttered a cry and ran full-tilt into the stalk of a blackened, draggled toadstool.

There was a curious crackling as of wet punk. The toadstool collapsed upon itself with a strange splashing sound. A great many creatures had laid their eggs in it, until now it was a seething mass of corruption and ill-smelling liquid.

When the toadstool crashed to the ground, it crumbled into a dozen pieces, spattering the earth for yards all about with stinking stuff in which tiny, headless maggots writhed convulsively.

The deep-toned buzzing of the flies took on a note of solemn satisfaction. They settled down upon this feast. Burl staggered to his feet and darted off again. Now he was nothing but a minor attraction to the flies, only three or four bothering to come after him. The others settled by the edges of the splashing fluid, quickly absorbed in an ecstasy of feasting. The few still hovering about his head, Burl killed,—but he did not have to smash them all. The remaining few descended to feast on their fallen comrades twitching feebly at his feet.

He ran on and passed beneath the wide-spreading leaves of an isolated giant cabbage. A great grasshopper crouched on the ground, its tremendous radially-opening jaws crunching the rank vegetation. Half a dozen great worms ate steadily of the leaves that supported them. One had swung itself beneath an overhanging leaf—which would have thatched houses for men—and was placidly anchoring itself for the spinning of a cocoon in which to sleep the sleep of metamorphosis.

A mile away, the great black tide of army ants advanced relentlessly. The great cabbage, the huge grasshopper, and all the stupid caterpillars on the leaves would presently be covered with small, black demons. The cocoon would never be spun. The caterpillars would be torn into thousands of furry fragments and devoured. The grasshopper would strike out with his terrific, unguided strength, crushing its assailants with blows of its great hind-legs and powerful jaws. But it would die, making terrible sounds of torments as the ants consumed it piecemeal.

The sound of the ants' advance overwhelmed all other noises now. Burl ran madly, his breath coming in great gasps, his eyes wide with panic. Alone of the world about him, he knew the danger that followed him. The insects he passed went about their business with that terrifying, abstracted efficiency found only in the insect world.

Burl's heart pounded madly from his running. The breath whistled in his nostrils—and behind him the flood of army ants kept pace. They came upon the feasting flies. Some took to the air and escaped. Others were too absorbed in their delicious meal. The twitching maggots, stranded by the scattering of their soupy broth, were torn to shreds and eaten. The flies who were seized vanished into tiny maws. And the serried ranks of ants moved on.

Burl could hear nothing else, now, but the clickings of their limbs and the stridulating challenges and cross-challenges they uttered. Now and then another sound pierced the noises made by the ants themselves: a cricket, perhaps, seized and dying, uttering deep-bass cries of agony.

Before the horde there was a busy world which teemed with life. Butterflies floated overhead on lazy wings; grubs waxed fat and huge; crickets feasted; great spiders sat quietly in their lairs, waiting with implacable patience for prey to fall into the trap-doors and snares; great beetles lumbered through the mushroom forests, seeking food and making love in monstrous, tragic fashion.

Behind the wide front of the army ants was—chaos. Emptiness. Desolation. All life save that of the army ants was exterminated, though some bewildered flying creatures still fluttered helplessly over the silent landscape. Yet even behind the army ants little bands of stragglers from the horde marched busily here and there, seeking some trace of life that had been overlooked by the main body.

Burl put forth his last ounce of strength. His limbs trembled. His breathing was agony. Sweat stood out upon his forehead. He ran for his life with the desperation of one who knows that death is at his heels. He ran as if his continued existence among the million tragedies of the single day were the purpose for which the universe had been created.

There was redness in the west and in the cloud-bank overhead. To the east gray sky became a deeper gray—much deeper. It was not yet time for the creatures of the day to seek their hiding-places, nor for the night-insects to come forth. But in many secret spots there were vague and sleepy stirrings.

Heedless of the approaching darkness Burl sped over an open space a hundred yards across. A thicket of beautifully golden mushrooms barred his way. Danger lay there. He dogged aside and saw in the gray dusk a glistening sheet of white, barely a yard above the ground. It was the web of the morning-spider which, on Earth, was noted only in hedges and such places when the dew of earliest dawn exposed it as a patternless plate of diamond-dust. There were anchor-cables, of course, but no geometry. Tidy housewives—also on Earth—used to mop it out of corners as a filmy fabric of irritating gossamer. On the forgotten planet it was a net with strength and bird-lime qualities that increased day by day, as its spinner moved restlessly over the surface, always trailing sticky cord behind itself.

Burl had no choice but to avoid it, even though he lost ground to the ant-horde roaring behind him. And night was definitely on the way. It was inconceivable that a human should travel in the lowlands after dark. It literally could not be done over the normal nightmare terrain. Burl had not only to escape the army ants, but find a hiding-place quickly if he was to see tomorrow's light. But he could not think so far ahead, just now.

He blundered through a screen of puffballs that shot dusty powder toward the sky. Ahead, a range of strangely colored hills came into view—purple, green, black and gold—melting into each other and branching off, inextricably mingled. They rose to a height of perhaps sixty or seventy feet. A curious grayish haze had gathered above them. It seemed to be a layer of thin vapor, not like mist or fog, clinging to certain parts of the hills, rising slowly to coil and gather into an indefinitely thicker mass above the ridges.

The hills themselves were not geological features, but masses of fungus that had grown and cannibalized, piling up upon themselves to the thickness of carboniferous vegetation. Over the face of the hills grew every imaginable variety of yeast and mould and rust. They grew within and upon themselves, forming freakish conglomerations that piled up into a range of hills, stretching across the lunatic landscape for miles.

Burl blundered up the nearest slope. Sometimes the surface was a hard rind that held him up. Sometimes his feet sank—perhaps inches, perhaps to mid-leg. He scrambled frantically.

Panting, gasping, staggering from the exhaustion of moving across the fungus quicksand, he made his way to the top of the first hill, plunged down into a little valley on the farther side, and up another slope. He left a clear trail behind him of disturbed and scurrying creatures that had inevitably found a home in the mass of living stuff. Small sinuous centipedes scuttled here and there, roused by his passage. At the bottom of his footprints writhed fat white worms. Beetles popped into view and vanished again...

A half mile across the range and Burl could go no farther. He stumbled and fell and lay there, gasping hoarsely. Overhead the gray sky had become a deep-red which was rapidly melting into that redness too deep to be seen except as black. But there was still some light from the west.

Burl sobbed for breath in a little hollow, his sharp-toothed club still clasped in his hands. Something huge, with wings like sails, soared in silhouette against the sunset. Burl lay motionless, breathing in great gasps, his limbs refusing to lift him.

The sound of the army ants continued. At last, above the crest of the last hillock he had surmounted, two tiny glistening antennae appeared, then the small, deadly shape of an army ant. The forerunner of its horde, it moved deliberately forward, waving its antennae ceaselessly. It made its way toward Burl, tiny clickings coming from its limbs.

A little wisp of vapor swirled toward the ant. It was the vapor that had gathered over the whole range of hills as a thin, low cloud. It enveloped the ant which seemed to be thrown into a strange convulsion, throwing itself about, legs moving aimlessly. If it had been an animal instead of an insect, it would have choked and gasped. But ants breathe through air-holes in their abdomens. It writhed helplessly on the spongy stuff across which it had been moving.

Burl was conscious of a strange sensation. His body felt remarkably warm. It felt hot. It was an unparalleled sensation, because Burl had no experience of fire or the heat of the sun. The only warmth he had ever known was when huddling together with his tribesmen in some hiding-place to avoid the damp chill of the night.

Then, the heat of their breath and flesh helped to combat discomfort. But this was a fiercer heat. It was intolerable. Burl moved his body with a tremendous effort and for a moment the fungus soil was cool beneath him. Then the sensation of hotness began again and increased until Burl's skin was reddened and inflamed.

The tenuous vapor, too, seemed to swirl his way. It made his lungs smart and his eyes water. He still breathed in painful gasps, but even that short period of rest had done him some good. But it was the heat that drove him to his feet again. He crawled painfully to the crest of the next hill. He looked back.

This was the highest hill he had come upon and he could see most of the purple range in the deep, deep dusk. Now he was more than halfway through the hills. He had barely a quarter-mile to go, northward. But east and west the range of purple hills was a ceaseless, undulating mass of lifts and hollows, of ridges and spurs of all imaginable colorings.

And at the tips of most of them were wisps of curling gray.

From his position he could see a long stretch of the hills not hidden by the surrounding darkness. Back along the way he had come, the army ants now swept up into the range of hills. Scouts and advance-guard parties scurried here and there. They stopped to devour the creatures inhabiting the surface layers. But the main body moved on inexorably.

The hills, though, were alive, not upheavals of the ground but festering heaps of insanely growing fungus, hollowed out in many places by tunnels, hiding-places, and lurking-places. These the ants invaded. They swept on, devouring everything...

Burl leaned heavily upon his club and watched dully. He could run no more. The army ants were spreading everywhere. They would reach him soon.

Far to the right, the vapor thickened. A thin column of smoke arose in the dim half-light. Burl did not know smoke, of course. He could not conceivably guess that deep down in the interior of the insanely growing hills, pressure had killed and oxidation had carbonized the once-living material. By oxidation the temperature down below had been raised. In the damp darkness of the bowels of the hills spontaneous combustion had begun.

The great mounds of tinderlike mushroom had begun to burn very slowly, quite unseen. There had been no flames because the hills' surface remained intact and there was no air to feed the burning. But when the army ants dug ferociously for fugitive small things, air was admitted to tunnels abandoned because of heat.

Then slow combustion speeded up. Smoulderings became flames. Sparks became coals. A dozen columns of fume-laden smoke rose into the heavens and gathered into a dense pall above the range of purple hills. And Burl apathetically watched the serried ranks of army ants march on toward the widening furnaces that awaited them.

They had recoiled from the river instinctively. But their ancestors had never known fire. In the Amazon basin, on Earth, there had never been forest fires. On the forgotten planet there had never been fires at all, unless the first forgotten colonists tried to make them. In any case the army ants had no instinctive terror of flame. They marched into the blazing openings that appeared in the hills. They snapped with their mandibles at the leaping flames, and sprang to grapple with the burning coals.

The blazing areas widened as the purple surface was consumed. Burl watched without comprehension—even without thankfulness. He stood breathing more and more easily until the glow from approaching flames reddened his skin and the acrid smoke made tears flow from his eyes. Then he retreated slowly, leaning on his club and often looking back.

Night had fallen, but yet it was light to the army ants. They marched on, shrilling their defiance. They poured devotedly—and ferociously—into the inferno of flame. At last there were only small groups of stragglers from the great ant-army scurrying here and there over the ground their comrades had stripped of all life. The bodies of the main army made a vast malodor, burning in the furnace of the hills.

There had been pain in that burning, agony such as no one would willing dwell upon. But it came of the insane courage of the ants, attacking the burning stuff with their horny jaws, rolling over and over with flaming lumps of charcoal clutched in their mandibles. Burl heard them shrilling their war-cry even as they died. Blinded, antennae singed off, legs shriveling, they yet went forward to attack their impossible enemy.

Burl made his way slowly over the hills. Twice he saw small bodies of the vanished army. They had passed between the widening furnaces and furiously devoured all that moved as they forged ahead. Once Burl was spied, and a shrill cry sounded, but he moved on and only a single ant rushed after him. Burl brought down his club and a writhing body remained to be eaten by its comrades when they came upon it.

And now the last faint traces of light had vanished in the west. There was no real brightness anywhere except the flames of the burning hills. The slow, slow nightly rain that dripped down all through the dark hours began. It made a pattering noise upon the unburnt part of the hills.

Burl found firm ground beneath his feet. He listened keenly for sounds of danger. Something rustled heavily in a thicket of toadstools a hundred feet away. There were sounds of preening, and of feet delicately placed here and there upon the ground. Then a great body took to the air with the throbbing beat of mighty wings.

A fierce down-current of air smote Burl, and he looked upward in time to glimpse the outline of a huge moth passing overhead. He turned to watch the line of its flight, and saw the fierce glow filling all the horizon. The hills burned brighter as the flames widened.

He crouched beneath a squat toadstool and waited for the dawn. The slow-dripping rain kept on, falling with irregular, drum-like beats upon the tough top of the toadstool.

He did not sleep. He was not properly hidden, and there was always danger in the dark. But this was not the darkness Burl was used to. The great fires grew and spread in the masses of ready-carbonized mushroom. The glare on the horizon grew brighter through the hours. It also came nearer.

Burl shivered a little, as he watched. He had never even dreamed of fire before, and even the overhanging clouds were lighted by these flames. Over a stretch at least a dozen miles in length and from half a mile to three miles across, the seething furnaces and columns of flame-lit smoke sent illumination over the world. It was like the glow the lights of a city can throw upon the sky. And like the flitting of aircraft above a city was the assembly of fascinated creatures of the night.

Great moths and flying beetles, gigantic gnats and midges grown huge upon this planet, fluttered and danced above the flames. As the fire came nearer, Burl could see them: colossal, delicately-formed creatures sweeping above the white-hot expanse. There were moths with riotously-colored wings of thirty-foot spread, beating the air with mighty strokes, their huge eyes glowing like garnets as they stared intoxicatedly at the incandescence below them.

Burl saw a great peacock-moth soaring above the hills with wings all of forty feet across. They fluttered like sails of unbelievable magnificence. And this was when all the separate flames had united to form a single sheet of white-hot burning stuff spread across the land for miles.

Feathery antennae of the finest lace spread out before the head of the peacock-moth; its body was of softest velvet. A ring of snow-white fur marked where its head began. The glare from below smote the maroon of its body with a strange effect. For one instant it was outlined clearly. Its eyes shone more redly than any ruby's fire. The great, delicate wings were poised in flight. Burl caught the flash of flame upon the two great irridescent spots on the wings. Shining purple and bright red, all the glory of chalcedony and of chrysoprase was reflected in the glare of burning fungi.

And then Burl saw it plunge downward, straight into the thickest and fiercest of the leaping flames. It flung itself into the furnace as a willing, drunken victim of their beauty.

Flying beetles flew clumsily above the pyre also, their horny wing-cases stiffly outstretched. In the light from below they shone like burnished metal. Their clumsy bodies, with spurred and fierce-toothed limbs, darted through the flame-lit smoke like so many grotesque meteors.

Burl saw strange collisions and still stranger meetings. Male and female flying creatures circled and spun in the glare, dancing their dance of love and death. They mounted higher than Burl could see, drunk with the ecstasy of living, and then descended to plunge headlong in the roaring flames below.

From every side the creatures came. Moths of brightest yellow, with furry bodies palpitant with life, flew madly to destruction. Other moths of a deepest black, with gruesome symbols on their wings, swiftly came to dance above the glow like motes in sunlight.

And Burl crouched beneath a toadstool, watching while the perpetual, slow raindrops fell and fell, and a continuous hissing noise came from where the rain splashed amid the flames.

CHAPTER FOUR
A Killer of Monsters

The night wore on, while the creatures above the firelight danced and died, their numbers ever reinforced by fresh arrivals. Burl sat tensely still, his eyes watching everything while his mind groped for an explanation of what he saw. At last the sky grew dimly gray, then brighter, and after a long time it was day. The flames of the burning hills seemed to dim and die as all world became bright. After a long while Burl crawled from his hiding-place and stood erect.

No more than two hundred paces from where he stood, a straight wall of smoke rose from the still-smouldering fungus-range. Burl could see the smoke rising for miles on either hand. He turned to continue on his way, and saw the remains of one of the tragedies of the night.

A great moth had flown into the flames, been horribly scorched, and floundered out again. Had it been able to fly, it would have returned to its devouring deity; but now it lay upon the ground, its antennae hopelessly seared. One beautiful wing was nothing but gaping holes. The eyes had been dimmed by flame. The exquisitely tapering limbs lay broken and crushed by the violence of landing. The creature was helpless on the ground, only the stumps of its antennae moving restlessly and the abdomen pulsating slowly as it drew pain-racked breaths.

Burl drew near. He raised his club.

When he moved on there was a velvet cloak cast over his shoulders, gleaming with all the colors of the rainbows. A gorgeous mass of soft blue moth-fur was about his middle, and he had bound upon his forehead two yard-long fragments of the moth's magnificent antennae.

He strode on slowly, clad as no man had been clad in all the ages before him. After a while another victim of the holocaust—similarly blundered out to die—yielded him a spear that was longer and sharper and much more deadly than his first. So he took up his journey to Saya looking like a prince of Ind upon a bridal journey—though surely no mere prince ever wore such raiment.

For many miles, Burl threaded his way through an extensive forest of thin-stalked toadstools. They towered high over his head, colorful, parasitic moulds and rusts all about their bases. Twice he came upon open glades where bubbling pools of green slime festered in corruption. Once he hid himself as a monster scarabeus beetle lumbered by three yards away, clanking like some mighty machine.

Burl saw the heavy armor and inward-curving jaws of the monster. He almost envied him his weapons. The time was not yet come, though, when Burl and his kind would hunt such giants for the juicy flesh within its armored limbs. Burl was still a savage, still ignorant, still essentially timid. His only significant advance had been that where at first he had fled without reasoning, now he paused to see if he need flee.

He was a strange sight, moving through the shadowed lanes of the forest in his cloak of velvet. The fierce-toothed leg of a fighting beetle rested in a strip of sinew about his waist, ready for use. His new spear was taller than himself. He looked like a conqueror. But he was still a fearful and feeble creature, no match for the monstrous creatures about him. He was weak—and in that lay his greatest hope. Because if he were strong, he would not need to think.

Hundreds of thousands of years before, his ancestors had been forced to develop brains as penalty for the lack of claws or fangs. Burl was sunk as low as any of them, but he had to combat more horrifying enemies, more inexorable dangers, and many times more crafty antagonists. His ancestors had invented knives and spears and flying missiles, but the creatures about Burl had weapons a thousand times more deadly than the ones that had defended the first humans.

The fact, however, simply put a premium on the one faculty Burl had which the insect world has not.

In mid-morning he heard a discordant, deep-bass bellow, coming from a spot not twenty yards from where he moved. He hid in panic, waiting for an instant, listening.

The bellow came again, but this time with a querulous note. Burl heard a crashing and plunging as of some creature caught in a snare. A mushroom tumbled with a spongelike sound, and the thud was followed by a tremendous commotion. Something was fighting desperately against something else, but Burl did not know what creatures were in combat.

He waited, and the noise died gradually away. Presently his breath came more slowly and his courage returned. He stole from his hiding-place and would have made away, but new curiosity held him back. Instead of creeping from the scene, he moved cautiously toward the source of the noise.

Peering between two cream-colored stalks he saw a wide, funnel-shaped snare of silk spread out before him, some twenty yards across and as many deep. The individual threads could be plainly seen, but in the mass it seemed a fabric of sheerest, finest texture. Held up by tall mushrooms, it was anchored to the ground below and drew away to a small point through which a hole led to some as yet unseen recess. All the space of the wide snare was hung with threads: fine, twisted threads no more than half the thickness of Burl's finger.

This was the trap of a labyrinth spider. Not one of the interlacing strands was strong enough to hold any but the feeblest prey, but the threads were there by thousands. A cricket had become entangled in the sticky maze. Its limbs thrashed out and broke threads with every stroke, but each time became entangled in a dozen more. It struggled mightily, emitting at intervals—again— its horrible bass roar.

Burl breathed more easily. He watched with fascinated eyes. Mere death among insects—even tragic death—held no great interest for him. It was too common an occurrence. And there were few insects which deliberately sought man. Most insects have their allotted prey and will seek no others.

But this involved a spider, and spiders have a terrifying impartiality. A spider devouring some luckless insect was but an example of what might happen to Burl. So he watched alertly, his eyes traveling from the enmeshed cricket to the strange opening at the back of the funnel-shaped labyrinth.

That opening darkened. Two shining, glistening eyes had been watching from the tunnel in which the spider had been waiting. Now it swung out lightly, revealing itself as a gray spider, with twin black ribbons upon its thorax and two stripes of curiously speckled brown and white upon its abdomen. Burl saw, also, two curious appendages like a tail, as it came nimbly out of its hiding-place and approached the trapped creature.

The cricket was struggling weakly, now, and the cries it uttered were but feeble, because of the cords that fettered its limbs. Burl saw the spider throw itself upon the cricket which gave one final, convulsive shudder as fangs pierced its armor.

Shortly after, the spider fed. With bestial enjoyment it sucked all the succulence, all the fluid, from its victim's carcass.

Then the breath left Burl in a peculiar, frightened gasp. It was not from anything he saw or heard. It was something that he thought.

For a second, his knees knocked together in self-induced panic. It occurred to him that he, Burl, had killed a hunting spider—a tarantula—upon the red-clay cliff. True, the killing had been an accident and had nearly cost him his own life in the web-spider's snare. But—he had killed a spider and of the most deadly kind. Now it occurred to Burl that he could kill another.

Spiders were the ogres of the human tribes on the forgotten planet. Knowledge of them was hard to come by, because to study them was death. But all men knew that web-spiders never left their traps. Never! And Burl had imagined himself making an impossibly splendid, incredibly daring use of that fact.

Denying to himself that he intended any action so suicidal, he nevertheless drew back from the front of the snare and made his way to the back, where the spider's tunnel was no more than ten feet away.

Then he found himself waiting.

Presently, through the interstices of the silk, he saw the gray bulk of the spider. It had left the drained and shrunken carcass of the cricket to return to its resting-place, settling itself carefully upon the soft walls of the fabric tunnel. From the yielding, globular nest at the tunnel's end it fixed maniacal eyes once more upon the threads of its snare, seen down the length of the passage-way.

Burl's hair stood on end from sheer fright, but he was the slave of an idea.

The tunnel and the nest at its end did not rest on the ground, but were suspended in air by cables like those that spread the gin itself. The gray labyrinth-spider bulged the fabric. It lay in luxurious comfort, waiting for victims to approach.

There was sweat on Burl's face as he raised his spear. The bare idea of attacking a spider was horrifying. But actually he was in no danger whatever before the instant of the spear-thrust, because web-spiders never, never, leave their webs to hunt.

So Burl sweated, and grasped his spear with agonized firmness—and thrust it into the bulge that was the spider's body in its nest. He thrust with hysterical fury.

And then he ran as if the devil were after him.

It was a long time before he dared come back, his heart in his throat. All was still. He had missed the horrid convulsions of the wounded spider; he had not heard the frightful gnashings of its fangs at the piercing weapon, nor seen the silken threads of the tunnel ripped and torn in the spider's death-struggle. Burl came back to quietness. There was a great rent in the silken tunnel, and a puddle of ill-smelling stuff lay upon the ground. From time to time another droplet fell from the spear to join it. And the great spider had fallen half through its own enlargement of the rent made by the spear in the wall of the nest.

Burl stared. Even when he saw it, the thing was not easy to believe. The dead eyes of the spider looked at him with mad, frozen malignity. The fangs were still raised to kill. The hairy legs were still braced as if to enlarge further the gaping hole through which it had partly fallen.

Then Burl felt exultation. His tribe had been furtive vermin for almost forty generations, fleeing from the mighty insects, hiding from them, and when caught waiting helplessly for death, screaming shrilly in horror. But he, Burl, had turned the tables. He, a man, had killed a spider! His breast expanded. Always his tribesmen went quietly and fearfully, making no sound. But a sudden, surprising, triumphant yell burst from Burl's lips—the first hunting-cry of man upon the forgotten planet in two thousand years.

Next second, of course, his pulse almost stopped in sheer terror because he had made such a noise. He listened fearfully. The insect world was oblivious to him. Presently, shuddering but infinitely proud, he drew near his prey. He carefully withdrew his spear, poised to flee if the spider stirred. It did not. It was dead. The blood upon the spear was revolting. Burl wiped it off on a leathery toadstool. Then...

He thought of Saya and his tribesmen. Trembling even as he gloated over his own remarkable self, he shifted the spider and worked it out of the nest. Presently he moved off with the belly of the spider upon his back and two of its hairy legs over his shoulders. The other limbs of the monster hung limp, trailing on the ground behind him.

Marching, then he was the first such spectacle in history. His velvet cloak shining with its irridescent spots, the yard-long scraps of golden antennae bound to his forehead, a spear in his hand, and the hideous bulk of a gray spider for burden—Burl was a very strange sight indeed.

He believed that other creatures fled before him because of the thing he carried. He tended to grow haughty. But actually, of course, insects do not know fear. They recognize their own specific enemies. That is necessary. But the his of the lowlands on the forgotten planet went on abstractedly, despite the splendid feat of one man.

Burl marched. He came upon a valley full of torn and tattered mushrooms. There was not a single yellow top among them. Every one had been infested with maggots that had liquefied the tough meat of the mushroom-tops, causing it to drip to the ground below. The liquid was gathered in a golden pool in the center of the small depression. Burl heard a loud and deep-toned humming before he saw the valley. Then he stopped and looked down.

He saw the golden pond, its surface reflecting the gray sky and the darkened stumps of mushrooms on the hillside which looked as if they had been blackened by a running flame. A small brooklet of golden liquid trickled over a rocky ledge, and all round the edges of the pond and brook, in ranks and rows, by hundreds and by thousands and it seemed by millions, were the green-gold bodies of great flies.

They were small compared to other insects. The flesh-flies laid their eggs by the hundreds in decaying carcasses. The others chose mushrooms to lay their eggs in. To feed the maggots that would hatch, a relatively great quantity of food was needed; therefore, the flies must remain comparatively small, or the body of a single grasshopper would furnish food for only a few maggots instead of the hundreds it must support. There must also be a limit to the size of worms if hundreds were to feast upon a single fungus.

But there was no limitation to the greediness of the adult creatures. There were bluebottles and green-bottles and all the flies of metallic lustre, gathered at a Lucullan feast of corruption. The buzzing of those swarming above the golden pool was a tremendous sound. The flying bodies flashed and glittered as they flew back and forth, seeking a place to alight and join in the orgy.

The glittering bodies clustered in already-found places were motionless as if carved from metal. Burl watched them. And then he saw motion overhead.

A slender, brilliant shape appeared, darting swiftly through the air, enlarging into a needle-like body with transparent, shining wings and two huge eyes. It circled and enlarged again, becoming a shimmering dragonfly, twenty feet and more in length. It poised itself abruptly above the pool, and then darted down, its jaws snapping viciously. They snapped again and again. Burl could not follow their slashings. And with each snap the glittering body of a fly vanished.

A second dragonfly appeared and a third. They swooped above the golden pool, snapping in mid-air, making their abrupt and angular turns, creatures of incredible ferocity and beauty. In that mass of buzzing creatures, even the most voracious appetite must soon have been sated, but the slender creatures still darted about in frenzied destruction.

And all this while the loud, contented, deep-bass humming went on as before. Their comrades were slaughtered by the hundreds not forty feet above their heads, but still the glittering rows of red-eyed flies gorged themselves upon the fluid of the pond. The dragonflies feasted until they were unable to devour even a single one more of their chosen prey. But even then they continued to sweep madly above the pool, striking down the buzzing flies though their bodies must perforce remain uneaten.

Some of the dead flies, crushed to pulp by the angry dragonflies, dropped among their feasting brothers. Presently, one of them placed its disgusting proboscis upon the mangled creature. It sipped daintily from the contents of the broken armor. Another joined it and another. In a little while a cluster of them pushed against each other for a chance to join them in a cannibalistic feast.

Burl turned aside and went on, leaving the dragonflies still at their massacre and the flies absorbed and ecstatic at their feast. The feast, indeed, was improved by the rain of murdered brethren from overhead.

Only a few miles farther on, Burl came upon a familiar landmark. He knew it well, but had always kept at a safe distance from it. A mass of rock had heaved itself up from the almost level plain over which he traveled to form an out-jutting cliff. At one point the rock overhung, forming an inverted ledge—a roof over nothingness—which had been preempted by a hairy monster and made into a fairy-like dwelling. A white hemisphere clung to the rock, firmly anchored by long cables.

Burl knew the place as one to be feared. A clotho spider had built itself a nest there, from which it emerged to hunt the unwary. Within the silken globe was a monstrosity, resting upon cushions of softest silk. The exterior had been beautiful once. But if one went too near one of the little inverted arches seemingly closed by panels of silk—it would open and out would rush a creature from a dream of hell.

Surely Burl knew this place. Hung upon the walls of the fairy palace were trophies. They had a purpose, of course. Stones and boulders hung there, too, to hold the structure firm against the storm-winds that rarely blew. But amid the stones and fragments of insect-armor there was a very special decoration: the shrunken, dessicated skeleton of a man.

The death of that man had saved Burl's life two years before. They had been together, seeking a new source of edible mushroom. The clotho spider was a hunter, not a spinner of webs. It had sprung suddenly from behind a great puffball as the two men froze in horror. Then it had come forward and deliberately chosen its victim. It did not choose Burl.

Now he looked with half-frightened speculation at the lair of his ancient enemy. Some day, perhaps...

But now he passed on. He went past the thicket in which the great moths hid by day, past the slimy pool in which something unknown but terrible lurked. He penetrated the little forest of mushrooms that glowed at night and the place where the truffle-hunting beetles chirped thunderously during the dark hours.

And then he saw Saya. He caught a flash of pink skin vanishing behind a squat toadstool, and he ran forward calling her name. She emerged, and saw the figure with the horrible bulk of the spider on its back. She cried out in horror, and Burl understood. He let his burden fall, running swiftly to her.

They met. Saya waited timidly until she saw who this man was, and then she was astounded indeed. With golden plumes rising from his head, a velvet cloak about his shoulders, blue moth-fur about his middle, and a spear in his hand—and a dead spider behind him!—this was not the Burl she had known.

He took her hands, babbling proudly. She stared at him and at his victim—but the language of men had diminished sadly—struggling to comprehend. Presently her eyes glowed. She pulled at his wrists.

When they found the other tribesmen, they were carrying the dead spider between them, Saya looking more proud than Burl.

CHAPTER FIVE
Meat of Man's Killing

In their climb up from savagery, the principal handicap from which men have always suffered is the fact that they are human. Or it can be said that human beings always have to struggle against the obstacle which is simply that they are men. To Burl his splendid return to the tribe called for a suitable reaction. He expected them to take note that he was remarkable, unparalleled, and in all ways admirable. He expected them to look at him with awe. He rather hoped that the sight of him would involve something like ecstasy.

And as a matter of fact, it did. For fully an hour they gathered around him while he used his—and their—scanty vocabulary to tell them of his unique achievements and adventures during the past two days and nights. They listened attentively and with appropriate admiration and vicarious pride.

This in itself was a step upward. Mostly their talk was of where food might be found and where danger lurked. Strictly practical data connected with the pressing business of getting enough to eat and staying alive. The sheer pressure of existence was so great that the humans Burl knew had altogether abandoned such luxuries as boastful narrative. They had given up tradition. They did not think of art in even its most primitive forms, and the only craft they knew was the craftiness which promoted simple survival. So for them to listen to a narrative which did not mean either food or even a lessening of danger to themselves was a step upward on the cultural scale.

But they were savages. They inspected the dead spider, shuddering. It was pure horror. They did not touch it—the adults not at all, and even Dik and Tet not for a very long time. Nobody thought of spiders as food. Too many of them had been spiders' food.

But presently even the horror aroused by the spider palled. The younger children quailed at sight of it, of course; but the adults came to ignore it. Only the two gangling boys tried to break off a furry leg with which to charge and terrify the younger ones still further. They failed to get it loose because they did not think of cutting it. But they had nothing to cut it with anyhow.

Old Jon went wheezing off, foraging. He waved a hand to Burl as he went. Burl was indignant. But it was true that he had brought back no food. And people must eat.

Tama went off, her tongue clacking, with Lona the half-grown girl to help her find and bring back something edible. Dor, the strongest man in the tribe, went away to look where he thought there might be edible mushrooms full-grown again. Cori left with her children—very carefully on watch for danger to them—to see what she could find.

In little more than an hour Burl's audience had diminished to Saya. Within two hours ants found the spider where it had been placed for the tribe to admire. Within three hours there was nothing left of it. During the fourth hour—as Burl struggled to dredge up some new, splendid item to tell Saya for the tenth time, or thereabouts—during the fourth hour one of the tribeswomen beckoned to Saya. She left with a flashing backward smile for Burl. She went, actually, to help dig up underground fungi—much like truffles—discovered by the older woman. She undoubtedly expected to share them with Burl.

But in five hours it was night and Burl was very indignant with his tribesfolk. They had shifted the location of the hiding-place for the night, and nobody had thought to tell him. And if Saya wished to come for Burl, to lead him to that place, she did not dare for the simple reason that it was night.

For a long time after he found a hiding-place, Burl fumed bitterly to himself. He was very much of a human being, differing from his fellows—so far—mainly because he had been through experiences not shared by them. He had resolved a subjective dilemma of sorts by determining to return to his tribe. He had discovered a weapon which, at first, had promised—and secured—foodstuff, and later had saved him from a tarantula. His discovery that fish-oil was useful when applied to spider-snares and things sticking to the feet was of vast importance to the tribe. Most remarkable of all, he had deliberately killed a spider. And he had experienced triumph. Temporarily he had even experienced admiration.

The adulation was a thing which could never be forgotten. Human appetites are formed by human experiences. One never had an appetite for a thing one has not known in some fashion. But no human being who has known triumph is ever quite the same again, and anybody who has once been admired by his fellows is practically ruined for life—at least so far as being independent of admiration is concerned.

So during the dark hours, while the slow rain dipped in separate, heavy drops from the sky, Burl first coddled his anger—which was a very good thing for a member of a race grown timorous and furtive—and then began to make indignant plans to force his tribesmen to yield him more of the delectable sensations he alone had begun to know.

He was not especially comfortable during the night. The hiding-place he had chosen was not water-tight. Water trickled over him for several hours before he discovered that his cloak, though it would not keep him dry—which it would have done if properly disposed—would still keep the same water next to his skin where his body could warm it. Then he slept. When morning came he felt singularly refreshed. For a savage, he was unusually clean, too.

He woke before dawn with vainglorious schemes in his head. The sky grew gray and then almost white. The overhanging cloud bank seemed almost to touch the earth, but gradually withdrew. The mist among the mushroom-forests grew thinner, and the slow rain ceased reluctantly. When he peered from his hiding-place, the mad world he knew was, as far as he could see, quite mad, as usual. The last of the night-insects had vanished. The day-creatures began to venture out.

Not too far from the crevice where he'd hidden was an ant-hill, monstrous by standards on other planets. It was piled up not of sand but gravel and small boulders. Burl saw a stirring. At a certain spot the smooth, outer surface crumbled and fell into an invisible opening. A spot of darkness appeared. Two slender, thread-like antennae popped out. They withdrew and popped out again. The spot enlarged until there was a sizeable opening. An ant appeared, one of the warrior-ants of this particular breed. It stood fiercely over the opening, waving its antennae agitatedly as if striving to sense some danger to its metropolis.

He was fourteen inches long, this warrior, and his mandibles were fierce and strong. After a moment, two other warriors thrust past him. They ran about the whole extent of the ant-hill, their legs clicking, antennae waving restlessly.

They returned, seeming to confer with the first, then went back down into the city with every appearance of satisfaction. As if they made a properly reassuring report, within minutes afterward, a flood of black, ill-smelling workers poured out of the opening and dispersed about their duties.

The city of the ants had begun its daily toil. There were deep galleries underground here: graineries, storage-vaults, refectories, and nurseries, and even a royal apartment in which the queen-ant reposed. She was waited upon by assiduous courtiers, fed by royal stewards, and combed and caressed by the hands of her subjects and children. A dozen times larger than her loyal servants, she was no less industrious than they in her highly specialized fashion. From the time of waking to the time of rest she was queen-mother in the most literal imaginable sense. At intervals, to be measured only in minutes, she brought forth an egg, perhaps three inches in length, which was whisked away to the municipal nursery. And this constant, insensate increase in the population of the city made all its frantic industry at once possible and necessary.

Burl came out and spread his cloak on the ground. In a little while he felt a tugging at it. An ant was tearing off a bit of the hem. Burl slew the ant angrily and retreated. Twice within the next half-hour he had to move swiftly to avoid foragers who would not directly attack him because he was alive—unless he seemed to threaten danger—but who lusted after the fabric of his garments.

This annoyance—and Burl would merely have taken it as a thing to be accepted a mere two days before—this annoyance added to Burl's indignation with the world about him. He was in a very bad temper indeed when he found old Jon, wheezing as he checked on the possibility of there being edible mushrooms in a thicket of poisonous, pink-and-yellow amanitas.

Burl haughtily commanded Jon to follow him. Jon's untidy whiskers parted as his mouth dropped open in astonishment. Burl's tribe was so far from being really a tribe that for anybody to give a command was astonishing. There was no social organization, absolutely no tradition of command. As a rule life was too uncertain for anybody to establish authority.

But Jon followed Burl as he stamped on through the morning mist. He saw a small movement and shouted imperatively. This was appalling! Men did not call attention to themselves! He gathered up Dor, the strongest of the men. Later, he found Jak who some day would wear an expression of monkey-like wisdom. Then Tet and Dik, the half-grown boys, came trooping to see what was happening.

Burl led onward. A quarter of a mile and they came upon a great, gutted shell which had been a rhinoceros beetle the day before. Today it was a disassembled mass of chitinous armor. Burl stopped, frowning portentously. He showed his quaking followers how to arm themselves. Dor picked up the horn hesitantly, Burl showing him how to use it. He stabbed out awkwardly with the sharp fragment of armor. Burl showed others how to use the leg-sections for clubs. They tested them without conviction. In any sort of danger, they would trust to their legs and a frantically effective gift for hiding.

Burl snarled at his tribesmen and led them on. It was unprecedented. But because of that fact there was no precedent for rebellion. Burl led them in a curve. They glanced all about apprehensively.

When they came to an unusually large and attractive clump of golden edible mushrooms, there were murmurings. Old Jon was inclined to go and load himself and retire to some hiding-place for as long as the food lasted. But Burl snarled again.

Numbly they followed on—Dor and Jon and Jak and the two youngsters. The ground inclined upward. They came upon puffballs. There was a new kind visible, colored a lurid red, that did not grow like the others. It seemed to begin and expand underground, then thrust away the soil above in its development. Its taut, angry-red parchment envelope seemed to swell from a reservoir of subterranean material. Burl and the others had never seen anything like it.

They climbed higher. As other edible mushrooms came into view Burl's followers cheered visibly. This was a new tribal ground anyhow and it had not been fully explored. But Burl was leading them to quantities of food they had never suspected before.

Quaintly, it was Burl himself who began to feel an uncomfortable dryness in his throat. He knew what he was about. His followers did not suspect because to them what he intended was simply inconceivable. They couldn't suspect it because they couldn't imagine anybody doing such a thing. It simply couldn't be thought of at all.

It is rather likely that Burl began to regret that he had thought of it. It had come to him first as an angry notion in the night. Then the idea had developed as a suitable punishment for his abandonment. By dawn it was an ambition so terrifying that it fascinated him. Now he was committed to it in his own mind, and the only way to keep his knees from knocking together was to keep moving. If his followers had protested now, he would have allowed himself to be persuaded. But he heard more pleased murmurs. There was more edible stuff, in quantity. But there were no ant-trails here, no sounds of foraging beetles. This was an area which Burl's tribesmen could clearly see was almost devoid of dangerous life. They seemed to brighten a little. This, they seemed to think, would be a good place to move to.

But Burl knew better. There were few ground-insects here because the area was hunted out. And Burl knew what had done the hunting.

He expected the others to realize where they were when they dodged around a clump of the new red puffballs and saw bald rock before them and a falling-away to emptiness beyond. Even then they could have retreated, but it did not enter their heads that Burl could do anything like this.

They didn't know where they were until Burl held up his hand for silence almost at the edge of the rock-knob which rose a hundred feet sheer, curving out a little near its top. They looked out uncomprehendingly at the mist-filled air and the nightmare landscape fading into its grayness. A tiny spider, the very youngest of hatchlings and barely four inches across, stealthily stalked another vastly smaller mite. The other was the many-legged larva of the oil-beetle. The larva itself had been called—on other planets by other men—the bee-louse. It could easily hide in the thick furl of a giant bumble-bee. But this one small creature never practiced that ability. The hatchling spider sprang and the small midge died. When the spider had grown and, being grown, spun a web, it would slay great crickets with the same insane ferocity.

Burl's followers saw first this and then certain three-quarter-inch strands of dirty silk that came up over the edge of the precipice. As one man after another realized where he was, he trembled violently. Dor turned gray. Jon and Jak were paralyzed with horror. They couldn't run.

Seeing the others even more frightened than himself filled Burl with a wholly unwarranted courage. When he opened his mouth, they cringed. If he shouted then at least one, more likely several, of them would die.

And this was because some forty or fifty feet down the mould-speckled precipice hung a drab-white object nearly hemispherical, some six feet in its half-diameter. A number of little semi-circular doors were fixed about its sides like arches. Though each one seemed to be a doorway, only one would open.

The thing had been oddly beautiful at first glance. It was held fast to the inward-sloping stone by cables, one or two of which stretched down toward the ground. Others reached up over the precipice-edge to hold it fast. It was a most unusual engineering feat, yet something more than that: this was also an ogre's castle. Ghastly trophies were fastened to the outer walls and hung by silken cords below it. Here was the hind-leg of one of the smaller beetles, there the wing-case of a flying creature. Here a snail-shell—the snails of Earth would hardly have recognized their descendant—and there a boulder weighing forty pounds or more. The shrunken head-armor of a beetle, the fierce jaws of a cricket, the pitiful shreds of dozens of creatures—all had once provided meals for the monster in the castle. And dangling by the longest cord of all was the shrunken, shriveled body of a long-dead man.

Burl glared at his tribesmen, clamping his jaws tight lest they chatter. He knew, as did the others, that any noise would bring the clotho spider swinging up its anchor-cables to the cliff-top. The men didn't dare move. But every one of them—and Burl was among the foremost—knew that inside the half-dome of gruesome relics the monster reposed in luxury and ease. It had eight furry, attenuated legs and a face that was a mask of horror. The eyes glittered malevolently above needle-sharp mandibles. It was a hunting-spider. At any moment it might leave the charnel-house in which it lived to stalk and pursue prey.

Burl motioned the others forward. He led one of them to the end of a cable where it curled up over the edge for an anchorage.

He ripped the end free—and his flesh crawled as he did so. He found a boulder and knotted the end of the cable about it. In a whisper that imitated a spider's ferocity, Burl gave the man orders. He plucked a second quaking tribesman by the arm. With the jerky, uncontrolled movements of a robot, Dor allowed himself to be led to a second cable.

Burl commanded in a frenzy. He worked with stiff fingers and a dry throat, not knowing how he could do this thing. He had formed a plan in anger which he somehow was carrying out in a panic. Although his followers were as responsive as dead men, they obeyed him because they felt like dead men, unable to resist. After all, it was simple enough. There were boulders at the top of the precipice and silken cables hung taut over the edge. As Burl fastened a heavy boulder to each cable he could find, he loosened the silken strand until it hung tight only at the very edge of the more-than-vertical fall.

He took his post—and his followers gazed at him with the despairing eyes of zombies—and made a violent, urgent gesture. One man dumped his boulder over the precipice's edge. Burl cried out shrilly to the others, half-mad with his own terror. There was a ripping sound. The other men dumped their boulders over, fleeing with the movement—the paralysis of horror relieved by that one bit of exertion.

Burl could not flee. He panted and gasped, but he had to see. He stared down the dizzy wall. Boulders ripped and tore their way down the cliff-wall, pulling the cables loose from the face of the precipice. They shot out into space and jerked violently at the half-globular nest, ripping it loose from its anchorage.

Burl cried out exultantly. And as he cried out the shout became a bubbling sound; for although the ogre's silken castle did swing clear, it did not drop the sixty feet to the hard ground below. There was one cable Burl had missed, hidden by rock-tripe and mould in a depressed part of the cliff-top. The spider's house was dangling crazily by that one strand, bobbing erratically to and fro in mid-air.

And there was a convulsive struggle inside it. One of the arch-doors opened and the spider emerged. It was doubtless confused, but spiders simply do not know terror. Their one response to the unusual is ferocity. There was still one cable leading up the cliff-face—the thing's normal climbing-rope to its hunting-ground above. The spider leaped for this single cable. Its legs grasped the cord. It swarmed upward, poison fangs unsheathed, mandibles clashing in rage. The shaggy hair of its body seemed to bristle with insane ferocity. The skinny articulated legs fairly twinkled as it rose. It made slavering noises, unspeakably horrifying.

Burl's followers were already in panic-stricken flight. He could hear them crashing through obstacles as they ran glassy-eyed from the horror they only imagined, but which Burl could not but encounter. Burl shivered, his body poised for equally frenzied but quite hopeless flight. But his first step was blocked. There was a boulder behind him, standing on end, reaching up to his knee. He could not take the first step without dodging it.

It was not the Burl of the terror-filled childhood who acted then. It was the throw-back, the atavism to a bolder ancestry. While the Burl who was a product of his environment was able to know only the stunned sensations of purest panic, the other Burl acted on a sounder basis of desperation. The emerging normal human seized the upright boulder. He staggered to the rock-face with it. He dumped it down the line of the descending cable.

Humans do have ancestral behavior-patterns built into their nervous systems. A frightened small child does not flee; it swarms up the nearest adult to be carried away from danger. At ten a child does not climb but runs. And there is an age when it is normal for a man to stand at bay. This last instinct can be conditioned away. In Burl's fellows and his immediate forbears it had been. But things had happened to Burl to break that conditioning.

He flung the pointed boulder down. For the fraction of a second he heard only the bubbling, gnashing sounds the spider made as it climbed toward him. Then there was a quite indescribable cushioned impact. After that, there were seconds in which Burl heard nothing whatever—and then a noise which could not be described either, but was the impact of the spider's body on the ground a hundred feet below, together with the pointed boulder it had fought insanely during all its fall. And the boulder was on top. The noise was sickening.

Burl found himself shaking all over. His every muscle was tense and strained. But the spider did not crawl over the edge of the precipice and something had hit far below.

A long minute later he managed to look.

The nest still dangled at the end of the single cable, festooned with its gruesome trophies. But Burl saw the spider. It was, of course, characteristically tenacious of life. Its legs writhed and kicked, but the body was crushed and mangled.

As Burl stared down, trying to breathe again, an ant drew near the shattered creature. It stridulated. Other ants came. They hovered restlessly at the edge of the death-scene. One loathesome leg did not quiver. An ant moved in on it.

The ants began to tear the dead spider apart, carrying its fragments to their city a mile away.

Up on the cliff-top Burl got unsteadily to his feet and found that he could breathe. He was drenched in sweat, but the shock of triumph was as overwhelming as any of the terrors felt by ancestors on this planet.

On no other planet in the Galaxy could any human experience such triumph as Burl felt now because never before had human beings been so completely subjugated by their environment. On no other planet had such an environment existed, with humans flung so helplessly upon its mercy.

Burl had been normal among his fellows when he was as frightened and furtive as they. Now he had been given shock treatment by fate. He was very close to normal for a human being newly come to the forgotten planet, save that he had the detailed information which would enable a normal man to cope with the nightmare environment. What he lacked now was the habit.

But it would be intolerable for him to return to his former state of mind.

He walked almost thoughtfully after his fled followers. And he was still a savage in that he was remarkably matter-of-fact. He paused to break off a huge piece of the edible golden mushrooms his fellow-men had noticed on the way up. Lugging it easily, he went back down over the ground that had looked so astonishingly free of inimical life—which it was because of the spider that had used it as a hunting-preserve.

Burl began to see that it was not satisfactory to be one of a tribe of men who ran away all the time. If one man with a spear or stone could kill spiders, it was ridiculous for half a dozen men to run away and leave that one man the job alone. It made the job harder.

It occurred to Burl that he had killed ants without thinking too much about it, but nobody else had. Individual ants could be killed. If he got his followers to kill foot-long ants, they might in time battle the smaller, two-foot beetles. If they came to dare so much, they might attack greater creatures and ultimately attempt to resist the real predators.

Not clearly but very dimly, the Burl who had been shocked back to the viewpoint which was normal to the race of men saw that human beings could be more than the fugitive vermin on which other creatures preyed. It was not easy to envision, but he found it impossible to imagine sinking back to his former state. As a practical matter, if he was to remain as leader his tribesmen would have to change.

It was a long time before he reached the neighborhood of the hiding-place of which he had not been told the night before. He sniffed and listened. Presently he heard faint, murmurous noises. He traced them, hearing clearly the sound of hushed weeping and excited, timid chattering. He heard old Tama shrilly bewailing fate and the stupidity of Burl in getting himself killed.

He pushed boldly through the toadstool-growth and found his tribe all gathered together and trembling. They were shaken. They chattered together—not discussing or planning, but nervously recalling the terrifying experience they had gone through.

Burl stepped through the screen of fungi and men gaped at him. Then they leaped up to flee, thinking he might be pursued. Tet and Dik babbled shrilly. Burl cuffed them. It was an excellent thing for him to do. No man had struck another man in Burl's memory. Cuffings were reserved for children. But Burl cuffed the men who had fled from the cliff-edge. And because they had not been through Burl's experiences, they took the cuffings like children.

He took Jon and Jak by the ear and heaved them out of the hiding-place. He followed them, and then drove them to where they could see the base of the cliff from whose top they had tumbled stones—and then run away. He showed them the carcass of the spider, now being carted away piecemeal by ants. He told them angrily how it had been killed.

They looked at him fearfully.

He was exasperated. He scowled at them. And then he saw them shifting uneasily. There were clickings. A single, foraging black ant—rather large, quite sixteen inches long—moved into view. It seemed to be wandering purposelessly, but was actually seeking carrion to take back to its fellows. It moved toward the men. They were alive, therefore, it did not think of them as food—though it could regard them as enemies.

Burl moved forward and struck with his club. It was butchery. It was unprecedented. When the creature lay still he commanded one of his typo for followers to take it up. Inside its armored legs there would be meat. He mentioned the fact, pungently. Their faces expressed amazed wonderment.

There was another clicking. Another solitary ant. Burl handed his club to Dor, pushing him forward. Dor hesitated. Though he was not afraid of one wandering ant, he held back uneasily. Burl barked at him.

Dor struck clumsily and botched the job. Burl had to use his spear to finish it. But a second bit of prey lay before the men.

Then, quite suddenly, this completely unprecedented form of foraging became understandable to Burl's followers. Jak giggled nervously.

An hour later Burl led them back to the tribe's hiding-place. The others had been terror-stricken, not knowing where the men had gone. But their terror changed to mute amazement when the men carried huge quantities of meat and edible mushroom into the hiding-place. The tribe held what amounted to a banquet.

Dik and Tet swaggered under a burden of ant-carcass. This was not, of course, in any way revolting. Back on Earth, even thousands of years before, Arabs had eaten locusts cooked in butter and salted. All men had eaten crabs and other crustaceans, whose feeding habits were similar to those of ants. If Burl and his tribesmen had thought to be fastidious, ants on the forgotten planet would still have been considered edible, since they had not lost the habits of extreme cleanliness which made them notable on Earth.

This feast of all the tribe, in which men had brought back not only mushroom to be eaten, but actual prey—small prey—of their hunting, was very probably the first such occasion in at least thirty generations of the forty-odd since the planet's unintended colonization. Like the other events, which began with Burl trying to spear a fish with a rhinoceros-beetle's horn, it was not only novel, on that world, but would in time have almost incredibly far-reaching consequences. Perhaps the most significant thing about it was its timing. It came at very nearly the latest instant at which it could have done any good.

There was a reason which nobody in the tribe would ever remember to associate with the significance of this banquet. A long time before—months in terms of Earth-time—there had been a strong breeze that blew for three days and nights. It was an extremely unusual windstorm. It had seemed the stranger, then, because during all its duration everyone in the tribe had been sick, suffering continuously. When the windstorm had ended, the suffering ceased. A long time passed and nobody remembered it any longer.

There was no reason why they should. Yet, since that time there had been a new kind of thing growing among the innumerable moulds and rusts and toadstools of the lowlands. Burl had seen them on his travels, and the expeditionary force against the clotho spider had seen them on the journey up to the cliff-edge. Red puffballs, developing first underground, were now pushing the soil aside to expose taut, crimson parchment spheres to the open air. The tribesmen left them alone because they were strange; and strange things were always dangerous. Puffballs they were familiar with—big, misshapen things which shot at a touch a powder into the air. The particles of powder were spores—the seed from which they grew. Spores had remained infinitely small even on the forgotten planet where fungi grew huge. Only their capacity for growth had increased. The red growths were puffballs, but of a new and different kind.

As the tribe ate and admired, the hunters boasting of their courage, one of the new red mushrooms reached maturity.

This particular growing thing was perhaps two feet across, its main part spherical. Almost eighteen inches of the thing rose above-ground. A tawny and menacing red, the sphere was contained in a parchment-like skin that was pulled taut. There was internal tension. But the skin was tough and would not yield, yet the inexorable pressure of life within demanded that it stretch. It was growing within, but the skin without had ceased to grow.

This one happened to be on a low hillside a good half-mile from the place where Burl and his fellows banqueted. Its tough, red parchment skin was tensed unendurably. Suddenly it ripped apart with an explosive tearing noise. The dry spores within billowed out and up like the smoke of a shell-explosion, spurting skyward for twenty feet and more. At the top of their ascent they spread out and eddied like a cloud of reddish smoke. They hung in the air. They drifted in the sluggish breeze. They spread as they floated, forming a gradually extending, descending dust-cloud in the humid air.

A bee, flying back toward its hive, droned into the thin mass of dust. It was preoccupied. The dust-cloud was not opaque, but only a thick haze. The bee flew into it.

For half a dozen wing-beats nothing happened. Then the bee veered sharply. Its deep-toned humming rose in pitch. It made convulsive movements in mid-air. It lost balance and crashed heavily to the ground. There its legs kicked and heaved violently but without purpose. The wings beat furiously but without rhythm or effect. Its body bent in paroxysmic flexings. It stung blindly at nothing.

After a little while the bee died. Like all insects, bees breathe through spiracles—breathing-holes in their abdomens. This bee had flown into the cloud of red dust which was the spore-cloud of the new mushrooms.

The cloud drifted slowly along over the surface of yeasts and moulds, over toadstools and variegated fungus monstrosities. It moved steadily over a group of ants at work upon some bit of edible stuff. They were seized with an affliction like that of the bee. They writhed, moved convulsively. Their legs thrashed about. They died.

The cloud of red dust settled as it moved. By the time it had travelled a quarter-mile, it had almost all settled to the ground.

But a half-mile away there was another skyward-spurting uprush of red dust which spread slowly with the breeze. A quarter-mile away another plumed into the air. Farther on, two of them spouted their spores toward the clouds almost together.

Living things that breathed the red dust writhed and died. And the red-dust puffballs were scattered everywhere.

Burl and his tribesmen feasted, chattering in hushed tones of the remarkable fact that men ate meat of their own killing.

CHAPTER SIX
Red Dust

It was very fortunate indeed that the feast took place when it did. Two days later it would probably have been impossible, and three days later it would have been too late to do any good. But coming when it did, it made the difference which was all the difference in the world.

Only thirty hours after the feasting which followed the death of the clotho spider, Burl's fellows—from Jon to Dor to Tet and Dik and Saya—had come to know a numb despair which the other creatures of his world were simply a bit too stupid to achieve.

It was night. There was darkness over all the lowlands, and over all the area of perhaps a hundred square miles which the humans of Burl's acquaintance really knew. He, alone of his tribe, had been as much as forty miles from the foraging-ground over which they wandered. At any given time the tribe clung together for comfort, venturing only as far as was necessary to find food. Although the planet possessed continents, they knew less than a good-sized county of it. The planet owned oceans, and they knew only small brooks and one river which, where they knew it, was assuredly less than two hundred yards across. And they faced stark disaster that was not strictly a local one, but beyond their experience and hopelessly beyond their ability to face.

They were superior to the insects about them only in the fact they realized what was threatening them.

The disaster was the red puffballs.

But it was night. The soft, blanketing darkness of a cloud-wrapped world lay all about. Burl sat awake, wrapped in his magnificent velvet cloak, his spear beside him and the yard-long golden plumes of a moth's antennae bound to his forehead for a headdress. About him and his tribesmen were the swollen shapes of fungi, hiding the few things that could be seen in darkness. From the low-hanging clouds the nightly rain dripped down. Now a drop and then another drop; slowly, deliberately, persistently moisture fell from the skies.

There was other sounds. Things flew through the blackness overhead—moths with mighty wing-beats that sometimes sent rhythmic wind-stirrings down to the tribe in its hiding-place. There were the deep pulsations of sound made by night-beetles aloft. There were the harsh noises of grasshoppers—they were rare—senselessly advertising their existence to nearby predators. Not too far from where Burl brooded came bright chirrupings where relatively small beetles roamed among the mushroom-forests, singing cheerfully in deep bass voices. They were searching for the underground tidbits which took the place of truffles their ancestors had lived on back on Earth.

All seemed to be as it had been since the first humans were cast away upon this planet. And at night, indeed, the new danger subsided. The red puffballs did not burst after sunset. Burl sat awake, brooding in a new sort of frustration. He and all his tribe were plainly doomed—yet Burl had experienced too many satisfying sensations lately to be willing to accept the fact.

The new red growths were everywhere. Months ago a storm-wind blew while somewhere, not too far distant, other red puffballs were bursting and sending their spores into the air. Since it was only a windstorm, there was no rain to wash the air clean of the lethal dust. The new kind of puffball—but perhaps it was not new: it could have thriven for thousands of years where it was first thrown as a sport from a genetically unstable parent—the new kind of puffball would not normally be spread in this fashion. By chance it had.

There were dozens of the things within a quarter-mile, hundreds within a mile, and thousands upon thousands within the area the tribe normally foraged in. Burl had seen them even forty miles away, as yet immature. They would be deadly at one period alone—the time of their bursting. But there were limitations even to the deadliness of the red puffballs, though Burl had not yet discovered the fact. But as of now, they doomed the tribe.

One woman panted and moaned in her exhausted sleep, a little way from where Burl tried to solve the problem presented by the tribe. Nobody else attempted to think it out. The others accepted doom with fatalistic hopelessness. Burl's leadership might mean extra food, but nothing could counter the doom awaiting them— so their thoughts seemed to run.

But Burl doggedly reviewed the facts in the darkness, while the humans about him slept the sleep of those without hope and even without rebellion. There had been many burstings of the crimson puffballs. As many as four and five of the deadly dust-clouds had been seen spouting into the air at the same time. A small boy of the tribe had breathlessly told of seeing a hunting-spider killed by the red dust. Lana, the half-grown girl, had come upon one of the gigantic rhinoceros-beetles belly-up on the ground, already the prey of ants. She had snatched a huge, meat-filled joint and run away, faster than the ants could follow. A far-ranging man had seen a butterfly, with wings ten yards across, die in a dust-cloud. Another woman—Cori—had been nearby when a red cloud settled slowly over long, solid lines of black worker-ants bound on some unknown mission. Later she saw other workers carrying the dead bodies back to the ant-city to be used for food.

Burl still sat wakeful and frustrated and enraged as the slow rain fell upon the toadstools that formed the tribe's lurking-place. He doggedly went over and over the problem. There were innumerable red puffballs. Some had burst. The others undoubtedly would burst. Anything that breathed the red dust died. With thousands of the puffballs around them it was unthinkable that any human in this place could escape breathing the red dust and dying. But it had not always been so. There had been a time when there were no red puffballs here.

Burl's eyes moved restlessly over the sleeping forms limned by a patch of fox-fire. The feathery plumes rising from his head were outlined softly by the phosphorescence. His face was lined with a frown as he tried to think his own and his fellows' way out of the predicament. Without realizing it, Burl had taken it upon himself to think for his tribe. He had no reason to. It was simply a natural thing for him to do so, now that he had learned to think—even though his efforts were crude and painful as yet.

Saya woke with a start and stared about. There had been no alarm,—merely the usual noises of distant murders and the songs of singers in the night. Burl moved restlessly. Saya stood up quietly, her long hair flowing about her. Sleepy-eyed, she moved to be near Burl. She sank to the ground beside him, sitting up—because the hiding-place was crowded and small—and dozed fitfully. Presently her head drooped to one side. It rested against his shoulder. She slept again.

This simple act may have been the catalyst which gave Burl the solution to the problem. Some few days before, Burl had been in a far-away place where there was much food. At the time he'd thought vaguely of finding Saya and bringing her to that place. He remembered now that the red puffballs flourished there as well as here—but there had been other dangers in between, so the only half-formed purpose had been abandoned. Now, though, with Saya's head resting against his shoulder, he remembered the plan. And then the stroke of genius took place.

He formed the idea of a journey which was not a going-after-food. This present dwelling-place of the tribe had been free of red puffballs until only recently. There must be other places where there were no red puffballs. He would take Saya and his tribesmen to such a place.

It was really genius. The people of Burl's tribe had no purposes, only needs—for food and the like. Burl had achieved abstract thought—which previously had not been useful on the forgotten planet and, therefore, not practised. But it was time for humankind to take a more fitting place in the unbalanced ecological system of this nightmare world, time to change that unbalance in favor of humans.

When dawn came, Burl had not slept at all. He was all authority and decision. He had made plans.

He spoke sternly, loudly—which frightened people conditioned to be furtive—holding up his spear as he issued commands. His timid tribesfolk obeyed him meekly. They felt no loyalty to him or confidence in his decisions yet, but they were beginning to associate obedience to him with good things. Food, for one.

Before the day fully came, they made loads of the remaining edible mushroom and uneaten meat. It was remarkable for humans to leave their hiding-place while they still had food to eat, but Burl was implacable and scowling. Three men bore spears at Burl's urging. He brandished his long shaft confidently as he persuaded the other three to carry clubs. They did so reluctantly, even though previously they had killed ants with clubs. Spears, they felt, would have been better. They wouldn't be so close to the prey then.

The sky became gray over all its expanse. The indefinite bright area which marked the position of the sun became established. It was part-way toward the center of the sky when the journey began. Burl had, of course, no determined course, only a destination— safety. He had been carried south, in his misadventure on the river. There were red puffballs to southward, therefore he ruled out that direction. He could have chosen the east and come upon an ocean, but no safety from the red spore-dust. Or he could have chosen the north. It was pure chance that he headed west.

He walked confidently through the gruesome world of the lowlands, holding his spear in a semblance of readiness. Clad as he was, he made a figure at once valiant and rather pathetic. It was not too sensible for one young man—even one who had killed two spiders—to essay leading a tiny tribe of fearful folk across a land of monstrous ferocity and incredible malignance, armed only with a spear from a dead insect's armor. It was absurd to dress up for the enterprise in a velvety cloak made of a moth's wing, blue moth-fur for a loin-cloth, and merely beautiful golden plumes bobbing above his forehead.

Probably, though, that gorgeousness had a good effect upon his followers. They surely could not reassure each other by their numbers! There was a woman with a baby in her arms—Cori. Three children of nine or ten, unable to resist the instinct to play even on so perilous a journey, ate almost constantly of the lumps of foodstuff they had been ordered to carry. After them came Dik, a long-legged adolescent boy with eyes that roved anxiously about. Behind him were two men. Dor with a short spear and Jak hefting a club, both of them badly frightened at the idea of fleeing from dangers they knew and were terrified by, to other dangers unknown and, consequently, more to be feared. The others trailed after them. Tet was rear-guard. Burl had separated the pair of boys to make them useful. Together they were worthless.

It was a pathetic caravan, in a way. In all the rest of the Galaxy, man was the dominant creature. There was no other planet from one rim to the other where men did not build their cities or settlements with unconscious arrogance—completely disregarding the wishes of lesser things. Only on this planet did men hide from danger rather than destroy it. Only here could men be driven from their place by lower life-forms. And only here would a migration be made on foot, with men's eyes fearful, their bodies poised to flee at sight of something stronger and more deadly than themselves.

They marched, straggling a little, with many waverings aside from a fixed line. Once Dik saw the trap-door of a trapdoor-spider's lair. They halted, trembling, and went a long way out of their intended path to avoid it. Once they saw a great praying-mantis a good half-mile off, and again they deviated from their proper route.

Near midday their way was blocked. As they moved onward, a great, high-pitched sound could be heard ahead of them. Burl stopped; his face grew pinched. But it was only a stridulation, not the cries of creatures being devoured. It was a horde of ants by the thousands and hundreds of thousands, and nothing else.

Burl went ahead to scout. And he did it because he did not trust anybody else to have the courage or intelligence to return with a report, instead of simply running away if the news were bad. But it happened to be a sort of action which would help to establish his position as leader of his tribe.

Burl moved forward cautiously and presently came to an elevation from which he could see the cause of the tremendous waves of sound that spread out in all directions from the level plain before him. He waved to his followers to join him, and stood looking down at the extraordinary sight.

When they reached his side—and Saya was first—the spectacle had not diminished. For quite half a mile in either direction the earth was black with ants. It was a battle of opposing armies from rival ant-cities. They snapped and bit at each other. Locked in vise-like embraces, they rolled over and over upon the ground, trampled underfoot by hordes of their fellows who surged over them to engage in equally suicidal combat. There was, of course, no thought of surrender or of quarter. They fought by thousands of pairs, their jaws seeking to crush each other's armor, snapping at each other's antennae, biting at each other's eyes...

The noise was not like that of army-ants. This was the agonizing sound of ants being dismembered while still alive. Some of the creatures had only one or two or three legs left, yet struggled fiercely to entangle another enemy before they died. There were mad cripples, fighting insanely with head and thorax only, their abdomens sheared away. The whining battle-cry of the multitude made a deafening uproar.

From either side of the battleground a wide path led back toward separate ant-cities which were invisible from Burl's position. These highways were marked by hurrying groups of ants—reinforcements rushing to the fight. Compared to the other creatures of this world the ants were small, but no lumbering beetle dared to march insolently in their way, nor did any carnivores try to prey upon them. They were dangerous. Burl and his tribesfolk were the only living things remaining near the battle-field—with one single exception.

That exception was itself a tribe of ants, vastly less in number than the fighting creatures, and greatly smaller in size as well. Where the combatants were from a foot to fourteen inches long, these guerilla-ants were no more than the third of a foot in length. They hovered industriously at the edge of the fighting, not as allies to either nation, but strictly on their own account. Scurrying among the larger, fighting ants with marvelous agility, they carried off piecemeal the bodies of the dead and valiantly slew the more gravely wounded for the same purpose.

They swarmed over the fighting-ground whenever the tide of battle receded. Caring nothing for the origin of the quarrel and espousing neither side, these opportunists busily salvaged the dead and still-living debris of the battle for their own purposes.

Burl and his followers were forced to make a two-mile detour to avoid the battle. The passage between bodies of scurrying reinforcements was a matter of some difficulty. Burl hurried the others past a route to the front, reeking of formic acid, over which endless regiments and companies of ants moved frantically to join in the fight. They were intensely excited. Antennae waving wildly, they rushed to the front and instantly flung themselves into the fray, becoming lost and indistinguishable in the black mass of fighting creatures.

The humans passed precariously between two hurrying battalions—Dik and Tet pausing briefly to burden themselves with prey—and hurried on to leave as many miles as possible behind them before nightfall. They never knew any more about the battle. It could have started over anything at all—two ants from the different cities may have disputed some tiny bit of carrion and soon been reinforced by companions until the military might of both cities was engaged. Once it had started, of course, the fighters knew whom to fight if not why they did so. The inhabitants of the two cities had different smells, which served them as uniforms.

But the outcome of the war would hardly matter. Not to the fighters, certainly. There were many red mushrooms in this area. If either of the cities survived at all, it would be because its nursery-workers lived upon stored food as they tended the grubs until the time of the spouting red dust had ended.

Burl's folk saw many of the red puffballs burst during the day. More than once they came upon empty, flaccid parchment sacs. More often still they came upon red puffballs not yet quite ready to emit their murderous seed.

That first night the tribe hid among the bases of giant puffballs of a more familiar sort. When touched they would shoot out a puff of white powder resembling smoke. The powder was harmless fortunately and the tribe knew that fact. Although not toxic, the white powder was identical in every other way to the terrible red dust from which the tribe fled.

That night Burl slept soundly. He had been without rest for two days and a night. And he was experienced in journeying to remote places. He knew that they were no more dangerous than familiar ones. But the rest of the tribe, and even Saya, were fearful and terrified. They waited timorously all through the dark hours for menacing sounds to crash suddenly through the steady dripping of the nightly rain around them.

The second day's journey was not unlike the first. The following day, they came upon a full ten-acre patch of giant cabbages bigger than a family dwelling. Something in the soil, perhaps, favored vegetation over fungi. The dozens of monstrous vegetables were the setting for riotous life: great slugs ate endlessly of the huge green leaves—and things preyed on them; bees came droning to gather the pollen of the flowers. And other things came to prey on the predators in their turn.

There was one great cabbage somewhat separate from the rest. After a long examination of the scene, Burl daringly led quaking Jon and Jak to the attack. Dor splendidly attacked elsewhere, alone. When the tribe moved on, there was much meat, and everyone—even the children—wore loin-cloths of incredibly luxurious fur.

There were perils, too. On the fifth day of the tribe's journey Burl suddenly froze into stillness. One of the hairy tarantulas which lived in burrows with a concealed trap-door at ground-level, had fallen upon a scarabeus beetle and was devouring it only a hundred yards ahead. The tribesfolk trembled as Burl led them silently back and around by a safe detour.

But all these experiences were beginning to have an effect. It was becoming a matter of course that Burl should give orders which others should obey. It was even becoming matter-of-fact that the possession of food was not a beautiful excuse to hide from all danger, eating and dozing until all the food was gone. Very gradually the tribe was developing the notion that the purpose of existence was not solely to escape awareness of peril, but to foresee and avoid it. They had no clear-cut notion of purpose as yet. They were simply outgrowing purposelessness. After a time they even looked about them with, dim stirrings of an attitude other than a desperate alertness for danger.

Humans from any other planet, surely, would have been astounded at the vistas of golden mushrooms stretching out in forests on either hand and the plains with flaking surfaces given every imaginable color by the moulds and rusts and tiny flowering yeasts growing upon them. They would have been amazed by the turgid pools the journeying tribe came upon, where the water was concealed by a thick layer of slime through which enormous bubbles of foul-smelling gas rose to enlarge to preposterous size before bursting abruptly.

Had they been as ill-armed as Burl's folk, though, visitors from other planets would have been at least as timorous. Lacking highly specialized knowledge of the ways of insects on this world even well-armed visitors would have been in greater danger.

But the tribe went on without a single casualty. They had fleeting glimpses of the white spokes of symmetrical spider-webs whose least thread no member of the tribe could break.

Their immunity from disaster—though in the midst of danger—gave them a certain all-too-human concentration upon discomfort. Lacking calamities, they noticed their discomforts and grew weary of continual traveling. A few of the men complained to Burl.

For answer, he pointed back along the way they had come. To the right a reddish dust-cloud was just settling, and to the rear rose another as they looked.

And on this day a thing happened which at once gave the complainers the rest they asked for, and proved the fatality of remaining where they were. A child ran aside from the path its elders were following. The ground here had taken on a brownish hue. As the child stirred up the surface mould with his feet, dust that had settled was raised up again. It was far too thin to have any visible color. But the child suddenly screamed, strangling. The mother ran frantically to snatch him up.

The red dust was no less deadly merely because it had settled to the ground. If a storm-wind came now—but they were infrequent under the forgotten planet's heavy bank of clouds—the fallen red dust could be raised up again and scattered about until there would be no living thing anywhere which would not gasp and writhe— and die.

But the child would not die. He would suffer terribly and be weak for days. In the morning he could be carried.

When night began to darken the sky, the tribe searched for a hiding-place. They came upon a shelf-like cliff, perhaps twenty or thirty feet high, slanting toward the line of the tribesmen's travel. Burl saw black spots in it—openings. Burrows. He watched them as the tribe drew near. No bees or wasps went in or out. He watched long enough to be sure.

When they were close, he was certain. Ordering the others to wait, he went forward to make doubly sure. The appearance of the holes reassured him. Dug months before by mining-bees, gone or dead now, the entrances to the burrows were weathered and bedraggled. Burl explored, first sniffing carefully at each opening. They were empty. This would be shelter for the night. He called his followers, and they crawled into the three-foot tunnels to hide.

Burl stationed himself near the outer edge of one of them to watch for signs of danger. Night had not quite fallen. Jon and Dor, hungry, went off to forage a little way beyond the cliff. They would be cautious and timid, taking no risks whatever.

Burl waited for the return of his explorers. Meanwhile he fretted over the meaning of the stricken child. Stirred-up red dust was dangerous. The only time when there would be no peril from it would be at night, when the dripping rainfall of the dark hours turned the surface of this world into thin shine. It occurred to Burl that it would be safe to travel at night, so far as the red dust was concerned. He rejected the idea instantly. It was unthinkable to travel at night for innumerable other reasons.

Frowning, he poked his spear idly at a tumbled mass of tiny parchment cup-like things near the entrance of a cave. And instantly movement became visible. Fifty, sixty, a hundred infinitesimal creatures, no more than half an inch in length, made haste to hide themselves among the thimble-sized paperlike cups. They moved with extraordinary clumsiness and immense effort, seemingly only by contortions of their greenish-black bodies. Burl had never seen any creature progress in such a slow and ineffective fashion. He drew one of the small creatures back with the point of his spear and examined it from a safe distance.

He picked it up on his spear and brought it close to his eyes. The thing redoubled its frenzied movements. It slipped off the spear and plopped upon the soft moth-fur he wore about his middle. Instantly, as if it were a conjuring-trick, the insect vanished. Burl searched for minutes before he found it hidden deep in the long, soft hairs of his garment, resting motionless and seemingly at ease.

It was the larval form of a beetle, fragments of whose armor could be seen near the base of the clayey cliffside. Hidden in the remnants of its egg-casings, the brood of minute things had waited near the opening of the mining-bee tunnel. It was their gamble with destiny when mining-bee grubs had slept through metamorphosis and come uncertainly out of the tunnel for the first time, that some or many of the larvae might snatch the instant's chance to fasten to the bees' legs and writhe upward to an anchorage in their fur. It happened that this particular batch of eggs had been laid after the emergence of the grubs. They had no possible chance of fulfilling their intended role as parasites on insects of the order hymenoptera. They were simply and matter-of-factly doomed by the blindness of instinct, which had caused them to be placed where they could not possibly survive.

On the other hand, if one or many of them had found a lurking-place, the offspring of their host would have been doomed. The place filled by oil-beetle larvae in the scheme of things is the place—or one of the places—reserved for creatures that limit the number of mining-bees. When a bee-louse-infested mining-bee has made a new tunnel, stocked it with honey for its young, and then laid one egg to float on that pool of nourishment and hatch and feed and ultimately grow to be another mining-bee—at that moment of egg-laying, one small bee-louse detaches itself. It remains zestfully in the provisioned cell to devour the egg for which the provisions were accumulated. It happily consumes those provisions and, in time, an oil-beetle crawls out of the tunnel a mining-bee so laboriously prepared.

Burl had no difficulty in detaching the small insect and casting it away, but in doing so he discovered that others had hidden themselves in his fur without his knowledge. He plucked them away and found more. While savages can be highly tolerant of vermin too small to be seen, they feel a peculiar revolt against serving as host to creatures of sensible size. Burl reacted violently—as once he had reacted to the discovery of a leech clinging to his heel. He jerked off his loin-cloth and beat it savagely with his spear.

When it was clean, he still felt a wholly unreasonable sense of humiliation. It was not clearly thought out, of course. Burl feared huge insects too much to hate them. But that small creatures should fasten upon him produced a completely irrational feeling of outrage. For the first time in very many years or centuries a human being upon the forgotten planet felt that he had been insulted. His dignity had been assailed. Burl raged.

But as he raged, a triumphant shout came from nearby. Jon and Dor were returning from their foraging, loaded down with edible mushroom. They, also, had taken a step upward toward the natural dignity of men. They had so far forgotten their terror as to shout in exultation at their find of food. Up to now, Burl had been the only man daring to shout. Now there were two others.

In his overwrought state this was also enraging. The result of hurt vanity on two counts was jealousy, and the result of jealousy was a crazy foolhardiness. Burl ground his teeth and insanely resolved to do something so magnificent, so tremendous, so utterly breathtaking that there could be no possible imitation by anybody else. His thinking was not especially clear. Part of his motivation had been provided by the oil-beetle larvae. He glared about him at the deepening dusk, seeking some exploit, some glamorous feat, to perform immediately, even in the night.

He found one.

CHAPTER SEVEN
Journey through Death

It was late dusk and the reddened clouds overhead were deepening steadily toward black. Dark shadows hung everywhere. The clay cliff cut off all vision to one side, but elsewhere Burl could see outward until the graying haze blotted out the horizon. Here and there, bees droned homeward to hive or burrow. Sometimes a slender, graceful wasp passed overhead, its wings invisible by the swiftness of their vibration.

A few butterflies lingered hungrily in the distance, seeking the few things they could still feast upon. No moth had wakened yet to the night. The cloud-bank grew more sombre. The haze seemed to close in and shrink the world that Burl could see.

The RED DUST

By Murray Leinster

A Sequel to "The Mad Planet."

Burl raised his spear, and plunged down on the back of the moving thing, thrusting his spear with all the force he could command. He had fallen upon the shining back of one of the huge, meat-eating beetles, and his spear had slid across the horny armor and then stuck fast, having pierced only the leathery tissue between the insect's head and thorax.

He watched, raging, for the sight that would provide him with the triumph to end all triumphs among his followers. The soft, down-reaching fingers of the night touched here and there and the day ended at those spots. Then, from the heart of the deep redness to the west a flying creature came. It was a beautiful thing—a yellow emperor butterfly—flapping eastward with great sail-like velvet wings that seemed black against the sunset. Burl saw it sweep across the incredible sky, alight delicately, and disappear behind a mass of toadstools clustered so thickly they seemed nearly a hillock and not a mass of growing things.

Then darkness closed in completely, but Burl still stared where the yellow emperor had landed. There was that temporary, utter quiet when day-things were hidden and night-things had not yet ventured out. Fox-fire glowed. Patches of pale phosphorescence—luminous mushrooms—shone faintly in the dark.

Presently Burl moved through the night. He could imagine the yellow emperor in its hiding-place, delicately preening slender limbs before it settled down to rest until the new day dawned. He had noted landmarks, to guide himself. A week earlier and his blood would have run cold at the bare thought of doing what he did now. In mere cool-headed detachment he would have known that what he did was close to madness. But he was neither cool-headed nor detached.

He crossed the clear ground before the low cliff. But for the fox-fire beacons he would have been lost instantly. The slow drippings of rain began. The sky was dead black. Now was the time for night-things to fly, and male tarantulas to go seeking mates and prey. It was definitely no time for adventuring.

Burl moved on. He found the close-packed toadstools by the process of running into them in the total obscurity. He fumbled, trying to force his way between them. It could not be done; they grew too close and too low. He raged at this impediment. He climbed.

This was insanity. Burl stood on spongy mushroom-stuff that quivered and yielded under his weight. Somewhere something boomed upward, rising on fast-beating wings into blackness. He heard the pulsing drone of four-inch mosquitos close by. He moved forward, the fungus support swaying, so that he did not so much walk as stagger over the close-packed mushroom heads. He groped before him with spear and panted a little. There was a part of him which was bitterly afraid, but he raged the more furiously because if once he gave way even to caution, it would turn to panic.

Burl would have made a strange spectacle in daylight gaudily clothed as he was in soft blue fur and velvet cloak, staggering over swaying insecurity, coddling ferocity in himself against the threat of fear.

Then his spear told him there was emptiness ahead. Something moved, below. He heard and felt it stirring the toadstool-stalks on which he stood.

Burl raised his spear, grasping it in both hands. He plunged down with it, stabbing fiercely.

The spear struck something vastly more resistant than any mushroom could be. It penetrated. Then the stabbed thing moved as Burl landed upon it, flinging him off his feet, but he clung to the firmly imbedded weapon. And if his mouth had opened for a yell of victory as he plunged down, the nature of the surface on which he found himself, and the kind of movement he felt, turned that yell into a gasp of horror.

It wasn't the furry body of a butterfly he had landed on; his spear hadn't pierced such a creature's soft flesh. He had leaped upon the broad, hard back of a huge, meat-eating, nocturnal beetle. His spear had pierced not the armor, but the leathery joint-tissue between head and thorax.

The giant creature rocketed upward with Burl clinging to his spear. He held fast with an agonized strength. His mount rose from the blackness of the ground into the many times more terrifying blackness of the air. It rose up and up. If Burl could have screamed, he would have done so, but he could not cry out. He could only hold fast, glassy-eyed.

Then he dropped. Wind roared past him. The great insect was clumsy at flying. All beetles are. Burl's weight and the pain it felt made its flying clumsier still. There was a semi-liquid crashing and an impact. Burl was torn loose and hurled away. He crashed into the spongy top of a mushroom and came to rest with his naked shoulder hanging halfway over some invisible drop. He struggled.

He heard the whining drone of his attempted prey. It rocketed aloft again. But there was something wrong with it. With his weight applied to the spear as he was torn free, Burl had twisted the weapon in the wound. It had driven deeper, multiplying the damage of the first stab.

The beetle crashed to earth again, nearby. As Burl struggled again, the mushroom-stalk split and let him gently to the ground.

He heard the flounderings of the great beetle in the darkness. It mounted skyward once more, its wing-beats no longer making a sustained note. It thrashed the air irregularly and wildly.

Then it crashed again.

There was seeming silence, save for the steady drip-drip of the rain. And Burl came out of his half-mad fear: he suddenly realized that he had slain a victim even more magnificent than a spider, because this creature was meat.

He found himself astonishedly running toward the spot where the beetle had last fallen.

But he heard it struggle aloft once more. It was wounded to death. Burl felt certain of it this time. It floundered in mid-air and crashed again.

He was within yards of it before he checked himself. Now he was weaponless, and the gigantic insect flung itself about madly on the ground, striking out with colossal wings and limbs, fighting it knew not what. It struggled to fly, crashed, and fought its way off the ground—ever more weakly—then smashed again into mushrooms. There it floundered horribly in the darkness.

Burl drew near and waited. It was still, but pain again drove it to a senseless spasm of activity.

Then it struck against something. There was a ripping noise and instantly the close, peppery, burning smell of the red dust was in the air. The beetle had floundered into one of the close-packed red puffballs, tightly filled with the deadly red spores. The red dust would not normally have been released at night. With the nightly rain, it would not travel so far or spread so widely.

Burl fled, panting.

Behind him he heard his victim rise one last time, spurred to impossible, final struggle by the anguish caused by the breathed-in red dust. It rose clumsily into the darkness in its death-throes and crashed to the ground again for the last time.

In time to come, Burl and his followers might learn to use the red-dust puffballs as weapons—but not how to spread them beyond their normal range. But now, Burl was frightened. He moved hastily sidewise. The dust would travel down-wind. He got out of its possible path.

There could be no exultation where the red dust was. Burl suddenly realized what had happened to him. He had been carried aloft an unknown though not-great distance, in an unknown direction. He was separated from his tribe, with no faintest idea how to find them in the darkness. And it was night.

He crouched under the nearest huge toadstool and waited for the dawn, listening dry-throated for the sound of death coming toward him through the night.

But only the wind-beats of night-fliers came to his ears, and the discordant notes of gray-bellied truffle-beetles as they roamed the mushroom thickets, seeking the places beneath which—so their adapted instincts told them—fungoid dainties, not too much unlike the truffles of Earth, awaited the industrious miner. And, of course, there was that eternal, monotonous dripping of the raindrops, falling at irregular intervals from the sky.

Red puffballs did not burst at night. They would not burst anyhow, except at one certain season of their growth. But Burl and his folk had so far encountered the over-hasty ones, bursting earlier than most. The time of ripeness was very nearly here, though. When day came again, and the chill dampness of the night was succeeded by the warmth of the morning, almost the first thing Burl saw in the gray light was a tall spouting of brownish-red stuff leaping abruptly into the air from a burst red parchment-like sphere.

He stood up and looked anxiously all around. Here and there, all over the landscape, slowly and at intervals, the plumes of fatal red sprang into the air. There was nothing quite like it anywhere else. An ancient man, inhabiting Earth, might have likened the appearance to that of a scattered and leisurely bombardment. But Burl had no analogy for them.

He saw something hardly a hundred yards from where he had hidden during the night. The dead beetle lay there, crumpled and limp. Burl eyed it speculatively. Then he saw something that filled him with elation. The last crash of the beetle to the ground had driven his spear deeply between the joints of the corselet and neck. Even if the red dust had not finished the creature, the spear-point would have ended its life.

He was thrilled once more by his superlative greatness. He made due note that he was a mighty slayer. He took the antennae as proof of his valor and hacked off a great barb-edged leg for meat. And then he remembered that he did not know how to find his fellow-tribesmen. He had no idea which way to go.

Even a civilized man would have been at a loss, though he would have hunted for an elevation from which to look for the cliff hiding-place of the tribe. But Burl had not yet progressed so far. His wild ride of the night before had been at random, and the chase after the wounded beetle no less dictated by chance. There was no answer.

He set off anxiously, searching everywhere. But he had to be alert for all the dangers of an inimical world while keeping, at the same time, an extremely sharp eye out for bursting red puffballs.

At the end of an hour he thought he saw familiar things. Then he recognized the spot. He had come back to the dead beetle. It was already the center of a mass of small black bodies which pulled and hacked at the tough armor, gnawing out great lumps of flesh to be carried to the nearest ant-city.

Burl set off again, very carefully avoiding any place that he recognized as having been seen that morning. Sometimes he walked through mushroom-thickets—dangerous places to be in—and sometimes over relatively clear ground colored exotically with varicolored fungi. More than once he saw the clouds of red stuff spurting in the distance. Deep anxiety filled him. He had no idea that there were such things as points of the compass. He knew only that he needed desperately to find his tribesfolk again.

They, of course, had given him up for dead. He had vanished in the night. Old Tama complained of him shrilly. The night, to them, meant death. Jon quaked watchfully all through it. When Burl did not come to the feast of mushroom that Jon and Dor had brought back, they sought him. They even called timidly into the darkness. They heard the throbbing of huge wings as a great creature rose desperately into the sky, but they did not associate that sound with Burl. If they had, they would have been instantly certain of his fate.

As it was, the tribe's uneasiness grew into terror which rapidly turned to despair. They began to tremble, wondering what they would do with no bold chieftain to guide them. He was the first man to command allegiance from others in much too long a period, on the forgotten planet, but the submission of his followers had been the more complete for its novelty. His loss was the more appalling. Burl had mistaken the triumphant shout of the foragers. He'd thought it independence of him—rivalry. Actually, the men dared to shout only because they felt secure under his leadership. When they accepted the fact that he had vanished—and to disappear in the night had always meant death—their old fears and timidity returned. To them it was added despair.

They huddled together and whispered to one another of their fright. They waited in trembling silence through all the long night. Had a hunting-spider appeared, they would have fled in as many directions as there were people, and undoubtedly all would have perished. But day came again, and they looked into each other's eyes and saw the self-same fear. Saya was probably the most pitiful of the group. Her face was white and drawn beyond that of any one else.

They did not move when day brightened. They remained about the bee-tunnels, speaking in hushed tones, huddled together, searching all the horizon for enemies. Saya would not eat, but sat still, staring before her in numbed grief. Burl was dead.

Atop the low cliff a red puffball glistened in the morning light. Its tough skin was taut and bulging, resisting the pressure of the spores within. Slowly, as the morning wore on, some of the moisture that kept the skin stretchable dried. The parchment-like stuff contracted. The tautness of the spore-packed envelope grew greater. It became insupportable.

With a ripping sound, the tough skin split across and a rush of the compressed spores shot skyward.

The tribesmen saw and cried out and fled. The red stuff drifted down past the cliff-edge. It drifted toward the humans. They ran from it. Jon and Tama ran fastest. Jak and Cori and the other were not far behind. Saya trailed, in her despair.

Had Burl been there, matters would have been different. He had already such an ascendancy over the minds of the others that even in panic they would have looked to see what he did. And he would have dodged the slowly drifting death-cloud by day, as he had during the night. But his followers ran blindly.

As Saya fled after the others she heard shrieks of fright to the left and ran faster. She passed by a thick mass of distorted fungi in which there was a sudden stirring and panic lent wings to her feet. She fled blindly, panting. Ahead was a great mass of stuff—red puffballs—showing here and there among great fanlike growths, some twelve feet high, that looked like sponges.

She fled past them and swerved to hide herself from anything that might be pursuing by sight. Her foot slipped on the slimy body of a shell-less snail and she fell heavily, her head striking a stone. She lay still.

Almost as if at a signal a red puffball burst among the fanlike growths. A thick, dirty-red cloud of dust shot upward, spread and billowed and began to settle slowly toward the ground again. It moved as it settled flowing over the inequalities of die ground as a monstrous snail or leach might have done, sucking from all breathing creatures the life they had within them. It was a hundred yards away, then fifty, then thirty...

Had any member of the tribe watched it, the red dust might have seemed malevolently intelligent. But when the edges of the dust-cloud were no more than twenty yards from Saya's limp body, an opposing breeze sprang up. It was a vagrant, fitful little breeze that halted the red cloud and threw it into some confusion, sending it in a new direction. It passed Saya without hurting her, though one of its misty tendrils reached out as if to snatch at her in slow-motion. But it passed her by.

Saya lay motionless on the ground. Only her breast rose and fell shallowly. A tiny pool of red gathered near her head.

Some thirty feet from where she lay, there were three miniature toadstools in a clump, bases so close together that they seemed but one. From between two of them, however, two tufts of reddish thread appeared. They twinkled back and forth and in and out. As if reassured, two slender antennae followed, then bulging eyes and a small, black body with bright-red scalloped markings upon it.

It was a tiny beetle no more than eight inches long—a sexton or burying-beetle. Drawing near Saya's body it scurried onto her flesh. It went from end to end of her figure in a sort of feverish haste. Then it dived into the ground beneath her shoulder, casting back a little shower of hastily-dug dirt as it disappeared.

Ten minutes later, another small creature appeared, precisely like the first. Upon the heels of the second came a third. Each made the same hasty examination and dived under her unmoving form.

Presently the ground seemed to billow at a spot along Saya's side and then at another. Ten minutes after the arrival of the third beetle, a little rampart had reared itself all about Saya's body, following her outlines precisely. Then her body moved slightly, in little jerks, seeming to settle perhaps half an inch into the ground.

The burying-beetles were of that class of creatures which exploited the bodies of the fallen. Working from below, they excavated the earth. When there was a hollow space below they turned on their backs and thrust up with their legs, jerking at the body until it sank into the space they had made ready. The process would be repeated until at last all their dead treasures had settled down below the level of the surrounding ground. The loosened dirt then fell in at the sides, completing the inhumation. Then, in the underground darkness, it was the custom for the beetles to feast magnificently, gorging themselves upon the food they had hidden from other scavengers—and of course rearing their young also upon its substance.

Ants and flies were rivals of these beetles and not infrequently the sexton-beetles came upon carrion after ants had taken their toll, and when it already swarmed with maggots. But in this case Saya was not dead. The fact that she still lived, though unconscious, was the factor that had given the sexton-beetles this splendid opportunity.

She breathed gently and irregularly, her face drawn with the sorrow of the night before, while the desperately hurrying beetles swarmed about beneath her body, channelling away the soil so she would sink lower and lower into it. She descended slowly, a half-inch by a half-inch. The bright-red tufts of thread appeared again and a beetle made its way to the open air. It moved hastily about, inspecting the progress of the work.

It dived below again. Another inch and, after a long time, another, were excavated.

Matters still progressed when Burl stepped out from a group of overshadowing toadstools and halted. He cast his eyes over the landscape and was struck by its familiarity. He was, in fact, very near the spot he had left the night before in that maniacal ride on the back of a flying beetle. He moved back and forth, trying to account for the feeling of recognition.

He saw the low cliff, then, and moved eagerly toward it, passing within fifty feet of Saya's body, now more than half-buried in the ground. The loose dirt around the outline of her figure was beginning to topple in little rivulets upon her. One of her shoulders was already half-screened from view. Burl passed on, unseeing.

He hurried a little. In a moment he recognized his location exactly. There were the mining-bee burrows. There was a thrown-away lump of edible mushroom, cast aside as the tribesfolk fled.

His feet stirred up a fine dust, and he stopped short. A red puffball had burst here. It fully accounted for the absence of the tribe, and Burl sweated in sudden fear. He thought instantly of Saya. He went carefully to make sure. This was, absolutely, the hiding place of the tribe. There was another mushroom-fragment. There was a spear, thrown down by one of the men in his flight. Red dust had settled upon the spear and the mushroom-fragments.

Burl turned back, hurrying again, but taking care to disturb the dust no more than he could possibly help.

The little excavation into which Saya was sinking inch by inch was not in his path. Her body no longer lay above the ground, but in it. Burl went by, frantic with anxiety about the tribe, but about Saya most of all.

Her body quivered and sank a fraction into the ground. Half a dozen small streams of earth were tumbling upon her. In minutes she would be wholly hidden from view.

Burl went to beat among the mushroom-thickets, in quest of the bodies of his tribesfolk. They could have staggered out of the red dust and collapsed beyond. He would have shouted, but the deep sense of loneliness silenced him. His throat ached with grief. He searched on…

There was a noise. From a huge clump of toadstools—perhaps the very one he had climbed over in the night—there came the sound of crashings and the breaking of the spongy stuff. Twin tapering antennae appeared, and then a monster beetle lurched into the open space, its ghastly mandibles gaping sidewise.

It was all of eight feet long and supported by six crooked, saw-toothed legs. Huge, multiple eyes stared with preoccupation at the world. It advanced deliberately with clankings and clashings as of a hideous machine. Burl fled on the instant, running directly away from it.

A little depression lay in the ground before him. He did not swerve, but made to jump over it. As he leaped he saw the color of bare flesh, Saya, limp and helpless, sinking slowly into the ground with tricklings of dirt falling down to cover her. It seemed to Burl that she quivered a little.

Instantly there was a terrific struggle within Burl. Behind him was the giant meat-eating beetle; beneath him was Saya whom he loved. There was certain death lurching toward him on evilly crooked legs—and the life he had hoped for lay in a shallow pit. Of course he thought Saya dead.

Perhaps it was rage, or despair, or a simple human madness which made him act otherwise than rationally. The things which raise humans above brute creation, however, are only partly reasonable. Most human emotions—especially the creditable ones—cannot be justified by reason, and very few heroic actions are based upon logical thought.

Burl whirled as he landed, his puny spear held ready. In his left hand he held the haunch of a creature much like the one which clanked and rattled toward him. With a yell of insane defiance—completely beyond justification by reason—Burl flung that meat-filled leg at the monster.

It hit. Undoubtedly, it hurt. The beetle seized it ferociously. It crushed it. There was meat in it, sweet and juicy.

The beetle devoured it. It forgot the man standing there, waiting for death. It crunched the leg-joint of a cousin or brother, confusing the blow with the missile that had delivered it. When the tidbit was finished it turned and lumbered off to investigate another mushroom thicket. It seemed to consider then an enemy had been conquered and devoured and that normal life could go on.

Then Burl stopped quickly, and dragged Saya from the grave the sexton-beetles had labored so feverishly to provide for her. Crumbled soil fell from her shoulders, from her face, and from her body. Three little eight-inch beetles with black and red markings scurried for cover in terrified haste. Burl carried Saya to a resting-place of soft mould to mourn over her.

He was a completely ignorant savage, save that he knew more of the ways of insects than anybody anywhere else—the Ecological Service, which had stocked this planet, not being excepted. To Burl the unconsciousness of Saya was as death itself. Dumb misery smote him, and he laid her down gently and quite literally wept. He had been beautifully pleased with himself for having slain one flying beetle. But for Saya's seeming death, he would have been almost unbearable with pride over having put another to flight. But now he was merely a broken-hearted, very human young man.

But a long time later Saya opened her eyes and looked about bewilderedly.

They were in considerable danger for some time after that, because they were oblivious to everything but each other. Saya rested in half-incredulous happiness against Burl's shoulder as he told her jerkily of his attempt on a night-bound butterfly, which turned out to be a flying beetle that took him aloft. He told of his search for the tribe and then his discovery of her apparently lifeless body. When he spoke of the monster which had lurched from the mushroom thicket, and of the desperation with which he had faced it, Saya looked at him with warm, proud eyes. But Burl was abruptly struck with the remarkable convenience of that discovery. If his tribesmen could secure an ample supply of meat, they might defend themselves against attack by throwing it to their attackers. In fact, insects were so stupid that almost any object thrown quickly enough and fast enough, might be made to serve as sacrifices instead of themselves.

A timid, frightened whisper roused them from their absorption. They looked up. The boy Dik stood some distance away, staring at them wide-eyed, almost convinced that he looked upon the living dead. A sudden movement on the part of either of them would have sent him bolting away. Two or three other bobbing heads gazed affrightedly from nearby hiding-places. Jon was poised for flight.

The tribe had come back to its former hiding-place simply as a way to reassemble. They had believed both Burl and Saya dead, and they accepted Burl's death as their own doom. But now they stared.

Burl spoke—fortunately without arrogance—and Dik and Tet came timorously from their hiding-places. The others followed, the tribe forming a frightened half-circle about the seated pair. Burl spoke again and presently one of the bravest—Cori—dared to approach and touch him. Instantly a babble of the crude labial language of the tribe broke out. Awed exclamations and questions filled the air.

But Burl, for once, showed some common sense. Instead of a vainglorious recital, he merely cast down the long tapering antennae of the flying-beetle. They looked, and recognized their origin.

Then Burl curtly ordered Dor and Jak to make a chair of their hands for Saya. She was weak from her fall and the loss of blood. The two men humbly advanced and obeyed. Then Burl curtly ordered the march resumed.

They went on, more slowly than on previous days, but none-the-less steadily. Burl led them across-country, marching in advance with a matter-of-fact alertness for signs of danger. He felt more confidence than ever before. It was not fully justified, of course. Jon now retrieved the spear he had discarded. The small party fairly bristled with weapons. But Burl knew that they were liable to be cast away as impediments if flight seemed necessary.

As he led the way Burl began to think busily in the manner that only leaders find necessary. He had taught his followers to kill ants for food, though they were still uneasy about such adventures. He had led them to attack great yellow grubs upon giant cabbages. But they had not yet faced any actual danger, as he had done. He must drive them to face something...

The opportunity came that same day, in late afternoon. To westward the cloud-bank was barely beginning to show the colors that presage nightfall, when a bumble-bee droned heavily overhead, making for its home burrow. The little, straggling group of marching people looked up and saw the scanty load of pollen packed in the stiff bristles of the bee's hind-legs. It sped onward heavily, its almost transparent wings mere blurs in the air.

It was barely fifty feet above the ground. Burl dropped his glance and tensed. A slender-waisted wasp was shooting upward from an ambush among the noisome fungi of this plain.

The bee swerved and tried to escape. The wasp over-hauled it. The bee dodged frantically. It was a good four feet in length,—as large as the wasp, certainly—but it was more heavily built and could not make the speed of which the wasp was capable. It dodged with less agility. Twice, in desperation, it did manage to evade the plunging dives of the wasp, but the third time the two insects grappled in mid-air almost over the heads of the humans.

They tumbled downward in a clawing, biting, tangle of bodies and legs. They hit the ground and rolled over and over. The bee struggled to insert her barbed sting in the more supple body of her adversary. She writhed and twisted desperately.

But there came an instant of infinite confusion and the bee lay on her back. The wasp suddenly moved with that ghastly skilled precision of a creature performing an incredible feat instinctively, apparently unaware that it is doing so. The dazed bee was swung upright in a peculiarly artificial pose. The wasp's body curved, and its deadly, rapier-sharp sting struck...

The bee was dead. Instantly. As if struck dead by lightning. The wasp had stung in a certain place in the neck-parts where all the nerve-cords pass. To sting there, the wasp had to bring its victim to a particular pose. It was precisely the trick of a *desnucador*, the butcher who kills cattle by severing the spinal cord. For the wasp's purposes the bee had to be killed in this fashion and no other.

Burl began to give low-toned commands to his followers. He knew what was coming next, and so did they. When the sequel of the murder began he moved forward, his tribesmen wavering after him. This venture was actually one of the least dangerous they could attempt, but merely to attack a wasp was a hair-raising idea. Only Burl's prestige plus their knowledge made them capable of it.

The second act of the murder-drama was gruesomeness itself. The pirate-wasp was a carnivore, but this was the season when the wasps raised young. Inevitably there was sweet honey in the half-filled crop of the bee. Had she arrived safely at the hive, the sweet and sticky liquid would have been disgorged for the benefit of bee-grubs. The wasp avidly set to work to secure that honey. The bee-carcass itself was destined for the pirate-wasp's own offspring, and that squirming monstrosity is even more violently carnivorous than its mother. The parent wasp set about abstracting the dead bee's honey, before taking the carcass to its young one, because honey is poisonous to the pirate-wasp's grub. Yet insects cannot act from solicitude or anything but instinct. And instinct must be maintained by lavish rewards.

So the pirate-wasp sought its reward—an insane, insatiable, gluttonous satisfaction in the honey that was poison to its young. The wasp foiled its murdered victim upon its back again and feverishly pressed on the limp body to force out the honey. And this was the reason for its precise manner of murder. Only when killed by the destruction of all nerve-currents would the bee's body be left limp like this. Only a bee killed in this exact fashion would yield its honey to manipulation.

The honey appeared, flowing from the dead bee's mouth. The wasp, in trembling, ghoulish ecstasy, devoured it as it appeared. It was lost to all other sights or sensations but its feast.

And this was the moment when Burl signalled for the attack. The tribesmen's prey was deaf and blind and raptured. It was aware of nothing but the delight it savored. But the men wavered, nevertheless, when they drew near. Burl was first to thrust his spear powerfully into the trembling body.

When he was not instantly destroyed the others took courage. Dor's spear penetrated the very vitals of the ghoul. Jak's club fell with terrific force upon the wasp's slender waist. There was a crackling, and the long, spidery limbs quivered and writhed. Then Burl struck again and the creature fell into two writhing halves.

They butchered it rather messily, but Burl noticed that even as it died, sundered and pierced with spears, its long tongue licked out in one last rapturous taste of the honey that had been its undoing.

Some time later, burdened with the pollen laden legs of the great bee, the tribe resumed its journey.

Now Burl had men behind him. They were still timid and prone to flee at the least alarm, but they were vastly more dependable than they had been. They had attacked and slain a wasp whose sting would have killed any of them. They had done battle under the leadership of Burl, whose spear had struck the first blow. They were sharers of his glory and, therefore, much more nearly like the followers of a chieftain ought to be.

Their new spirit was badly needed. The red puffballs were certainly no less numerous in the new territory the tribe traversed than in the territory they had left. And the season of their ripening' was further advanced. More and more of the ground showed the deadly rime of settled death-dust. To stay alive was increasingly difficult. When the full spore-casting season arrived, it would be impossible. And that season could not be far away.

The very next day after the killing of the wasp, survival despite the red dust had begun to seem unimaginable. Where, earlier, one saw a red-dust cloud bursting here and there at intervals, on this day there was always a billowing mass of lethal vapor in the air. At no time was the landscape free of a moving mist of death. Usually there were three or four in sight at once. Often there were half a dozen. Once there were eight. It could be guessed that in one day more they would ripen in such monstrous numbers that anything which walked or flew or crawled must breathe in the spores and perish.

And that day, just at sunset, the tribe came to the top of a small rise in the ground. For an hour they had been marching and countermarching to avoid the suddenly-billowing clouds of dust. Once they had been nearly hemmed in when three of the dull-red mists seemed to flow together, enclosing the three sides of a circle. They escaped then only by the most desperate of sprinting.

But now they came to the little hillock and halted. Before them stretched a plain, all of four miles wide, colored a brownish brick-red by the red puffballs. The tribe had seen mushroom forests—they had lived in them—and knew of the dangers that lurked there. But the plain before them was not simply dangerous; it was fatal. To right and left it stretched as far as the eye could see, but away on its farther edge Burl caught a glimpse of flowing water.

Over the plain itself a thin red haze seemed to float. It was simply a cloud of the deadly spores, dispersed and indefinite, but constantly replenished by the freshly bursting puffballs. While the tribesfolk stood and watched, thick columns of dust rose here and there and at the other place, too many to count. They settled again but left behind enough of the fine powder to keep a thin red haze over all the plain. This was a mass of literally millions of the deadly growths. Here was one place where no carnivorous beetles roamed and where no spiders lurked. There were nothing here but the sullen columns of dust and the haze that they left behind.

And of course it would be nothing less than suicide to try to go back.

CHAPTER EIGHT
A Flight Continues

Burl kept his people alive until darkness fell. He had assigned watchers for each direction and when flight was necessary the adults helped the children to avoid the red dust. Four times they changed direction after shrill-voiced warnings. When night settled over the plain they were forced to come to a halt.

But the puffballs were designed to burst by day. Stumbled into, they could split at any time, and the humans did hear some few of the tearing noises that denoted a spore-spout in the darkness. But after slow nightly rain began they heard no more.

Burl led his people into the plain of red puffballs as soon as the rain had lasted long enough to wash down the red haze still hanging in the air and turn the fallen spores to mud.

It was an enterprise of such absolute desperation that very likely no civilized man would have tried it. There were no stars, for guidance, nor compasses to show the way. There were no lights to enable them to dodge the deadly things they strove to escape, and there was no possibility of their keeping a straight course in the darkness. They had to trust to luck in perhaps the longest long-shot that humans every accepted as a gamble.

Quaintly, they used the long antennae of a dead flying-beetle as sense-organs for themselves. They entered the red plain in a long single file, Burl leading the way with one of the two feathery whips extended before him. Saya helped him check on what lay in the darkness ahead, but made sure not to leave his side. Others trailed behind, hand in hand.

Progress was slow. The sky was utter blackness, of course, but nowhere in the lowlands is there an absolute black. Where fox-fire doesn't burn without consuming, there are mushrooms with glows of their own. Rusts sometimes shone faintly. Naturally there were no fireflies or glow-worms of any sort; but neither were there any living things to hunt the tiny tribe as it moved half-blindly in single file through the plain of red puffballs. Within half an hour even Burl did not believe he had kept to his original line. An hour later they realized despairingly that they were marching helpless through puffballs which would make the air unbreathable at dawn. But they marched on.

Once they smelled the rank odor of cabbages. They followed the scent and came upon them, glowing palely with parasitic moulds on their leaves. And there were living things here: huge caterpillars eating and eating, even in the dark, against the time of metamorphosis. Burl could have cried out infuriatedly at them because they were—so he assumed—immune to the death of the red dust. But the red dust was all about, and the smell of cabbages was not the smell of life.

It could have been, of course. Caterpillars breathe like all insects at every stage of their development. But furry caterpillars breathe through openings which are covered over with matted fur. Here, that matted fur acted to filter the air. The eggs of the caterpillars had been laid before the puffballs were ready to burst. The time of spore-bearing would be over before the grubs were butterflies or moths. These creatures were safe against all enemies—even men. But men groped and blundered in the darkness simply because they did not think to take the fur garments they wore and hold them to their noses to serve as gas-masks or air-filters. The time for that would come, but not yet.

With the docility of despair, Burl's tribe followed him through all the night. When the sky began to pale in the east, they numbly resigned themselves to death. But still they followed.

And in the very early gray light—when only the very ripest of the red puffballs spouted toward a still-dark sky—Burl looked harassedly about him and could have groaned. He was in a little circular clearing, the deadly red things all about him. There was not yet light enough for colors to appear. There was merely a vast stillness everywhere, and a mocking hint of the hot and peppery scent of death-dust—now turned to mud—all about him.

Burl dropped in bitter discouragement. Soon the misty dust-clouds would begin to move about; the reddish haze would form above all this space...

Then, quite suddenly, he lifted his head and whooped. He had heard the sound of running water.

His followers looked at him with dawning hope. Without a word to them, Burl began to run. They followed hastily and quickened their pace when his voice came back in a shout of triumph. In a moment they had emerged from the tangle of fungus growths to stand upon the banks of a wide river—the same river whose gleam Burl had seen the day before, from the farther side of the red puffball plain.

Once before, Burl had floated down a river upon a mushroom raft. That journey had been involuntary. He had been carried far from his tribe and Saya, his heart filled with desolation. But now he viewed the swiftly-running current with delight.

He cast his eyes up and down the bank. Here and there it rose in a low bluff and thick shelf-fungi stretched out above the water. They were adaptations of the fungi that once had grown on trees and now fed upon the incredibly nourishing earth-banks formed of dead growing things. Burl was busy in an instant, stabbing the relatively hard growths with his spear and striving to wrench them free. The tribesmen stared blankly, but at a snapped order they imitated him.

Soon two dozen masses of firm, light fungus lay upon the shore. Burl began to explain what they were for, but Dor remonstrated. They were afraid to part from him. If they might embark on the same fungus-raft, it would be a different matter. Old Tama scolded him shrilly at the thought of separation. Jon trembled at the mere idea.

Burl cast an apprehensive glance at the sky. Day was rapidly approaching. Soon the red puffballs would burst and shoot their dust-clouds into the air. This was no time to make stipulations. Then Saya spoke softly.

Burl made the suggested great sacrifice. He took the gorgeous velvet cloak of moth-wing from his shoulder and tore it into a dozen long, irregular pieces along the lines of the sinews reinforcing it. He planted his spear upright in the largest raft, fastening the other cranky craft to it with the improvised lines.

In a matter of minutes the small flotilla of rafts bobbed in the stream. One by one, Burl settled the folk upon them with stern commands about movement. Then he shoved them out from the bank. The collection of uneasy, floating things moved slowly out from shore to where the current caught them. Burl and Saya sat on the same section of fungus, the other trustful but frightened tribes-people clustered timorously about.

As they began to move between the mushroom-lined banks of the river, and as the mist of nighttime lifted from its surface, columns of red dust spurted sullenly upward on the plain. In the light of dawn the deadly red haze was forming once more over the puffball plain.

By that time, however, the unstable rafts were speeding down the river, bobbing and whirling in the stream, with wide-eyed people as their passengers gazing in wonderment at the shores.

Five miles downstream, the red growths became less numerous and other forms of fungus took their places. Moulds and rusts covered the ground as grass did on more favored planets. Toadstools showed their creamy, rounded heads, and there were malformed things with swollen trunks and branches mocking the trees that were never seen in these lowlands. Once the tribesmen saw the grisly bulk of a hunting-spider outlined on the river-bank.

All through the long day they rode the current, while the insect life that had been absent in the neighborhood of the death-plain became abundant again. Bees once more droned overhead, and wasps and dragonflies. Four-inch mosquitoes appeared, to be driven off with blows. Glittering beetles made droning or booming noises as they flew. Flies of every imaginable metallic hue flew about. Huge butterflies danced above the steaming land and running river in seeming ecstasy at simply being alive.

All the thousand-and-one forms of insect life flew and crawled and swam and dived where the people of the rafts could see them. Water-beetles came lazily to the surface to snap at other insects on the surface. The shell-covered boats of caddis-flies floated in the eddies and backwaters.

The day wore on and the shores flowed by. The tribesmen ate of their food and drank of the river. When afternoon came the banks fell away and the current slackened. The shores became indefinite. The river merged itself into a vast swamp from which came a continual muttering.

The water seemed to grow dark when black mud took the place of the clay that had formed its bed. Then there appeared floating green things which did not move with the flowing water. They were the leaves of the water-lilies that managed to survive along with cabbages and a very few other plants in the midst of a fungus world. Twelve feet across, any one of the green leaves might have supported the whole of Burl's tribe.

They became so numerous that only a relatively narrow, uncovered stream flowed between tens of acres of the flat, floating leaves. Here and there colossal waxen blossoms could be seen. Three men could hide in those enormous flowers. They exhaled an almost overpowering fragrance into the air.

And presently the muttering sound that had been heard far away grew in volume to an intermittent deep-bass roar. It seemed to come from the banks on either side. It was the discordant croaking of frogs, eight feet in length, which lived and throve in this swamp. Presently the tribesfolk saw them: green giants sitting immobile upon the banks, only opening their huge mouths to croak.

Here in the swamps there was such luxuriance of insect life that a normal tribal hunting-ground—in which tribesmen were not yet accustomed to hunt—would seem like a desert by comparison. Myriads of little midges, no more than three or four inches across their wings, danced above the water. Butterflies flew low, seemingly enamoured of their reflections in the glassy water.

The people watched as if their eyes would become engorged by the strange new things they saw. Where the river split and split and divided again, there was nothing with which they were familiar. Mushrooms did not grow here. Moulds, yes. But there were cattails, with stalks like trees, towering thirty feet above the waterways.

After a long, long time though, the streams began to rejoin each other. Then low hills loomed through the thicker haze that filled the air here. The river flowed toward and through them. And here a wall of high mountains rose toward the sky, but their height could not be guessed. They vanished in the mist even before the cloud-bank swallowed them.

The river flowed through a river-gate, a water-gap in the mountains. While day still held fully bright, the bobbing rafts went whirling through a narrow pass with sheer walls that rose beyond all seeing in the mist. Here there was even some white water. Above it, spanning a chasm five hundred feet across, a banded spider had flung its web. The rafts floated close enough to see the spider, a monster even of its kind, its belly swollen to a diameter of yards. It hung motionless in the center of the snare as the humans swept beneath it.

Then the mountains drew back and the tribe was in a valley where, look as they might, there was no single tawny-red puffball from whose spreading range the tribesmen were refugees. The rafts grounded and they waded ashore while still the day held. And there was food here in plenty.

But darkness fell before they could explore. As a matter of precaution Burl and his folk found a hiding-place in a mushroom-thicket and hid until morning. The night-sounds were wholly familiar to them. The noise of katydids was louder than usual—the feminine sound of that name gives no hint of the sonorous, deep-toned notes the enlarged creatures uttered—and that implied more vegetation as compared with straight fungoid flora. A great many fireflies glowed in the darkness shrouding the hiding-place, indicating that the huge snails they fed on were plentiful. The snails would make very suitable prey for the tribesmen also. But men were not yet established in their own minds as predators.

They were, though, definitely no longer the furtive vermin they had been. They knew there were such things as weapons. They had killed ants for food and a pirate-wasp as an exercise in courage. To some degree they were acquiring Burl's own qualities. But they were still behind him—and he still had some way to go.

The next day they explored their new territory with a boldness which would have been unthinkable a few weeks before. The new haven was a valley, spreading out to a second swamp at its lower end. They could not know it, but beyond the swamp lay the sea. Exploring, because of strictly practical purposes and not for the sake of knowledge, they found a great trap-door in the earth, sure sign of the lair of a spider. Burl considered that before many days the monster would have to be dealt with. But he did not yet know how it could be done.

His people were rapidly becoming a tribe of men, but they still needed Burl to think for them. What he could not think out, so far, could not be done. But a part of the proof that they needed Burl to think for them lay in the fact that they did not realize it. They gathered facts about their environment. The nearest ant-city was miles away. That meant that they would encounter its scouting foragers rather than working-parties. The ant-city would be a source of small prey—a notion that would have been inconceivable a little while ago. There were numerous giant cabbages in the valley and that meant there were big, defenseless slugs to spear whenever necessary.

They saw praying-mantises—the adults were eighteen feet tall and as big as giraffes, but much less desirable neighbors—and knew that they would have to be avoided. But there were edible mushrooms on every hand. If one avoided spiders and praying-mantises and the meat-eating beetles; if one were safely hidden at night against the amorous male spiders who took time off from courtship to devour anything living that came their way; and if one lived at high-tension alertness, interpreting every sound as possible danger and every unknown thing as certain peril—then one could live quite comfortably in this valley.

For three days the tribesmen felt that they had found a sort of paradise. Jon had his belly full to bursting all day long. Tet and Dik became skilled ant-hunters. Dor found a better spear and practiced thoughtfully with it.

There were no red puffballs here. There was food. Burl's folk could imagine no greater happiness. Even old Tama scolded only rarely. They surely could not conceive of any place where a man might walk calmly about with no danger at all of being devoured. This was paradise!

And it was a deplorable state of affairs. It is not good for human beings to feel secure and experience contentment. Men achieve only by their wants or through their fears. Back at their former foraging-ground, the tribe would never have emulated Burl with any passion so long as they could survive by traditional behavior. Before the menace of the red puffballs developed, he had brought them to the point of killing ants, with him present and ready to assist. They would have stayed at about that level. The red dust had forced their flight. During that flight they had achieved what was—compared to their former timidity—prodigies of valor.

But now they arrived at paradise. There was food. They could survive here in the fashion of the good old days before they learned the courage of desperation. They did not need Burl to keep them alive or to feed them. They tended to disregard him. But they did not disperse. Social grouping is an instinct in human beings as it is in cattle or in schools of fish. Also, when Burl was available there was a sense of pleasant confidence. He had gotten them out of trouble before. If more trouble came, he would get them out of it again. But why look for trouble?

Burl's tribesmen sank back into a contented lethargy. They found food and hid themselves until it was all consumed. A part of the valley was found where they were far enough from visible dangers to feel blissfully safe. When they did move, though still with elaborate caution, it was only to forage for food. And they did not need to go far because there was plenty of food. They slipped back. Happier than they had ever been, the foragers finally began to forget to take their new spears or clubs with them. They were furtive vermin in a particularly favorable environment.

And Burl was infuriated. He had known adulation. He was cherished, to be sure, but adulation no longer came his way. Even Saya...

An ironically natural change took place in Saya. When Burl was a chieftain, she looked at him with worshipful eyes. Now that he was as other men, she displayed coquetry. And Burl was of that peculiarly direct-thinking sort of human being who is capable of leadership but not of intrigue. He was vain, of course. But he could not engage in elaborate maneuvers to build up a romantic situation. When Saya archly remained with the women of the tribe, he considered that she avoided him. When she coyly avoided speech with him, he angrily believed that she did not want his company.

When they had been in the valley for a week Burl went off on a bitter journey by himself. Part of his motivation, probably, was a childish resentment. He had been the great man of the tribe. He was no longer so great because his particular qualities were not needed. And—perhaps with some unconscious intent to punish them for their lessened appreciation—he went off in a pet.

He still carried spear and club, but the grandeur of his costume had deteriorated. His cloak was gone. The moth-antennae he had worn bound to his forehead were now so draggled that they were ridiculous. He went off angrily to be rid of his fellows' indifference.

He found the upward slopes which were the valley's literal boundaries. They promised nothing. He found a minor valley in which a labyrinth spider had built its shining snare. Burl almost scorned the creature. He could kill it if he chose, merely by stabbing it though the walls of its silken nest as it waited for unlucky insects to blunder into the intricate web. He saw praying-mantises. Once he came upon that extraordinary egg-container of the mantis tribe: a gigantic leaf-shaped mass of solidified foam, whipped out of some special plastic compound which the mantis secretes, and in which the eggs are laid.

He found a caterpillar wrapped in its thick cocoon and, because he was not foraging and not particularly hungry, he inspected it with care. With great difficulty he even broke the strand of silk that formed it, unreeling several feet in curiosity. Had he meditated, Burl would have seen that this was cord which could be used to build snares as spiders did. It could also be used to make defenses in which—if built strongly and well—even hunting-spiders might be tangled and dispatched.

But again he was not knowingly looking for things to be of use. He coddled his sense of injury against the tribe. He punished them by leaving them.

He encountered a four-foot praying-mantis that raised its saw-toothed forelimbs and waited immobile for him to come within reach. He had trouble getting away without a fight. His spear would have been a clumsy weapon against so slender a target and the club certainly not quick enough to counter the insect's lightning-like movements.

He was bothered. That day he hunted ants. The difficulty was mainly that of finding individual ants, alone, who could be slaughtered without drawing hordes of others into the fight. Before nightfall he had three of them—foot-long carcasses—slung at his belt. Near sunset he came upon another fairly recent praying-mantis hatchling. It was almost an ambush. The young monster stood completely immobile and waited for him to walk into its reach.

Burl performed a deliberate experiment—something that had not been done for a very long time on the forgotten planet. The small, grisly creature stood as high as Burl's shoulders. It would be a deadly antagonist. Burl tossed it a dead ant.

It struck so swiftly that the motion of its horrible forearms could not be seen. Then it ignored Burl, devouring the tidbit.

It was a discovery that was immediately and urgently useful.

On the second day of his aimless journey Burl saw something that would be even more deadly and appalling than the red dust had been for his kind. It was a female black hunting-spider, the so-called American tarantula. When he glimpsed the thing the blood drained from Burl's face.

As the monster moved out of sight Burl, abandoning any other project he might have intended, headed for the place his tribe had more or less settled in. He had news which offered the satisfaction of making him much-needed again, but he would have traded that pleasure ten hundred times over for the simple absence of that one creature from this valley. That female tarantula meant simply and specifically that the tribe must flee or die. This place was not paradise!

The entry of the spider into the region had preceded the arrival of the people. A giant, even of its kind, it had come across some pass among the mountains for reasons only it could know. But it was deadliness beyond compare. Its legs spanned yards. The fangs were needle-sharp and feet in length—and poisoned. Its eyes glittered with insatiable, insane blood-lust. Its coming was ten times more deadly to the humans—as to the other living creatures of the valley—than a Bengal tiger loosed in a human city would have been. It was bad enough in itself, but it brought more deadly disaster still behind it.

Bumping and bouncing behind its abdomen as it moved, fastened to its body by dirtied silken ropes, this creature dragged a burden which was its own ferocity many times multiplied. It was dragging an egg-bag larger than its body—which was feet in diameter. The female spider would carry this ghastly burden—cherishing it—until the eggs hatched. And then there would be four to five hundred small devils loose in the valley. From the instant of their hatching they would be as deadly as their parent. Though the offspring would be small—with legs spanning no more than a foot—their bodies would be the size of a man's fist and able to leap two yards. Their tiny fangs would be no less envenomed than their mother's. In stark, maniacal hatred of all other life they would at least equal the huge gray horror which had begot them.

Burl told his tribesmen. They listened, eyes large with fright but not quite afraid. The thing had not yet happened. When Burl insistently commanded that they follow him on a new journey, they nodded uneasily but slipped away. He could not gather the tribe together. Always there were members who hid from him—and when he went in search of them, the ones he had gathered vanished before he could return.

There were days of bright light and murder, and nights of slow rain and death in the valley. The great creatures under the cloud-bank committed atrocities upon each other and blandly dined upon their victims. Unthinkingly solicitous parents paralyzed creatures to be left living and helpless for their young to feed on. There were enormities of cruelty done in the matter-of-fact fashion of the insect world. To these things the humans were indifferent. They were uneasy, but like other humans everywhere they would not believe the worst until the worst arrived.

Two weeks after their coming to the valley, the worst was there. When that day came the first gray light of dawn found the humans in a shivering, terrified group in a completely suicidal position. They were out in the open—not hidden but in plain view. They dared not hide any more. The furry gray monster's brood had hatched. The valley seemed to swarm with small gray demons which killed and killed, even when they could not devour. When they encountered each other they fought in slavering fury and the victors in such duels dined upon their brethren. But always they hunted for more things to kill. They were literally maniacs—and they were too small and too quick to fight with spears or clubs.

So now, at daybreak, the humans looked about despairingly for death to come to them. They had spent the night in the open lest they be trapped in the very thickets that had formerly been their protection. They were in clear sight of the large gray murderer, if it should pass that way. And they did not dare hide because of that ogreish creature's brood.

The monster appeared. A young girl saw it and cried out chokingly. It had not seen them. They watched it leap upon and murder a vividly-colored caterpillar near the limit of vision in the morning-mist. It was in the tribe's part of the valley. Its young swarmed everywhere. The valley could have been a paradise, but it was doomed to become a charnel-house.

And then Burl shook himself. He had been angry when he left his tribe. He had been more angry when he returned and they would not obey him. He had remained with them, petulantly silent, displaying the offended dignity he felt and elaborately refusing to acknowledge any overtures, even from Saya. Burl had acted rather childishly. But his tribesmen were like children. It was the best way for him to act.

They shivered, too hopeless even to run away while the shaggy monster feasted a half-mile away. There were six men and seven women besides himself, and the rest were children, from gangling adolescents to one babe in arms. They whimpered a little. Then

Saya looked imploringly at Burl—coquetry forgotten now. The other whimpered more loudly. They had reached that stage of despair, now, when they could draw the monster to them by blubbering in terror.

This was the psychological moment. Burl said dourly:

"Come!"

He took Saya's hand and started away. There was but one direction in which any human being could think to move in this valley, at this moment. It was the direction away from the grisly mother of horrors. It happened to be the way up the valley wall. Burl started up that slope. Saya went with him.

Before they had gone ten yards Dor spoke to his wife. They followed Burl, with their three children. Five yards more, and Jak agitatedly began to bustle his family into movement. Old Jon, wheezing, frantically scuttled after Burl, and Cori competently set out with the youngest of her children in her arms and the others marching before her. Within seconds more, all the tribe was in motion.

Burl moved on, aware of his following, but ignoring it. The procession continued in his wake simply because it had begun to do so. Dik, his adolescent brashness beaten down by terror, nevertheless regarded Burl's stained weapon with the inevitable envy of the half-grown for achievement. He saw something half-buried in the soil and—after a fearful glance behind—he moved aside to tug at it. It was part of the armor of a former rhinoceros beetle. Tet joined him. They made an act of great daring of lingering to find themselves weapons as near as possible to Burl's.

A quarter-mile on, the fugitives passed a struggling milkweed plant, no more than twenty feet high and already scabrous with scale and rusts upon its lower parts. Ants marched up and down its stalk in a steady single file, placing aphids from their nearby ant-city on suitable spots to feed,—and to multiply as only parthenogenic aphids can do. But already, on the far side of the milkweed, an ant-lion climbed up to do murder among them. The ant-lion, of course, was the larval form of a lace-wing fly. The aphids were its predestined prey.

Burl continued to march, holding Saya's hand. The reek of formic acid came to his nostrils. He ignored it. Ants were as much prey to his tribesmen, now, as crabs and crayfish to other, shore-dwelling tribesmen on long-forgotten Earth. But Burl was not concerned with food, now. He stalked on toward the mountain-slopes.

Dik and Tet brandished their new weapons. They looked fearfully behind them. The monster from whom they fled was lost in its gruesome feasting,—and they were a long way from it, now. There was a steady, single-file procession of ants, with occasional gaps in the line. The procession passed the line through one of those gaps.

Beyond it, Tet and Dik conferred. They dared each other. They went scrambling back to the line of ants. Their weapons smote. The slaughtered ants died instantly and were quickly dragged from the formic-acid-scented path. The remaining ants went placidly on their way. The weapons struck again.

The two adolescents had to outdo each other. But they had as much food as they could carry. Gloating—each claiming to have been most daring and to have the largest bag of game—they ran panting after the tribe. They grandly distributed their take of game. It was a form of boasting. But the tribesfolk accepted the gifts automatically. It was, after all, food.

The two gangling boys, jabbering at each other, raced back once more. Again they returned with dangling masses of foodstuff,—half-scores of foot-long creatures whose limbs, at least, contained firm meat.

Behind, the ant-lion made his onslaught into the stupidly feasting aphids, and warrior-ants took alarm and thrust forward to offer battle. Tumult arose upon the milkweed.

But Burl led his followers toward the mountainside. He reached a minor eminence and looked about him. Caution was the price of existence on this world.

Two hundred feet away, a small scurrying horror raged and searched among the rough-edged layers of what on other worlds was called paper-mould or rock-tripe. Here it was thick as quilting, and infinitesimal creatures denned under it. The sixteen-inch spider devoured them, making gluttonous sounds. But it was busy, and all spiders are relatively short-sighted.

Burl turned to Saya, and realized that all his tribe had followed him fearfully even to this small height he'd climbed only to look around from. Dor had taken advantage of Burl's pause. There was an empty cricket-shell partly overwhelmed by the fungoid soil. He tore free a now-hollow, sickle-shaped jaw. It was curved and sharp and deadly if properly wielded. Dor had seen Burl kill things. He had even helped. Now, very grimly, he tried to imagine killing something all alone. Jak saw him working on the sickle-shaped weapon. He tugged at the cricket's ransacked carcass for another weapon. Dik and Tet vaingloriously pretended to fight between themselves with their recently acquired instruments for killing. Jon wheezed and panted. Old Tama complained to herself in whispers, not daring to make sounds in the daylight. The rest waited until Burl should lead them further.

When Burl turned angry eyes upon them—he was beginning to do such things deliberately, now—they all regarded him humbly. Now they remembered that they had been hungry and he had gotten food for them, and they had been paralyzed by terror, and he dared to move. They definitely had a feeling of dependence upon him, for the present moment only. Later, their feeling of humbleness would diminish. In proportion as he met their needs for leadership, they would tend to try to become independent of him. His leadership would be successful in proportion as he taught them to lead themselves. But Burl perceived this only dimly. At the moment it was pleasing to have all his tribe regard him so worshipfully, even if not in quite the same fashion as Saya. He was suddenly aware that now—at any rate while they were so frightened—they would obey him. So he invented an order for them to obey.

"I carry sharp things," he said sternly. "Some of you have gotten sharp things. Now everybody must carry sharp things, to fight with."

Humbly, they scattered to obey. Saya would have gone with them, but Burl held her back. He did not quite know why. It could have been that the absolute equality of the sexes in cravenness was due to end, and for his own vanity Burl would undertake the defense of Saya. He did not analyze so far. He did not want her to leave him, so he prevented it.

The tribesfolk scattered. Dor went with his wife, to help her arm herself. Jak uneasily followed his. Jon went timorously where the picked-over remnant of the cricket's carcass might still yield an instrument of defense. Cori laid her youngest child at Burl's feet while she went fearfully to find some toothed instrument meeting Burl's specification of sharpness.

There was a stifled scream. A ten-year-old boy—he was Dik's younger brother—stood paralyzed. He stared in an agony of horror at something that had stepped from behind a misshapen fungoid object fifty yards from Burl, but less than ten yards from him.

It was a pallidly greenish creature with a small head and enormous eyes. It stood upright, like a man,—and it was a few inches taller than a man. Its abdomen swelled gracefully into a leaflike form. The boy faced it, paralyzed by horror, and it stood stock-still. Its great, hideously spined arms were spread out in a pose of hypocritical benediction.

It was a partly-grown praying mantis, not too long hatched. It stood rigid, waiting benignly for the boy to come closer or try to flee. If he had fled, it would fling itself after him with a ferocity beside which the fury of a tiger would be kittenish. If he approached, its fanged arms would flash down, pierce his body, and hold him terribly fast by the needle-sharp hooks that were so much worse than trap-claws. And of course it would not wait for him to die before it began its meal.

All the small party of humans stood frozen. It may be questioned whether they were filled with horror for the boy, or cast into a deeper abyss of despair by the sight of a half-grown mantis. Only Burl, so far, had any notion of actually leaving the valley. To the rest, the discovery of one partly mature praying mantis meant that there would be hundreds of others. It would be impossible to evade the tiny, slavering demons which were the brood of the great spider. It would be impossibility multiplied to live where a horde of small—yet vastly larger—fiends lived, raising their arms in a semblance of blessing before they did murder.

Only Burl was capable of thought, and this was because vanity filled him. He had commanded and had been obeyed. Now obedience was forgotten because there was this young mantis. If the men had dreamed of fighting it, it could have destroyed any number of them by sheer ferocity and its arsenal of knives and daggers. But Burl was at once furious and experienced. He had encountered such a middle-sized monster, when alone, and deliberately had experimented with it. In consequence he could dare to rage. He ran toward the mantis. He swung the small corpse of an ant—killed by Tet only minutes since—and hurled it past the terror-fascinated boy. He had hurled it at the mantis.

It struck. And insects simply do not think. Something hurtled at the ghastly young creature. Its arms struck ferociously to defend itself. The ant was heavy. Poised upright in its spectral attitude, the mantis was literally flung backward. But it rolled over, fighting the dead ant with that frenzy which is not so much ferocity as mania.

The small boy fled, hysterically, once the insect's attention was diverted.

The human tribe gathered around Burl many hundreds of yards away,—again uphill. He was their rendezvous because of the example set by Cori. She had left her baby with Burl. When Burl dashed from the spot, Saya had quite automatically followed the instinct of any female for the young of its kind. She'd snatched up the baby before she fled. And—of course—she'd joined Burl when the immediate danger was over.

The floor of the valley seemed a trifle indistinct, from here. The mist that hung always in the air partly veiled the details of its horrors. It was less actual, not quite as deadly as it once had seemed.

Burl said fiercely to his followers:

"Where are the sharp things?"

The tribesfolk looked at one another, numbly. Then Jon muttered rebelliously, and old Tama raised her voice in shrill complaint. Burl had led them to this! There had been only the red dust in the place from which they had come, but here was a hunting-spider and its young and also a new hatching of mantises! They could dodge the red dust, but how could they escape the deaths that waited them here? Ai! Ai! Burl had persuaded them to leave their home and brought them here to die...

Burl glared about him. It was neither courage nor resolution, but he had come to realize that to be admired by one's fellows was a splendid sensation. The more one was admired, the better. He was enraged that anyone dared to despair instead of thinking admiringly about his remarkableness.

"I," said Burl haughtily, "am not going to stay here. I go to a place where there are neither spiders nor mantises. Come!"

He held out his hand to Saya. She gave the child to Cori and confidently moved to follow him. Burl stalked grandly away and she went with him. He went uphill. Naturally! There were spiders and mantises in the valley,—so many that to stay there meant death. So he moved to go somewhere else.

And this was the climactic event that changed the whole history of humanity upon the forgotten planet. Up to this point, there may have been other individuals who had accomplished somewhat of Burl's kind of leadership. A few may have learned courage. It is possible that some even led their tribesfolk upon migrations in search of safer lands to live in. But until Burl led his people out of a valley filled with food, up a mountainside toward the unknown, it was simply impossible for humans to rise permanently above the status of hunted vermin; at the mercy of monstrous mindless creatures; whose forbears had most ironically been brought to this planet to prepare it for humans to live on.

Burl was the first man to lead his fellows toward the heights.

CHAPTER NINE
This is Such a Thing as Sunshine

The sun that shone upon the forgotten planet was actually very near. It shone on the top of the cloud-bank, and the clouds glowed with dazzling whiteness. It shone on the mountain-peaks where they penetrated the mist, and the peaks were warmed, and there was no snow anywhere despite the height. There were winds, here where the sun yielded sensible heat. The sky was very blue. At the edge of the plateau—from which the cloud-banks were down instead of up—the mountainsides seemed to descend into a sea of milk. Great undulations in the mist had the semblance of waves, which moved with great deliberation toward the shores.

They seemed sometimes to break in slow-motion against the mountain-walls where they were cliff-like, and sometimes they seemed to flow up gentler inclinations like water flowing up a beach. But all of this was very deliberate indeed, because the cloud-waves were sometimes twenty miles from crest to crest.

The look of things was different on the highlands. This part of the unnamed world, no less than the lowlands, had been seeded with life on two separate occasions. Once the seedings was with bacteria and moulds and lichens to break up the rocks and make soil of them, and once with seeds and insect-eggs and such living things as might sustain themselves immediately they were hatched. But here on the highlands the different climatic conditions had allowed other seedlings and creatures to survive together.

Here moulds and yeasts and rusts were stunted by the sunlight. Grasses and weeds and trees survived, instead. This was an ideal environment for plants that needed sunlight to form chlorophyl, with which to make use of the soil that had been formed. So on the highlands the vegetation was almost earthlike. And there was a remarkable side-effect on the fauna which had been introduced in the same manner and at the same time as the creatures down below. In coolness which amounted to a temperate climate, there developed no such frenzy of life as made the nightmare jungles under the clouds. Plants grow at a slower rate than fungi, and less luxuriantly. There was no vast supply of food for large-sized plant-eaters. Insects which were to survive, here, could not grow to be monsters. Moreover, the nights here were chill. Very many insects grow torpid in the cool of a temperate-zone night, but warm up to activity soon after sunrise. But a large creature, made torpid by cold, will not revive so quickly. If large enough, it will not become fully active until close to dark. On the plateau, the lowland monsters would starve in any case. But more;—they would have only a fraction of each day of full activity.

So there was a necessary limit to the size of the creatures that lived above the clouds. To humans from other planets, the life on the plateau would not have seemed horrifying at all. Save for the absence of birds to sing, and a lack of small mammals to hunt or merely to enjoy, the untouched, sunlit plateau with its warm days and briskly chill nights would have impressed most civilized men as an ideal habitation.

But Burl and his followers were hardly prepared to see it that way at first glance. If told about it in advance, they would have thought of it with despair.

But they did not know beforehand. They toiled upward, their leader moved by such ridiculous motives of pride and vanity as have caused men to achieve greatness throughout all history. Two great continents were discovered back on Earth by a man trying to get spices to hide the gamey flavor of half-spoiled meat, and the power that drives mile-long space-craft was first discovered and tamed by men making bombs to destroy their fellows. There were precedents for foolish motives producing results far from foolishness.

The trudging, climbing folk crawled up the hillside. They reached a place high above the valley Burl had led them to. That valley grew misty in appearance. Presently it could no longer be seen at all. The mist they had taken for granted, all their lives, hid from them everything but the slanting stony wall up which they climbed. The stone was mostly covered by bluish-green rock-tripe in partly overlapping sheets. Such stuff is always close behind the bacteria which first attack a rock-face. On a slope, it clings while soil is washed downward as fast as it is formed. The people never ate rock-tripe, of course. It produces frightening cramps. In time they might learn that when thoroughly dried it can be cooked to pliability again and eaten with some satisfaction. But so far they neither knew dryness nor fire.

Nor had they ever known such surroundings as presently enveloped them. A slanting rocky mountainside, which stretched up frighteningly to the very sky. Grayness overhead. Grayness also to one side,—the side away from the mountain. And equal grayness below. The valley from which they had come could no longer be seen even as a different shading of the mist. And as they scrambled and trudged after Burl, his followers gradually became aware of the utter strangeness of all about them. For one result, they grew sick and dizzy. To them it seemed that all solidity was slowly tilting. Had they been superstitious, they might have thought of demons preparing to punish them for daring to come to such a place. But—quaintly enough—Burl's followers had developed no demonology. Your typical savage is resolved not to think, but he does have leisure to want. He makes gods and devils out of his nightmares, and gambles on his own speculations to the extent of offering blackmail to demons if they will only let him alone or—preferably—give him more of the things he wants.

But the superstitions of savages involve the payment of blackmail in exact proportion to their prosperity. The Eskimos of Earth lived always on the brink of starvation. They could not afford the luxury of tabus and totem animals whose flesh must not be eaten, and forbidden areas which might contain food.

Religion there was, among Burl's people, but superstition was not. No humans, anywhere, can live without religion, but on Earth Eskimos did with a minimum of superstitions,—they could afford no more—and the humans of the forgotten planet could not afford any at all.

Therefore they climbed desperately despite the unparalleled state of things about them. There was no horizon, but they had never seen a horizon. Their feeling was that what had been "down" was now partly "behind" and they feared lest a toppling universe ultimately let them fall toward that grayness they considered the sky.

But all kept on. To lag behind would be to be abandoned in this place where all known sensations were turned topsy-turvy. None of them could imagine turning back. Even old Tama, whimpering in a whisper as she struggled to keep up, merely complained bitterly of her fate. She did not even think of revolt. If Burl had stopped, all his followers would have squatted down miserably to wait for death. They had no thought of adventure or any hope of safety. The only goodnesses they could imagine were food and the nearness of other humans. They had food—nobody had abandoned any of the dangling ant-bodies Tet and Dik had distributed before the climb began. They would not be separated from their fellows.

Burl's motivation was hardly more distinct. He had started uphill in a judicious mixture of fear and injured vanity and desperation. There was nothing to be gained by going back. The terrors at hand were no greater than those behind, so there was no reason not to go ahead.

They came to a place where the mountain-flank sank inward. There was a flat space, and behind it a winding cañon of sorts like a vast crack in the mountain's substance. Burl breasted the curving edge and found flatness beyond it. He stopped short.

The mouth of the cañon was perhaps fifty yards from the lip of the downward slope. So much space was practically level, and on it were toadstools and milkweed—two of them—and there was food. It was a small, isolated asylum for life such as they were used to. They could—it was possible that they could—have found a place of safety here.

But the possibility was not the fact. They saw the spider-web at once. It was slung between the opposite cañon-walls by cables all of two hundred feet long. The radiating cables reached down to anchorages on stone. The snare-threads, winding out and out in that logarithmic spiral whose properties men were so astonished to discover, were fully a yard apart. The web was for giant game. It was empty now, but Burl saw the telegraph-cord which ran from the very center of the web to the web-maker's lurking-place. There was a rocky shelf on the cañon-wall. On it rested the spider, almost invisible against the stone, with one furry leg touching the cable. The slightest touch on any part of the web would warn it instantly.

Burl's followers accumulated behind him. Old Jon's wheezing was audible. Tama ceased her complaints to survey this spot. It might be—it could be—a haven, and she would have to find new and different things to complain about in consequence. The spider-web itself, of course, was no reason for them to be alarmed. Web-spiders do not hunt. Their males do, but they are rarely in the neighborhood of a web save at mating-time. The web itself was no reason not to settle here. But there was a reason.

The ground before the web,—between the web and themselves—was a charnel-house of murdered creatures. Half-inch-thick wing-cases of dead beetles and the cleaned-out carapaces of other giants. The ovipositor of an ichneumon-fly,—see feet of springy, slender, deadly-pointed tube—and the abdomen-plates of bees and the draggled antennae of moths and butterflies.

Something very terrible lived in this small place. The mountainsides were barren of food for big flying things. Anything which did fly this high for any reason would never land on sloping foodless stone. It would land here. And very obviously it would die. Because something—Something—killed things as they came. It denned back in the cañon where they could not see it. It dined here.

The humans looked and shivered, all but Burl. He cast his eyes about for better weapons than he possessed. He chose for himself a magnificent lance grown by some dead thing for its own defense. He pulled it out of the ground.

It was utterly silent, here on the heights. No sounds from the valley rose so high. There was no noise except the small creakings made as Burl strove to free the new, splendid weapon for himself.

That was why he heard the gasp which somebody uttered in default of a scream that would not be uttered. It was a choked, a strangled, an inarticulate sobbing noise.

He saw its cause.

There was a thing moving toward the folk from the recesses of the cañon. It moved very swiftly. It moved upon stilt-like, impossibly attenuated legs of impossible length and inconceivable number. Its body was the thickness of Burl's own. And from it came a smell of such monstrous foetor that any man, smelling it, would gag and flee even without fear to urge him on. The creature was a monstrous millipede, forty feet in length, with features of purest, unadulterated horror.

It did not appear to plan to spring. Its speed of movement did not increase as it neared the tribesfolk. It was not rushing, like the furious charge of the murderers Burl's tribe knew. It simply flowed sinuously toward them with no appearance of haste, but at a rate of speed they could not conceivably outrun.

Sticklike legs twitched upward and caught the spinning body of an ant. The creature stopped, and turned its head about and seized the object its side-legs had grasped. It devoured it. Burl shouted again and again.

There was a rain of missiles upon the creature. But they were not to hurt it, but to divert its incredibly automaton-like attention. Its legs seized the things flung to it. It was not possible to miss.

Ten, fifteen,—twenty of the items of small-game were grasped in mid-air, as if they were creatures in flight.

Burl's shoutings took effect. His people fled to the side of the level lip of ground. They climbed frantically past the opening of the valley. They fled toward the heights.

Burl was the last to retreat. The monstrous millipede stood immobile, trapped for the moment by the gratification of all its desires. It was absorbed by the multitude of tiny tidbits with which it had been provided.

It was a fact to Burl's honor that he debated a frantic attack upon the monster in its insane absorption. But the strangling stench was deterrent enough. He fled,—the last of his band of fugitives to leave the place where the monstrous creature lived and preyed. As he left it, it was still crunching the small meals, one by one, with which the folk had supplied it.

They went on up the mountain-flank. It was not to be supposed, of course, that the creature could not move above the slanting rock-surface. Unquestionably it roamed far and wide, upon occasion. But its own foetid reek would make impossible any idea of trailing the humans by scent. And, climbing desperately as the humans did, it would be unable to see them when they were past the first protuberance of the mountain.

In twenty minutes they slackened their pace. Exhaustion prompted it. Caution ordered it. Because here they saw another small island of flatness in the slanting universe which was all they could see save mist. It was simply a place where boulders had piled up, and soil had formed, and there was a miniature haven for life other than moulds which could grow on naked stone.

Actually, there was a space a hundred feet by fifty on which wholly familiar mushrooms grew. It was a thicket like a detached section of the valley itself. Well-known edible fungi grew here. There were gray puffballs. And from it came the cheerful loud chirping of some small beetle, arrived at this spot nobody could possibly know how, but happily ensconsed in a separate bit of mushroom-jungle remote from the dangers of the valley. If it was small enough, it would even be safe from the reeking horror of the cañon just below it.

They broke off edible mushrooms here and ate. And this could have been safety for them—save for the giant millipede no more than half a mile below. Old Jon wheezed querulously that here was food and there was no need for them to go further, just now. Here was food...

Burl regarded him with knitted brows. Jon's reaction was natural enough. The tribesfolk had never tended to think for the future because it was impossible to make use of such planning. Even Burl could easily enough have accepted the fact that this was safety for the moment and food for the moment. But it happened that to settle down here until driven out would—and at this moment—have deprived him of the authority he had so recently learned to enjoy.

"You stay," he said haughtily, to Jon. "I go on, to a better place where nothing is to be feared at all!"

He held out his hand to Saya. He assailed the slope again, heading upward in the mist.

His tribe followed him. Dik and Tet, of course, because they were boys and Burl led on to high adventures in which so far nobody had been killed. Dor followed because—he being the strongest man in the tribe—he had thoughtfully realized that his strength was not as useful as Burl's brains and other qualities. Cori followed because she had children, and they were safer where Burl led than anywhere else. The others followed to avoid being left alone.

The procession toiled on and up. Presently Burl noticed that the air seemed clearer, here. It was not the misty, only half transparent stuff of the valley. He could see for miles to right and left. He realized the curvature of the mountain-face. But he could not see the valley. The mist hid that.

Suddenly he realized that he saw the cloud-bank overhead as an object. He had never thought of it specifically before. To him it had been simply the sky. Now he saw an indefinite lower surface which yet definitely hid the heights toward which he moved. He and his followers were less than a thousand feet below it. It appeared to Burl that presently he would run into an obstacle which would simply keep him from going any further. The idea was disheartening. But until it happened he obstinately climbed on.

He observed that the thing which was the sky did not stay still. It moved, though slowly. A little higher, he could see that there were parts of it which were actually lower than he was. They moved also, but they moved away from him as often as they moved toward him. He had no experience of any dangerous thing which did not leap at its victims. Therefore he was not afraid.

In fact, presently he noticed that the whiteness which was the cloud-layer seemed to retreat before him. He was pleased. Weak things like humans fled from enemies. Here was something which fled at his approach! His followers undoubtedly saw the same thing. Burl had killed spiders. He was a remarkable person. This unknown white stuff was afraid of him. Therefore it was wise to stay close to Burl. Burl found his vanity inflamed by the fact that always—even at its thickest—the white cloud-stuff never came nearer than some dozens of feet. He swaggered as he led his people up.

And presently there was brightness about them. It was a greater brightness than the tribesfolk had ever known. They knew daylight as a grayness in which one could see. Here was a brightness that shone. They were not accustomed to brightness.

They were not accustomed to silence, either. The noises of the valley were like all the noises of the lowlands. They had been in the ears of every one of the human beings since they could hear at all. They had gradually diminished as the valley dropped behind them. Now, in the radiant white mist which was the cloud-layer, there were no sounds at all, and the fact was suddenly startling.

They blinked in the brightness. When they spoke to each other, they spoke in whispers. The stone underfoot was not even lichen-covered, here. It was bare and bright and glistened with wetness. The light they experienced took on a golden tint. All of these things were utterly unparalleled, but the stillness was a hush instead of a menacing silence. The golden light could not possibly be associated with fear. The people of the forgotten planet felt, most likely, the sort of promise in this shining tranquility which before they had known only in dreams. But this was no dream.

They came up through the surface of a sea of mist, and they saw before them a shore of sunshine. They saw blue and sky and sunlight for the first time. The light smote their shins and brilliantly colored furry garments. It glittered in changing, ever-more-colorful flashes upon cloaks made of butterfly wings. It sparkled on the great lance carried by Burl in the lead, and the quite preposterous weapons borne by his followers.

The little party of twenty humans waded ashore through the last of the thinning white stuff which was cloud. They gazed about them with wondering, astonished eyes. The sky was blue. There was green grass. And again there was sound. It was the sound of wind blowing among trees, and of things living in the sunshine.

They heard insects, but they did not know what they heard. The shrill small musical whirrings; the high-pitched small cries which made an elfin melody everywhere,—these were totally strange. All things were new to their eyes, and an enormous exultation filled them. From deep-buried ancestral memories they somehow knew that what they saw was right, was normal, was appropriate and proper, and that this was the kind of world in which humans belonged, rather than the seething horror of the lowlands. They breathed clean air for the first time in many generations.

Burl shouted in his triumph, and his voice echoed among trees and hillsides.

It was time for the plateau to ring with the shouting of a man in triumph!

CHAPTER TEN
Men Climb up to Savagery

They had food for days. They had brought mushroom from the isolated thicket not too far beneath the clouds. There were the ants that Dik and Tet had distributed grandly, and not all of which had been used to secure escape from the cañon of the millipede. Had they found other food immediately, they would have settled down comfortably in the fashion normal to creatures whose idea of bliss is a secure hiding-place and food on hand so they do not have to leave it. Somehow they believed that this high place of bright light and new colors was secure. But they had no hiding-place. And though they did accept with the unreasoning faith of children and savages that there were no enemies here, they still wanted one.

They found a cave. It was small, so that it would be crowded with all of them in it, but as it turned out, this was fortunate. At some time it had been occupied by some other creature, but the dirt which floored it had settled flat and showed no tracks. It retained faint traces of a smell which was unfamiliar but not unpleasing,—it held no connotation of danger. Ants stank of formic acid plus the musky odor of their particular city. One could identify not only the kind of ant, but its home city, by sniffing at an ant-trail. Spiders had their own hair-raising odor. The smell of a praying-mantis was acrid, and all beetles reeked of decay. And of course there were those bugs whose main defense was an effluvium which tended to strangle all but the smell's happy possessor. This faint smell in the cave was different. The humans thought vaguely that it might possibly be another kind of man.

Actually, it was the smell of a warm-blooded animal. But Burl and his fellows knew of no warm-blooded creature but themselves.

They had come above the clouds a bare two hours before sunset,—of which they knew nothing. For an hour they marveled, staying close together. They were especially astounded by the sun, since they could not bear to look at it. But presently, being savages, they accepted it matter-of-factly.

They could not cease to wonder at the vegetation about them. They were accustomed only to gigantic fungi and the few straggling plants which tried so desperately to bear seed before they were devoured. Here they saw many plants and no fungi,—and they did not see anything they recognized as insects. They looked only for large things.

They were astounded by the slenderness and toughness of the plants. Grass fascinated them, and weeds. A large part of their courage came from the absence of debris upon the ground. The hunting-grounds of spiders were marked by grisly remnants of finished meals, and where mantises roamed there were bits of transparent beetle-wings and sharp spiny bits of armor not tasty enough to be consumed. Here, in the first hour of their exploration, they saw no sign that an insect like the lowland ones had ever been in this place at all. But they could not believe the monsters never came. They correctly—and pessimistically—assumed that their coming was only rare.

The cave was a great relief. Trees did not grow close enough to give them a feeling of safety,—though they were ludicrously amazed at the invincible hardness of tree trunks. They had never known anything but insect-armour and stone which was as hard as the trunks of those growing things. They found nothing to eat, but they were not yet hungry. They did not worry about food while they still had remnants from their climb.

When the sun sank low and crimson colorings filled the west, they were less happy. They watched the glory of their first sunset with scared, incredulous eyes. Yellows and reds and purples reared toward the zenith. It became possible to look at the sun directly. They saw it descend behind something they could not guess at. Then there was darkness.

The fact stunned them. So night came like this!

Then they saw the stars for the first time, as they came singly into being. And the folk from the lowland crowded frantically into the cave with its faint odor of having once been occupied by something else. They filled the cave tightly. But Burl had some reluctance to admit his terror. He and Saya were the last to enter.

And nothing happened. Nothing. The sounds of sunset continued. They were strange but soothing and somehow—again ancestral memory spoke comfortingly—they were the way night-sounds ought to be. Burl and the others could not possibly know it, but for the first time in forty generations on the forgotten planet, human beings were in an environment really suited to them. It had a rightness and a goodness which was obvious in spite of its novelty. And because of Burl's own special experiences, he was a little bit better able to estimate novelties than the rest. He listened to the night-noises from close by the cave's small entrance. He heard the breathing of his tribesfolk. He felt the heat of their bodies, keeping the crowded enclosure warm enough for all. Saya held fast to his hand, for the reassurance of the contact. He was wakeful, and thinking very busily and painfully, but Saya was not thinking at all. She was simply proud of Burl.

She felt, to be sure, a tumult which was fear of the unknown and relief from much greater fear of the familiar. She felt warm, prideful memories of the sight of Burl leading and commanding the others. She had absorbing fresh memories of the look and feel of sunshine, and mental pictures of sky and grass and trees which she had never seen before. Confusedly she remembered that Burl had killed a spider, no less, and he had shown how to escape a praying-mantis by flinging it at an ant, and he had grandly led the others up a mountainside it had never occurred to anybody else to climb. And the giant millipede would have devoured them all, but that Burl gave commands and set the example, and he had marched magnificently up the mountainside when it seemed that all the cosmos twisted and prepared to drop them into an inverted sky...

Saya dozed. And Burl sat awake, listening, and presently with fast-beating heart he slipped out of the entrance to the cave and stared about him in the night.

There was coolness such as he had never known before, but nightfall was not long past. There were smells in the air he had never before experienced,—green things growing, and the peculiar clean odor of wind that has been bathed in sunshine, and the oddly satisfying smell of resinous trees.

But Burl raised his eyes to the heavens. He saw the stars in all their glory, and he was the first human in two thousand years and more to look at them from this planet. There were myriads upon myriads of them, varying in brightness from stabbing lights to infinitesimal twinklings. They were of every possible color. They hung in the sky above him, immobile and unthreatening. They had not descended. They were very beautiful.

Burl stared. And then he noticed that he was breathing deeply, with a new zest. He was filling his lungs with clean, cool, fragrant air such as men were intended to breathe from the beginning, and of which Burl and many others had been deprived. It was almost intoxicating to feel so splendidly alive and unafraid.

There was a slight sound. Saya stood beside him, trembling a little. To leave the others had required great courage, but she had come to realize that if Burl was in danger she wished to share it.

They heard the nightwind and the orchestra of night-singers. They wandered aside from the cave-mouth and Saya found completely primitive and satisfying pride in the courage of Burl, who was actually not afraid of the dark! Her own uneasiness became something which merely added savor to her pride in him. She followed him wherever he went, to examine this and consider that in the nighttime. It gave her enormous satisfaction at once to think of danger and to feel so safe because of his nearness.

Presently they heard a new sound in the night. It was very far away, and not in the least like any sound they had ever heard before. It changed in pitch as insect-cries do not. It was a baying, yelping sound. It rose, and held the higher note, and abruptly dropped in pitch before it ceased. Minutes later it came again.

Saya shivered, but Burl said thoughtfully:

"That is a good sound."

He didn't know why. Saya shivered again. She said reluctantly:

"I am cold."

It had been a rare sensation in the lowlands. It came only after one of the infrequent thunderstorms, when wetted human bodies were exposed to the gusty winds that otherwise never blew. But here the nights grew cold after sundown. The heat of the ground would radiate to outer space with no clouds to intercept it, and before dawn the temperature might drop nearly to freezing. On a planet so close to its sun, however, there would hardly be more than light hoar-frost at any time.

The two of them went back to the cave. It was warm there, because of the close packing of bodies and many breaths. Burl and Saya found places to rest and dozed off, Saya's hand again trustfully in Burl's.

He still remained awake for a long time. He thought of the stars, but they were too strange to estimate. He thought of the trees and grass. But most of his impressions of this upper world were so remote from previous knowledge that he could only accept them as they were and defer reflecting upon them until later. He did feel an enormous complacency at having led his followers here, though.

But the last thing he actually thought about, before his eyes blinked shut in sleep, was that distant howling noise he had heard in the night. It was totally novel in kind, and yet there was something buried among the items of his racial heritage that told him it was good.

He was first awake of all the tribesmen and he looked out into the cold and pallid grayness of before-dawn. He saw trees. One side was brightly lighted by comparison, and the other side was dark. He heard the tiny singing noises of the inhabitants of this place. Presently he crawled out of the cave again.

The air was biting in its chill. It was an excellent reason why the giant insects could not live here, but it was invigorating to Burl as he breathed it in. Presently he looked curiously for the source of the peculiar one-sided light.

He saw the top of the sun as it peered above the eastern cloud-bank. The sky grew lighter. He blinked and saw it rise more fully into view. He thought to look upward, and the stars that had bewildered him were nearly gone.

He ran to call Saya.

The rest of the tribe waked as he roused her. One by one, they followed to watch their first sunrise. The men gaped at the sun as it filled the east with colorings, and rose and rose above the seemingly steaming layer of clouds, and then appeared to spring free of the horizon and swim on upward.

The women stared with all their eyes. The children blinked, and shivered, and crept to their mothers for warmth. The women enclosed them in their cloaks, and they thawed and peered out once more at the glory of sunshine and the day. Very soon, too, they realized that warmth came from the great shining body in the sky. The children presently discovered a game. It was the first game they had ever played. It consisted of running into a shaded place until they shivered, and then of running out into warm sunshine once more. Until this, dawning fear was the motive for such playing as they did. Now they gleefully made a game of sunshine.

In this first morning of their life above the clouds, the tribesmen ate of the food they had brought from below. But there was not an indefinite amount of food left. Burl ate, and considered darkly, and presently summoned his followers' attention. They were quite contented and for the moment felt no need of his guidance. But he felt need of admiration.

He spoke abruptly:

"We do not want to go back to the place we came from," he said sternly. "We must look for food here, so we can stay for always. Today we find food."

It was a seizure of the initiative. It was the linking of what the folk most craved with obedience to Burl. It was the device by which dictators seize power, and it was the instinctive action of a leader.

The eating men murmured agreement. There was a certain definite idea of goodness—not virtue, but of things desirable—associated with what Burl did and what he commanded. His tribe was gradually forming a habit of obedience, though it was a very fragile habit up to now.

He led them exploring as soon as they had eaten. All of them, of course. They straggled irregularly behind him. They came to a brook and regarded it with amazement. There were no leeches. No greenish algae. No foaming masses of scum. It was clear! Greatly daring, Burl tasted it. He drank the first really potable water in a very long time for his race on this planet. It was not fouled by drainage through moulds or rusts.

Dor drank after him. Jak. Cori tasted, and instantly bade her children drink. Even old Tama drank suspiciously, and then raised her voice in shrill complaint that Burl had not led them to this place sooner. Tet and Dik became convinced that there were no deadly things lurking in it, and splashed each other. Dik slipped and sat down hard on white stuff that yielded and almost splashed. He got up and looked fearfully at what he thought might be a deadly slime. Then he yelped shrilly.

He sat down on and crushed part of a bed of mushrooms. But they were tiny, clean, and appetizing. They were miniatures of the edible mushrooms the tribe fed on.

Burl smelled and finally tasted one. It was, of course, nothing more or less than a perfectly normal edible mushroom, growing to the size that mushrooms originally grew on Earth. It grew on a shaded place in enormously rich soil. It had been protected from direct sunlight by trees, but it had not had the means or the stimulus to become a monster.

Burl ate it. He carefully composed his features. Then he announced the find to his followers. There was food here, he told them sternly, but in this splendid world to which he had led them, food was small. There would be no great enemies here, but the food would have to be sought in small objects instead of great ones. They must look at this place and seek others like it, in order to find food...

The tribesmen were doubtful. But they plucked mushrooms—whole ones!—instead of merely breaking off parts of their tops. With deep astonishment they recognized the miniature objects as familiar things ensmalled. These mushrooms had the same savor, but they were not coarse or stringy or tough like the giants. They melted in the mouth; Life in this place to which Burl had led them was delectable! Truly the doings of Burl were astonishing!

When the oldest of Cori's children found a beetle on a leaf, and they recognized it, and instead of being bigger than a man and a thing to flee from, it was less than an inch in size and helpless against them—. They were entranced. From that moment onward they would really follow Burl anywhere, in the happy conviction that he could only bring good to everybody.

The opinion could have drawbacks, and it need not be always even true, but Burl did nothing to discourage it.

And then, near midday, they made a discovery even greater than that of familiar food in unfamiliar sizes. They were struggling, at the time, through a vast patch of bushes with thorns on them—they were not used to thorns—which they deeply distrusted. Eventually they would find out that the glistening dark fruit were blackberries, and would rejoice in them, but at this first encounter they were uneasy. In the midst of such an untouched berry-patch they heard noises in the distance.

The sound was made up of cries of varying pitch, some of which were loud and abrupt, and others longer and less loud. The people did not understand them in the least. They could have been cries of human beings, perhaps, but they were not cries of pain. Also they were not language. They seemed to express a tremendous, zestful excitement. They had no overtone of horror. And Burl and his folk had known of no excitement among insects except frenzy. They could not imagine what sort of tumult this could be.

But to Burl these sounds had something of the timbre of the yelping noises of the night before. He had felt drawn to that sound. He liked it. He liked this.

He led the way boldly toward the agitated noises. Presently— after a mile or so—he and his people came out of breast-high weeds. Saya was immediately behind him. The others trailed,— Tama complaining bitterly that there was no need to track down sounds which could only mean danger. They emerged in a space of bare stone above a small and grassy amphitheatre. The tumult came from its center.

A pack of dogs was joyously attacking something that Burl could not see clearly. They were dogs. They barked zestfully, and they yelped and snarled and yapped in a dozen different voices, and they were having a thoroughly good time,—though it might not be so good for the thing they attacked.

One of them sighted the humans. He stopped stock-still and barked. The others whirled and saw the humans as they came out into view. The tumult ceased abruptly.

There was silence. The tribesmen saw creatures with four legs only. They had never before seen any living thing with fewer than six,—except men. Spiders had eight. The dogs did not have mandibles. They did not have wing-cases. They did not act like insects. It was stupifying!

And the dogs saw men, whom they had never seen before. Much more important, they smelled men. And the difference between man-smell and insect-smell was so vast—because through hundreds of generations the dogs had not smelled anything with warm blood save their own kind—the difference in smell was so great in kind that the dogs did not react with suspicion, but with a fascinated curiosity. This was an unparalleled smell. It was, even in its novelty, an overwhelmingly satisfying smell.

The dogs regarded the men with their heads on one side, sniffing in the deepest possible amazement,—amazement so intense that they could not possibly feel hostility. One of them whined a little because he did not understand.

CHAPTER ELEVEN
Warm Blood is a Bond

Peculiarly enough, it was a matter of topography. The plateau which reached above the clouds rose with a steep slope from the valley from which a hunting-spider's brood had driven the men. This was on the eastern edge of the plateau. On the west, however, the highland was subject to an indentation which almost severed it. No more than twenty miles from where Burl's group had climbed to sunshine, there was a much more gradual slope downward. There, mushroom-forests grew almost to the cloud-layer. From there, giant insects strayed up and onto the plateau itself.

They could not live above the clouds, of course. There was not food enough for their insatiable hunger. Especially at night, it was too cold to allow them to stay active. But they did stray from their normal environment, and some of them did reach the sunshine, and perhaps some of them blundered back down to their mushroom-forests again. But those which did not stumble back were chilled to torpor during their first night underneath the stars. They were only partly active on the second day,—if, indeed, they were active at all. Few or none recovered from their second nights' coldness. None at all kept their full ferocity and deadliness.

And this was how the dogs survived. They were certainly descended from dogs on the wrecked space-ship—the *Icarus*—whose crew had landed on this planet some forty-odd human generations since. The humans of today had no memories of the ship, and the dogs surely had no traditions. But just because those early dogs had less intelligence, they had more useful instincts. Perhaps the first generations of castaways bred dogs in their first few desperate centuries, hoping that dogs could help them survive. But no human civilization could survive in the lowlands. The humans went back to the primitive state of their race and lived as furtive vermin among monsters. Dogs could not survive there, though humans did linger on, so somehow the dogs took to the heights. Perhaps dogs survived their masters. Perhaps some were abandoned or driven away. But dogs had reached the highlands. And they did survive because giant insects blundered up after them,—and could not survive in a proper environment for dogs and men.

There was even reason for the dogs remaining limited in number, and keenly intelligent. The food-supply was limited. When there were too many dogs, their attacks on stumbling insect giants were more desperate and made earlier, before the monsters' ferocity was lessened. So more dogs died. Then there was an adjustment of the number of dogs to the food-supply. There was also a selection of those too intelligent to attack rashly. Yet those who had insufficient courage would not eat.

In short, the dogs who now regarded men with bright, interested eyes were very sound dogs. They had the intelligence needed for survival. They did not attack anything imprudently, but they also knew that it was not necessary to be more than reasonably wary of insects in general,—not even spiders unless they were very newly arrived from the steaming lowlands. So the dogs regarded men with very much the same astonished interest with which the men regarded the dogs.

Burl saw immediately that the dogs did not act with the blind ferocity of insects, but with an interested, estimative intelligence strikingly like that of men. Insects never examined anything. They fled or they fought. Those who were not carnivorous had no interest in anything but food, and those who were meat-eaters lumbered insanely into battle at the bare sight of possible prey. The dogs did neither. They sniffed and they considered.

Burl said sharply to his followers:

"Stay here!"

He walked slowly down into the amphitheatre. Saya followed him instantly. Dogs moved warily aside. But they raised their noses and sniffed. They were long, luxurious sniffs. The smell of human kind was a good smell. Dogs had lived hundreds of their generations without having it in their nostrils, but before that there were thousands of generations to whom that smell was a necessity.

Burl reached the object the dogs had been attacking. It lay on the grass, throbbing painfully. It was the larva of an azure-blue moth which spread ten-foot wings at nightfall. The time for its metamorphosis was near, and it had traveled blindly in search of a place where it could spin its cocoon safely and change to its winged form. It had come to another world,—the world above the clouds. It could find no proper place. Its stores of fat had protected it somewhat from the chill. But the dogs had found it as it crawled blindly—.

Burl considered. It was the custom of wasps to sting creatures like this at a certain special spot,—apparently marked for them by a tuft of dark fur.

Burl thrust home with his lance. The point pierced that particular spot. The creature died quickly and without agony. The thought to kill was an inspiration. Then instinct followed. Burl cut off meat for his tribesmen. The dogs offered no objection. They were well-fed enough. Burl and Saya, together, carried the meat back to the other tribesfolk. On the way Burl passed within two yards of a dog which regarded him with extreme intentness and almost a wistful expression. Burl's smell did not mean game. It meant—something the dog struggled helplessly to remember. But it was good.

"I have killed the thing," said Burl to the dog, in the tone of one addressing an equal. "You can go and eat it now. I took only part of it."

Burl and his people ate of what he had brought back. Many of the dogs—most of them—went to the feast Burl had left. Presently they were back. They had no reason to be hostile. They were fed. The humans offered them no injury, and the humans smelled of something that appealed to the deepest well-springs of canine nature.

Presently the dogs were close about the humans. They were fascinated. And the humans were fascinated in return. Each of the people had a little of the feeling that Burl had experienced as the tribal leader. In the intent, absorbed and wholly unhostile regard of the dogs, even children felt flattered and friendly. And surely in a place where everything else was so novel and so satisfactory, it was possible to imagine friendliness with creatures which were not human, since assuredly they were not insects.

A similar state of mind existed among the dogs.

Saya had more meat than she desired. She glanced among the members of the tribe. All were supplied. She tossed it to a dog.

He jerked away alertly, and then sniffed at it where it had dropped. A dog can always eat. He ate it.

"I wish you would talk to us," said Saya hopefully.

The dog wagged his tail.

"You do not look like us," said Saya interestedly, "but you act like we do. Not like the—Monsters."

The dog looked significantly at meat in Burl's hand. Burl tossed it. The dog caught it with a quick snap, swallowed it, wagged his tail briefly and came closer. It was a completely incredible action, but dogs and men were blood-kin on this planet. Besides, there was racial-memory rightness in friendship between men and dogs. It was not hindered by any past experience of either. They were the only warm-blooded creatures on this world. It was a kinship felt by both.

Presently Burl stood up and spoke politely to the dog. He addressed him with the same respect he would have given to another man. In all his life he had never felt equal to an insect, but he felt no arrogance toward this dog. He felt superior only to other men.

"We are going back to our cave," he said politely. "Maybe we will meet again."

He led his tribe back to the cave in which they had spent the previous night. The dogs followed, ranging on either side. They were well-fed, with no memory of hostility to any creature which smelled of warm blood. They had an instinct without experience to dull it. The latter part of the journey back to the tribal cave was—if anybody had been qualified to notice it—remarkably like a group of dogs taking a walk with a group of people. It was companionable. It felt right.

That night Burl left the cave, as before, to look at the stars. This time Saya went with him matter-of-factly. But as they came out of the cave-entrance there was a stirring. A dog rose and stretched himself elaborately, yawning the while. When Burl and Saya moved away, he trotted amiably with them.

They talked to it, and the dog seemed pleased. It wagged its tail.

When morning came, the dogs were still waiting hopefully for the humans to come out. They appeared to expect the people to take another nice long walk, on which they would accompany them. It was a brand-new satisfaction they did not want to miss. After all, from a dog's standpoint, humans are made to take long walks with, among other things. The dogs greeted the people with tail-waggings and cordiality.

The dogs made a great difference in the adjustment of the tribe to life upon the plateau. Their friendship assured the new status of human life. Burl and his fellows had ceased to be fugitive game for any insect murderer. They had hoped to become unpursued foragers,—because they could hardly imagine anything else. But when the dogs joined them, they were immediately raised to the estate of hunters. The men did not domesticate the dogs. They made friends with them. The dogs did not subjugate themselves to the men. They joined them,—at first tentatively, and then with worshipful enthusiasm. And the partnership was so inevitably a right one that within a month it was as if it had always been.

Actually, save for a mere two thousand years, it had been.

At the end of a month the tribe had a permanent encampment. There were caves at a suitable distance from the slope up which most wanderers from the lowlands came. Cori's oldest child found the chrysalis of a giant butterfly, whose caterpillar form had so offensive an odor that the dogs had not attacked it. But when it emerged from the chrysalis, men and dogs together assailed it before it could take flight. They ended the enterprise with warm mutual approval. The humans had acquired great wings with which to make warm cloaks,—very useful against the evening chill. Dogs and men, alike, had feasted.

Then, one dawning, the dogs made a vast outcry which awoke the tribesmen. Burl led the rush to the spot. They did battle with a monster nocturnal beetle, less chilled than most such invaders. In the gray dawnlight Burl realized that the darting, yapping dogs kept the creature's full attention. He crippled, and then killed it with his spear. The feat appeared to earn him warm admiration from the dogs. Burl wore a moth's feathery antenna again, bound to his forehead like a knight's plumes. He looked very splendid.

The entire pattern of human life changed swiftly, as if an entire revelation had been granted to men. The ground was often thorny. One man pierced his foot. Old Tama, scolding him for his carelessness, bound a strip of wing-fabric about it so he could walk. The injured foot was more comfortable than the one still unhurt. Within a week the women were busily contriving diverse forms of footgear to achieve greater comfort for everybody. One day Saya admired glistening red berries and tried to pluck one, and they stained her fingers. She licked her fingers to clean them,—and berries were added to the tribe's menu. A veritable orgy of experiment began, which is a state of things which is extremely rare in human affairs. A race with an established culture and tradition does not abandon old ways of doing things without profound reason. But men who have abandoned their old ways can discover astonishingly useful new ones.

Already the dogs were established as sentries and watchmen, and as friends to every member of the tribe. By now mothers did not feel alarmed if a child wandered out of sight. There would be dogs along. No danger could approach a child without vociferous warning from the dogs. Men went hunting, now, with zestful tail-wagging dogs as companions in the chase. Dor killed a torpid minotaur-beetle alone, save for assisting dogs, and Burl felt a twinge of jealousy. But then Burl, himself, battled a black male spider in a lone duel,—with dogs to help. By the time a stray monster from the lowlands reached this area, it was dazed and half-numbed by one night of continuous chill. Even the black spider could not find the energy to leap. It fought like a fiend, yet sluggishly. Burl killed this one while the dogs kept it busy,—and the dogs were reproachful because he carried it back to the tribal headquarters before dividing it among his assistants. Afterward, he realized that though he could have avoided the fight he would have been ashamed to do so, while the dogs barked and snapped at its furry legs.

It was while things were in this state that the way of life for human beings on the forgotten planet was settled for all time. Burl and Saya went out early one morning with the dogs, to hunt for meat for the village. Hunting was easiest in the early hours, while creatures that strayed up the night before were still sluggish with cold. Often, hunting was merely butchery of an enfeebled monster to whom any effort at all was terribly difficult.

This morning they strode away briskly. The dogs roved exuberantly through the brush before them. They were some five miles from the village when the dogs bayed game. And Burl and Saya ran to the spot with ready spears,—which was something of a change from their former actions on notice of a carnivore abroad. They found the dogs dancing and barking around one of the most ferocious of the meat-eating beetles. It was not unduly large, to be sure. Its body might have been four feet long, or thereabouts. But its horrible gaping mandibles added a good three feet more.

Those scythelike weapons gaped wide—opening sidewise as insects' jaws do—as the beetle snapped hideously at its attackers, swinging about as the dogs dashed at it. Its legs were spurred and spiked and armed with dagger-like spines. Burl plunged into the fight.

The great mandibles clicked and clashed. They were capable of disemboweling a man or snapping a dog's body in half without effort. There were whistling noises as the beetle breathed through its abdominal spiracles. It fought furiously, making ferocious charges at the dogs who tormented and bewildered it. But they created the most zestfully excited of tumults.

Burl and Saya were, of course, at least as absorbed and excited as the dogs, or they would have noticed the thing that was to make so much difference to every human being, not only on the plateau but still down in the lowlands. This unnoticed thing was beyond their imagining. There had been nothing else like it on this world in many hundreds of years. It was half a dozen miles away and perhaps a thousand feet high when Burl and Saya prepared to intervene professionally on behalf of the dogs. It was a silvery needle, floating unsupported in the air. As they entered the battle, it swerved and moved swiftly in their direction.

It was silent, and they did not notice. They knew of no reason to scan the sky in daytime. And there was business on hand, anyhow.

Burl leaped in toward the beetle with a lance-thrust at the tough integument where an armored leg joined the creature's body. He missed, and the beetle whirled. Saya flashed her cloak before the monster so that it seemed a larger and a nearer antagonist. As the creature whirled again, Burl stabbed and a hind-leg crumpled.

Instantly the thing was limping. A beetle does not use its legs like four-legged creatures. A beetle moving shifts the two end legs on one side and the central leg on the other, so that it always stands on an adjustable tripod of limbs. It cannot adjust readily to crippling. A dog snatched at a spiny lower leg and crunched,—and darted away. The machine-like monster uttered a formless, deep-bass cry and was spurred to unbelievable fierceness. The fight became a thing of furious movement and joyous uproar, with Burl striking once at a multiple eye so the pain would deflect it from a charge at Saya, and Saya again deflecting it with her cloak and once breathlessly trying to strike it with her shorter spear.

They struck it again, and a third time, and it sank horribly to the ground, all three legs on one side crippled. The remaining three thrust and thrust and struggled senselessly,—and suddenly it was on its back, still striking its gigantic jaws frantically in the hope of murder. But then Burl struck home between two armor-plates where a ganglion was almost exposed. The blow killed it instantly.

Burl and Saya were smiling at each other when there was a monstrous sound of crashing trees. They whirled. The dogs pricked up their ears. One of them barked defiantly.

Something huge—truly huge!—had settled to the ground a bare two hundred yards away. It was metal, and there were ports in its sides, and it was quite beyond imagining. Because, of course, no space-ship had landed on this planet in forty-odd human generations.

A port opened as they stared at it. Men came out. Burl and Saya were barbarically attired, but they had been fighting some sort of local monster—the men on the space-ship could not quite grasp what they had seen—and they had been helped by dogs. Human beings and dogs, together, always mean some sort of civilization.

The dogs gave an impression of a very high level indeed. They trotted confidently over to the ship, and they sniffed cautiously at the men who had landed. Then their behavior was admirable. They greeted the new-come men with the self-confident cordiality of dogs who are on the best possible terms with human beings,—and there was no question of any suspicion by anybody. The attitude of a man toward a dog is a perfectly valid indication of his character, if not of his technical education. And the newcomers knew how to treat dogs.

So Burl and Saya went forward, with the confident pleasure with which well-raised children and other persons of innate dignity greet strangers.

The ship was the *Wapiti*, a private cruiser doing incidental exploration for the Biological Survey in the course of a trip after good hunting. It had touched on the forgotten planet, and it would never be forgotten again.

EPILOGUE

The survey-ship *Tethys* made the first landing on the forgotten planet, and the *Orana* followed, and some centuries later the *Ludred*. Then the planet was forgotten until the *Wapiti* arrived. The arrival of the *Wapiti* was as much an accident as the loss of the punched card which caused the planet to be overlooked for some thousands of years. Somebody had noticed that the sun around which it circled was of a type which usually has useful planets, but there was no record that it had ever been visited. So a request to the sportsmen on the *Wapiti* had caused them to turn aside. They considered, anyhow, that it would be interesting to land on a brand-new world or two. They considered it fascinating to find human beings there before them. But they could not understand the use of such primitive weapons or garments of such barbaric splendor. They had trouble, too, because in forty-odd generations the speech of the universe had changed, while Burl and Saya spoke a very archaic language indeed.

But there was an educator on the *Wapiti*. It was quite standard apparatus,—simply basic-education for a human child, so that one's school-years could be begun with a backlog of correct speech, and reading, with the practical facts of mathematics, sanitation, and the general information that any human being anywhere needs to know. Children use it before they start school, and they absorb its information quite painlessly. It is rare that an adult needs it. But Burl and Saya did.

Burl was politely invited to wear the head-set, and he politely obliged. He found himself equipped with a new language and what seemed to him an astonishing amount of information. Among the information was the item that he was going to have—as an adult—a severe headache. Which he did. Also included was the fact that the making of records for such educators was so laborious a process that it took generations to compile one master-record for the instruments.

Burl, with a splitting headache, nevertheless urged Saya to join him in getting an education. And she did. And thereafter they were able to converse with the sportsmen on the *Wapiti* comfortably enough,—except for their headaches.

And all this led to extremely satisfactory arrangements. Sportsmen could not but be enthusiastic about the hunting of giant insects with dogs and spears. The sportsmen on the *Wapiti* wanted some of that kind of sport. Burl's fellow-tribesmen were delighted to oblige,—though they had not quite the zest of Burl. They had to acquire educations in their turn, so they could talk to their new hunting-companions. But the hunting was magnificent. The *Wapiti* abandoned its original plans and settled down for a stay.

Presently Burl's casual talk of the lowlands produced results. An atmosphere-flier came out of the ship's storage-compartments. And through the educator Burl was now a civilized man. He had not the specialized later information of his guests, but he had knowledge they could not dream of, and which it would take much of a century to put in recordable form for an educator.

So an atmosphere-flier went down into the lowlands through the cloud-banks. There were three men on board. They had good hunting. Magnificent hunting. Even more importantly, they found another cluster of human beings who lived as fugitives among the insect giants. They brought them to the plateau, a few at a time. Sportsmen stayed in the lowlands with modern weapons, hunting enthusiastically, while the transfer took place.

In all, the *Wapiti* stayed for two months Earth-time. When it left, its sportsmen had such trophies as would make them envied of all other hunters in three star-clusters. They left behind weapons and atmosphere-fliers and their library and tools. But they took with them enthusiasm for the sport on the once-forgotten planet, and rather warm feelings of friendship for Burl.

They sent their friends back. The next ship to come in found a small city on the plateau, with a population of three hundred souls,—all civilized by educator. Naturally, they'd had no trouble building civilized dwellings or practising sanitation, or developing a neatly adapted culture-pattern for their particular environment. This second ship brought more weapons and fliers and news from the first party about commercial demand for the incredibly luxurious moth-fur, to be found on only one planet in all the galaxy.

The fourth ship to land on the plateau was a trading-ship anxious to load such furs for recklessly bidding merchants in a dozen interplanetary marts. There were then nearly a thousand people living on the plateau. They had a natural monopoly,—not of moth-fur and butterfly-wing fabric, and panels of irridescent chitin for luxurious decoration, but—of the strictly practical and detailed knowledge of insect-habits which made it possible to obtain them. Off-planet visitors who tried to hunt without local knowledge did not come back from the lowlands. In time, Burl firmly enacted a planetary law which forbade the inexperienced to go below the cloud-layer.

Because, of course, a government had to be formed for the planet. But men with the basic education of citizens everywhere did not fumble it. They had a job to do which was more important than anybody's vanity. It was a job which gave deep and abiding satisfaction. When naked, trembling folk were found in the mushroom-jungles and brought to the plateau, they had one instant, feverish desire as soon as they got over the headache from the educator.

They wanted to go back to the lowlands. It was profitable, to be sure. But it was even more of a satisfaction to hunt and kill the monsters that had hunted and killed men for so long. It felt good, too, to find other humans and bring them out to sunshine.

So nowadays the forgotten planet has ceased to be forgotten. It is hardly necessary to name it, because its name is known through all the Galaxy. Its population is not large, so far, but it is an interesting place to live in. In the popular mind, it is the most glamorous of all possible worlds,—and for easily understandable reasons. The inhabitants of its capital city wear moth-fur garments and butterfly-wing cloaks for the benefit of their fellows in the lowlands. There is no day but fliers take off and dive down into the mists. When human hunters are in the lowlands, they dress as the lowlanders they used to be, so that lowlanders who may spy them will be sure that they are men, and friends, and come to them to be raised to proper dignity above the insects. It is not unusual for a man to be brought up to sunshine, and have his session with the educator, and be flying his own assigned atmosphere-flier within a week, diving back above what used to be the place where he was hunted, but where he has become the hunter.

It is a very pleasant arrangement. The search for more humans in the lowlands is a prosperous business, even when it is unsuccessful. The wings of white Morpho butterflies bring the highest prices, but even a common swallow-tail is riches, and the fur of caterpillars—duly processed—goes into the holds of the planet-owned space-line ships with the care given elsewhere to platinum and diamonds.

And also it is good sport. The planet is a sportsman's paradise. There are not too many visitors. Nobody may go hunting without an experienced host. And off-planet sportsmen tend to feel somewhat queasy after a session as guest of the folk who have made Burl their planet-president. Visitors are not so much alarmed at fighting flying beetles in mid-air, even though the beetles may compare with the hunters' craft in size and are terrifically tenacious of life. The thing that appalls strangers is the insistence of Burl's fellow-citizens—no longer only tribesmen—upon fighting spiders on the ground. With their memories, they like it that way. It's more satisfactory.

Not long ago the Planet President of Sumor XI was Burl's guest for a hunt. Sumor XI is a highly civilized planet, and life there has become tame. Its president is an ardent hunter. He liked Burl, who is still all hard muscle despite his graying hair. He and Saya have a very comfortable dwelling, and now that their children are grown they have room in it even for a planet president, if he comes as a sportsman guest. The Planet President of Sumor XI even liked the informal atmosphere of a house where pleasantly self-possessed dogs curl up comfortably on rugs of emperor-moth down that elsewhere are beyond price.

But the President of Sumor XI was embarrassed on his visit. He and Burl are both hunters, and they are highly congenial. But the President of Sumor XI was upset on his last flight to the lowlands. Burl got out of the atmosphere-flier alone, and for pure deep personal satisfaction he fought a mastodon-sized wolf spider with nothing but a spear.

He killed the creature, of course. But the President of Sumor XI was embarrassed. He wouldn't have dared try it. He felt that, however sporting it might be, it was too risky a thing for a Planet President to do.

But Saya took it for granted.

THE END